ENDANGERED

ENDANGERED

The Ballad of Bitterroot Bob

ALEX CAMPBELL

RESOURCE *Publications* · Eugene, Oregon

ENDANGERED
The Ballad of Bitterroot Bob

Resource Publications
An Imprint of Wipf and Stock Publishers
199 W. 8th Ave., Suite 3
Eugene, OR 97401

www.wipfandstock.com

PAPERBACK ISBN: 978-1-6667-4364-7
HARDCOVER ISBN: 978-1-6667-4365-4
EBOOK ISBN: 978-1-6667-4366-1

JULY 19, 2022 11:08 AM

For Ann

"Which would you prefer to have your life compared to, wind or dust? Why?"

—JOY WILLIAMS, *THE QUICK AND THE DEAD*

SPACE

1

Digging—me against the dirt of the Great Basin of the western United States—proved I had passed my prime. Although the hole barely punctured that corner of Oregon's southeastern desert, I was already dripping sweat and breathing hard.

I had come here to relearn my country from the ground up. Yet in this wide-open territory it seemed one could walk off in any direction without it mattering. To anchor myself, so to speak, to plant a stake, I had chosen to go down, directly *into* it. So, digger, dirt, and hole. Seemed commonplace.

But learning comes in many forms, I reminded myself.

Mine wasn't a project to dig through to China or any other happy childhood pastime like a backyard model of all the canals of Venice Out here, there is always one important consideration: where to get water? There'd never be enough to float a toy gondola.

Even after I'd broken through its baked crust, the flinty volcanic soil resisted the blades of my posthole digger. With sweat running down my ribs, I puffed and swore through an eternity of digging before dumping the entire bucket of water that I'd carted out here into the still shallow hole. The water disappeared as if there were no bottom. I pictured the liquid running through water-starved aquifers toward the center of the earth, straight to its molten core, turned to steam, reformed as part of the rivers, the lakes, the ocean of lava roiling miles below.

Imaging that slide and glide of water and seething fluid rock gave me pause. Within the interval of a hummingbird's heartbeat, my Mundane World had become the envelope of a churning caldron. Not so commonplace after all.

It was also possible I'd been in the sun too long.

I went about setting my eight-foot post.

When I figured I'd driven the four-by deep enough, I let the post driver fall a last time. *Bam.* Maybe some residue dampness had eased my pounding the post down. Maybe not.

After unsleeving the driver from the top of the post, I heaved the weighted iron to the ground. I back-filled around the post what I'd dug out, stomped the arid soil as best I could, and tacked up my sign with a few nails. Standing back, I read my hand-lettering:

Entering

PURGATORY
(unincorporated)

Elev. 4309 feet   Pop. 1

My sign didn't invite folks to stay away. Not exactly. Should its wording be less subtle? *No Trespassing* or *Keep Out* were succinct. They would also imply the "Or Else" hostility I had hoped to escape by coming here.

So far, so good, I reassured myself. But would my present success hold? Purgatory isn't purgatory if it's crowded. I'd traveled to this high desert for its distances between people. All I wanted—needed—was space, lots of it. My country had become unrecognizable.

The transformation left me frustrated, confused, and unsettled.

I was convinced that for me to learn anything useful about why my world had stopped being familiar, let alone some clue about how I could now live in it, my project had to be solo.

I had sensed they were there before I turned to see them, her and the horse she was on. They topped the low bluff that began its steep rise maybe fifty yards behind me. Outlined against the sky, looking down, she sat there as still as a blank page. The horse, a chestnut Appaloosa by its spotted markings, head up, ears trained in my direction, was as intent on me as she was.

I understood their curiosity. Some gray-haired geezer at the verge of a little-used track in an ignored splinter of this elements-scoured western landscape, teetering on a rock to get the height necessary to pound a weathered four-by into grit that gets less than ten inches of rain a year.

Maybe the rhythmic, dull thump of my post driver had drawn them. Both she and her horse might have recognized the sound—fence lines aren't unknown in the area. But in this mostly free range, she must have wondered, why here? And now she could see the post wasn't for a fence. And the sun was all heat and no clouds and the geezer was without a hat. One oddity after another for her.

With one hand, I shaded my eyes for a better look.

At first, I had taken the rider for a man. Well: horse, rider, big western hat. But still, why first assume a man? And why should my making that assumption surprise me, since I was aware of my mind's throwing up its best guesses about what I perceive? Often wrong guesses. And sure enough, this time, too. That, up there, was, indeed, a long braid that came over one shoulder and hung nearly to her waist. So: woman. Another guess that I quickly realized could be wrong, seeing as how there seemed to be as many Natives out here—some male, with braids—as other folks.

Strange what drifts to mind in wide-open landscape.

She raised no hand or otherwise acknowledged my gaze. Nor did I, hers. No need, come to that. Our shared awareness had been sufficiently communicated for mutual strangers.

I didn't hear her speak to the horse or see her hands or feet move, but the horse flicked one ear back toward her, turned its head, and walked the ridgeline before they disappeared over the backside of the bluff. Maybe she had seen enough.

Me, too.

I collected the handful of leftover nails, my post-hole digger and shovel, empty bucket, hammer, post driver, and the hatchet I'd used to rough out a point on the four-by. After tossing everything into the bed of my Ranchero pickup and hauling them up the road to the shack that crouched next to the steep face of a black rock outcropping, I stored them in the lean-to shed at the back. I could return the post driver to A-1 Equipment Rentals in Burns tomorrow.

The shed's door latch didn't have a lock. I wasn't worried much about theft around here.

Went on over to my dilapidated Airstream trailer parked under a cottonwood tree. Inside was still cool. Knocked back a big glass of tepid water. Delicious. Out of habit, I flapped my shirt tail to unstick the cloth from my back, but it wasn't necessary. Although I'd been sweating a bunch, the desiccated air dried the shirt and me about as fast as I got damp. I ran one hand across my shoulders. In time, the only sign I'd have of my ongoing perspiration would be a rough white band of salt there across the shirt's fabric.

On the pad on my desk, I jotted yet another note to get a line up outside so I could wash and rinse clothes and hang them to dry.

I tried to sit to writing. Words covering blank pages, that was my objective. But not just any words.

In my isolation, I hoped to find a pattern of words to cope with feeling like an outsider in my own country. Over the first couple of weeks at this work, which was how long since I'd taken up residency here, I had come to think of my process having three parts: seeing what had changed to make the country unrecognizable to me, sorting out the cause or causes of that difference, and deciding how to come to terms with it.

Determining the steps had been the easy business.

Corralling words for any of the three components matched the landscape around me: an uncomfortably long way between water and taking more time than it first looks like to traverse the distance. As with much else out here, I'd just have to see what would come of it.

This time around, not much. I was too restless.

I would have liked to think the horse rider—woman or whoever—had unsettled me. She had, but that wasn't my writing problem. I'd written myself into a box canyon.

I decided I should drive to town, that wide spot roughed-out on either side of the sparsely traveled Oregon State Route, and replenish my stores. I printed out what I'd typed before getting fidgety, turned off my laptop, and tossed the page on the desk.

Checking the half-fridge and cupboards didn't take long. Not much needed, just the normal food groups and staples of potato chips, beef jerky and Coors—Rocky Mountain Kool-Aid, according to many. That suited me fine right now. Maybe I'd get some lentils—there's optimism for you—or some other beans into which I could throw the bit of fatback left over in the fridge. Might even splash out and get a sausage and some spaghetti.

I figured there was no need of a grocery list.

Closing the screen door behind me without letting it slam, I felt a thrill of accomplishment.

I'd give my writing a think on the way into town.

Nearing the slower speed limit posted by the prudent Oregon State Department of Highways, I eased off on the gas. Eased off, too, on any thinking about the writing I had been pretending to take a run at. What had come of that so far, I concluded, still had the look and feel of a box canyon. At lot like Purgatory, in fact, with the same lack of clarity of how to get out.

Road signs at the north and south approaches to the town informed infrequent travelers that they were entering Fast Buck, population number obliterated. I've always been interested in how a place gets its name. Passing the southern sign and its assorted bullet holes, some rims glittering, some rusted, I assumed once more that the town's name hadn't come from somebody's thought about antelope, whose numbers were probably diminishing by the time the town's founding fathers decided on the label. At least the wise soul who picked the name had been more honest than most who'd projected their longings onto place-names in an environment they woefully misunderstood. Cornucopia, for instance, a way north of here. Who were they kidding, other than themselves? Plush? Not likely. The namers of Cuprum, further up the road from Cornucopia, may have found some humor in using the Latin word for copper while knowing the thirst of the aspiring prospectors. But those Silver Cities that dot the west are ghost towns now, most of them. Of course, there are honest town names: Brush, Wind River, Weed, Buttonwillow. Even Las Vegas—the Meadows—once sported grassy sweeps due to a water source. But Los Angeles? Somebody had been more lost in hope than noticing what surrounded them.

Tombstone, though, now there's a town name with merit. Seldom, is another, although it took folks in Newfoundland to assign it to a place.

In the rearview mirror, I watched the dust blow up behind my pickup as I pulled off the road to park. What had the Paiute or Shoshone named this place before the white men? Given that the local Cooked Creek drains north toward its confluence with the Owyhee River, maybe the Natives combined something with *pah* or *pa*, their word—according to place-name experts—for water. Maybe something like Pahrump, meaning Water-rock, not far from Las Vegas. Or like Tonopah—Greasewood spring water—towns in both Nevada and Arizona.

I switched off the engine and listened to its slow tick-tick as it cooled. The dust took its time to settle.

This haphazard collection of buildings scattered on both sides of the road looked more tossed up than constructed. On the far side, a string of bungalows formed a shallow arc. Fronting them, one slightly larger sported three signs of differing vintage, which declared in sequence: Motel, Office, Vacancy.

Nearby Milly's clapboard café sported a single gas pump out front and a freestanding tank with hose and nozzle for diesel off to one side. A General Store included a U.S. flag flapping from the pole outside to indicate the post office inside. It operated across the closed lower half of a Dutch door that was clear in the back of the store, at the end of the aisle with General Mills baking goods on one side and Purina feed and seed on the other.

Scrunched next to the General was the one-room house where the storeowners, Fred and Doris, watched TV in the evenings. Beyond, lay another small house, deserted.

And a bit down the road on my side, a double-doored building that had functioned as a stable before becoming a mechanic's garage. It now stood empty of anyone's hopes. Its weather-silvered boards showed daylight between them here and there. Once I'd peeked through the slots and found an old Dodge Power Wagon with air still in its tires. In the gloom, oddly, it appeared clean and waxed.

Outside the garage, most of the rails were down, askew, or missing from the corral posts that now all leaned away from the south side, as if laboring against a stiff wind.

Directly in front of where I was parked stood a saloon. I knew it was a saloon and not a bar or tavern because the sign said so: Saloon. The flickering yellow neon was generally the most active thing in town.

I got out, shoved the door closed, and raised my nose into the breeze, hoping to inhale the scent of sage. Got a whiff of the pickup's hot metal, the strip of sun-cooked asphalt, and the gas pump from across the road. A cold beer was the best answer to that. I set out for the steps to the abbreviated boardwalk that fronted the saloon.

My eyes took half a minute to adjust to the dim interior. Woody, the owner and barkeep, didn't believe in spending for lights in the middle of the day. He was behind his bar, polishing glasses. Seemed like he was always polishing. I didn't see him look up from under the camo-fabric baseball cap he always wore.

"You're going to drop from heatstroke," he said when I got close enough so he didn't have to generate much energy to raise his voice. "If you don't start wearing a hat."

"Hello, Woody," I said. "So you tell me every time I'm in here."

"Don't make it less true." He pulled a draft and slid the already sweating glass across the bar. "A woman came by earlier asking about you," he said.

"A woman? Here?"

He nodded, barely, and moved back to his glasses. He was what my grandfather would have called a long, tall drink of water. And thin enough you worried that if he turned sideways, he might disappear. Another grandfatherism. For all that, working behind the bar, he moved with a grace that suggested coiled strength.

"What'd she want?" I already had the feeling this conversation would be uphill work.

"You know, general wonderments about you." Woody held a glass at arm's length toward the brightness of the open door and squinted. He decided the glass needed work.

"What'd you tell her?"

"Don't know much to tell, do I? Gave her basic directions to where you live." He flapped one arm toward a wrong compass point. "She seemed to already know." He paused. "But maybe I got that wrong."

"She ask for my phone number?"

"You have a phone?"

"Of course, I have a phone." I smacked the beer back onto the bar, spilling some. "You think we're living in the middle of nowhere?"

Woody, wiping up the beer spill, paused long enough to raise his head and study me. I couldn't tell if his eyes were laughing or if he just had doubts about me. His face was always friendly enough, but, boy, it gave away about as much as a card shark's over a big pot.

I used another swig of beer to cool down. "Where'd she go?"

"Left."

"I'd noticed that. I meant which way did she head out?"

"Dunno."

"You don't—"

"She rode in on a horse. Went away on the same. Wasn't my business to notice East, West, North or South." He folded his wiping cloth and placed it by the sink. "Spotted," he added, "not her—the horse, all across a big patch of white over its hind quarters."

I didn't know what to think of that, and I didn't want to say much about it either. "She leave a message?"

"No."

"Name?"

"Didn't ask." He'd gone back to polishing, his mouth a straight line between two parentheses.

"Appaloosa," I said. No reaction. "The horse. Famously developed and favored by the Nez Perce."

"Most of them," he said, going after something that had him bothered on the glass, "the Nez Perce, not the horses, tend to live further north and east of here, across the state line and into Idaho."

I waited for anything else. There wasn't any. So: woman, confirmed—probably not Native. The information didn't seem to advance my understanding much.

I carried my now less-full glass of beer to a table near the big dusty window and sat down Wyatt Earp style, facing the door. Woody probably already knew about Appaloosas. If he knew that much about the Nez Perce, he knew about their horses. It occurred to me that he might know about the woman rider, too.

He'd had a step on me all along.

Awareness of my age pressed me like the heat beyond the plate glass I sat before, dry heat that sucked water through my thinning skin even as my fingers lapped at the condensation on the beer glass.

"How old are you?" Woody had once asked, in a moment of uncharacteristic bluntness.

"Somewhere north of forty-nine and south of a hundred," I'd allowed.

He had nodded in his slow way to let me know that despite how absurdly low that forty-nine might be, my true age could—with him—remain an open question.

Now on the other side of the bar, he polished and peered and polished, no doubt thinking up clever ways to say "I told you so" when I dropped from sunstroke. I'd be hard-pressed then for a catchy comeback.

I was worrying those options to keep from thinking about the horsewoman but left off to watch a vehicle pull up next to mine. It was a tricked-out Land Rover SUV, its high-polish green surface just getting a patina of dust. The fog and running lights across roof and at the bottom of the grill struck me as overkill. Whoever it was, probably didn't hail from a sophisticated metropolitan center like Burns or Winnemucca. I checked the license plate. California. Same as mine. That squirming sensation in my gut was discomfort at the thought this newcomer and I shared any similarity.

The driver's door opened, and I watched a young man—late-twenties, early-thirties—swing out and drop to the ground. Running shoes. No socks. On the top end, he sported a red baseball cap. Woody would approve of the hat. Rattlesnakes would appreciate the bare ankles. Although most rattlesnakes prefer to glide away rather than hang around for practice striking at legs, bare or otherwise.

The man reached back inside the Rover and retrieved a slim canvas briefcase. With one hand, he slipped the strap over his shoulder while with the other he pushed the door shut.

After climbing the steps to the boardwalk out front, he turned to survey this dust-painted outpost and arched his back like he'd been sitting in his SUV too long. Blue tee-shirt, camo cargo-shorts.

How does any sane person contemplate venturing out here with bare legs among stiff-branched sage, not to mention all the rest that grows thorns, hooks, points, saw edges, or stickers?

The pockets of his cargo-shorts bulged with civilization's ballast. He dropped the Rover's keys into a left pocket with room to spare.

Apparently sated with the vista's beauties, he walked inside and over to Woody at the bar.

"Whadda ya got cold to drink?" the man asked.

Woody barely flicked an eye over him before looking at the labeled handles of the two drafts on tap and then up to the blackboard behind him that listed a half-dozen bottled beers.

"Got any Heineken?"

Maybe the man's eyes hadn't adjusted from all the sunlight.

Woody finished a glass and slid it into precise row with others. "That the one in a green bottle?"

"Yeah. Green. That's the one."

After a long study of the tap labels and blackboard again, Woody said, "Nope. No green Heineken." He selected another glass.

The man looked down at the bar, twisted around and leaned back on it for a look around the saloon. He pushed his sunglasses onto his forehead. *Oh.* He spotted me over by the window, pointed, and said. "I'll have what he's drinking."

Woody pulled it.

After a sip and another glance at Woody, the guy must have decided to cut his losses. He adjusted the strap of his briefcase on his shoulder, picked up the beer, and came over to me.

"May I?" He gestured at the empty chair. I nodded.

He set the beer down, tossed his cap on the table, unslung the canvas briefcase, sat, and scraped the chair closer to the table. While he was going through all that, I took a read of his cap's inscription.

In bold chartreuse letters, the first line spelled out "Rod and Gun." Under that ran an italicized line: "*The Good Life.*"

He saw me looking and flashed a smile, one of those stunner smiles, by man or woman.

Without returning it, I said, "You hunt?"

"No."

"Fish?"

He shook his head. "No." He seemed to be enjoying himself.

"Why the billboard?" I gestured at the cap.

He twisted it to read it like he'd never seen it before. "Helps me make friends."

I absorbed that bit of information along with a last swallow of beer. "Seems like you're the type to strike up a conversation pretty easy."

"Well, yes."

"Think it's the cap?"

He considered the question before shaking his head again. "To be honest, no."

"Maybe it's your soft-spoken, easy-talking ways?"

"I think when folks hear how much I'm offering to buy their place, they get friendly real fast."

"You're in real estate?"

"Not exactly." He took another sip of beer. "I'm just a buyer."

"Who for?"

Instead of answering, he wiped his damp hand across his tee-shirt and reached out to me. "I'm Roger, by the way. Roger Stegman. You're . . .?"

Slowly, I took his hand and gave it a squeeze. "Bitterroot Bob."

He laughed. It was an easy laugh, I had to admit. He didn't need the cap.

"No, you're not. I know who you are, now that I've got you in this light. You're just the man I've come to see. This saves me a trip to the post office for directions to where you live."

While talking, he'd unzipped the canvas carrier and pulled a laptop from what I'd taken for a briefcase. He flipped up the top and pushed a button.

"Have I got a deal for you." It wasn't a question.

I got up, already fighting back my mounting aversion to this guy, and toted my empty glass to the bar. "Looks like I'll need another."

Woody took the glass over to the tap. He was shaking his head.

"'Bitterroot Bob?'" He cocked an eyebrow in my direction. "Really? Bitterroot? A flower? That's the best you could come up with?" He took his time pulling the beer, still shaking his head. "For someone who's been out here only a few weeks, you're sure getting to be Mr. Popular." He set the filled glass in front of me. "But maybe I got that wrong."

Woody didn't say much, but he didn't miss much either.

"I had the mountain range in mind," I said, hoping not to sound defensive about the flower tag.

I made the long trek back to Roger Stegman, bent over his laptop, tapping away.

Mr. Popular, indeed. This was getting dicey. I barely stake out a little solitude in Purgatory, and some unknown woman rides in snooping around. Next thing I know, this fella drives up claiming to know me. Here was the kind of crowd that would frustrate my search.

They'd both learn quickly enough that I was determined to defend my isolation. And I'd just as soon start with ol' Rog than the Appaloosa woman. She was *not* a recognized entity, but Roger sure as hell was.

2

alf-aware that I'd regained my chair, I stared out the saloon window. A couple of maverick dust devils kicked up beyond Milly's café and twirled off deeper into the Harney Basin. I yearned to go with them.

This other man at the table, with his technology, his boasted knowledge of my identity, his bare legs, bat-fanged personality and other traces of a society maladapted to this landscape, his threatened *deal*—whatever that was—represented a whole bunch of what I'd sought to escape by coming to Purgatory. Yet here he was on my doorstep.

The dust devils didn't get far before their twisting plumes whipped apart and vanished. My hankering to ride the wind with them also disappeared, leaving a haze of foreboding.

One beer shouldn't have made me so melodramatic.

Roger spun his laptop in my direction. "This is you, right?"

I recognized the picture on his screen as a mug shot for a security badge I'd worn while doing contract research for a large Silicon Valley corporation at least a decade ago.

Anger followed recognition. This was like finding a snapshot of me in the wallet of someone I hadn't given it to. I felt invaded.

Old Rog was grinning, I had probably startled when I saw the photo. His smile looked more wolfish this time than winning.

Or perhaps that was my anger's interpretation. He might only have been pleased with himself, with his tricks of due diligence and sleights of hand that revealed his find.

Beside and below my pic ran a couple of blocked columns of print that could have been particulars about me. At my distance from the screen and without glasses, I saw mostly blurred letters. He slid a finger across the touch pad before I could remedy any of that, gave a tap, and the screen renewed, now with a pic of my cabin and shed, absent the Airstream. So, the image had been taken before I'd had it towed in and parked there.

Another slide of his finger, a tap, and a new picture of the buildings and rock-face behind them, from above. Purgatory as seen from heaven, only a little closer. I realized it had been taken from the same bluff-ridge lately ridden by the Appaloosa woman. Across the top ran a series of numbers I took to be G.P.S. coordinates.

"Your place," Roger said. "The one near here. Not the one you have in the Bay Area." He sat back and eyed me. "See? I do know who you really are, Bitterroot Bob."

"What do you want?" It felt like I'd bitten off each word clean.

"I want to buy your place. This one." He pointed to the computer's picture a second before it dimmed to rest.

"I'm not selling."

"You'll sell when you hear how much I'm offering."

"That's the *deal* you mentioned?

He cocked his head like he was trying to remember where I'd gotten the word. "You might say we're now starting negotiation."

I shook my head.

"Okay, we can dicker about the price a bit," Roger said, unperturbed. "That's what folks out here say, isn't it, dicker?"

"Might." I gave his suggestion a nod. "Might could. If they were twice my age. Or trying to be folksy."

Ol' Roger considered that for a hot second. "Whatever language I'm using, I can't help noticing most folks don't even dicker about my first offer. No hesitation. Pretty much a lunge for it. Like Mr. Peterson not far from here, up the road a bit, between Rome and Jordan Valley." A smile tickled the corners of his mouth. "Don't you just love the names of towns around here?"

I was taken back by his reaction to place-names that was akin to my own just a short time earlier. Stunned, in fact.

"Maybe you know him? Mr. Peterson?" He'd misread my silence.

I shook my head.

"Well, at any rate, he came around real fast. Sold up and moved to Portland. May he and his wife live happily ever after near their daughter and grandson."

Amazing how fast hate fills a heart. That emotion was another thing I'd hoped to absent myself from in Purgatory. But smug had always gotten my goat. And Rog, sitting there all relaxed and easy, looked and sounded full of smug. Heat spread like a stain from my core to toes and eyebrows.

I slipped my hand from around the beer glass and smoothed its moisture on my cheeks to cool down a degree or two.

Maybe he took that as my way of thinking about things and left me to considering. He gazed out the window. After half a minute, asked, "Does that motel across the road have Wi-Fi?"

For a moment, I was distracted by the wistful softness that had taken up occupancy across his face. What longing, I wondered, lay behind it? Was it desire to escape this wide-open territory and regain the enfolding comforts of urban society? With dismay, I felt my dislike of him ebb. Hadn't I, when first returned here, hankered after every swath of green, each patch of color, with the hunger of a deprived exile from wetter climates? Adjusting took a while. Perhaps like me, he would someday switch where he felt more at home.

I'd stayed at the motel he'd asked about while waiting for the Airstream to arrive. I knew each room to be furnished with a bed covered by army surplus blankets, a side table, bentwood chair, and under a wooden shelf, a short dowel with a couple of wire hangers bent by use. No TV, only an old Delco radio that got one station out of Burns. There was a hook on the back of the door for a coat. And/or for a hat, if you were of Woody's persuasion. For a second, I imagined the Rod-and-Gun hat hanging from it. Or Rog, black tongue lolling, eyes bulging.

"You'll have to ask the registration clerk," I said.

Across the room, Woody fumbled a glass into the metal sink with a clunk and rattle, so maybe I'd beaten him by a step or two this time.

"How does two-fifty an acre sound?" Roger asked, still looking at the motel.

"Low to average," I said, "And you're wasting your time."

He spun the laptop so he could get at its keys. Fingers hip-hopped across them and he turned the screen so I could read it. He'd done the math. *$12,500* stared back at me.

"I'll round up to fifteen thou," his voice smooth with magnanimity.

"As of a few days ago, what you're angling for became an unincorporated population center. You're bidding on developed property, you know." I was pleased I'd managed to get all the words said without a trace of irony.

It was the first thing I'd said that got his eyes swiveled from the motel to me.

"You call a well with a hand pump and falling water table developed?"

I was starting to enjoy myself, but imagining myself channeling Woody, kept my face and voice as impassive as humanly possible. 'The hand pump is a classic exercise machine, and you're forgetting the power and phone lines as well as the road, house, and shed."

"Dirt track, shack, and lean-to more like," he shot back, maybe to flex his dickering muscles as much as anything.

"Now that I've met you, I'm considering making it a gated community." I had a feeling he was about to catch on.

"Double it," he said, "thirty grand. That'll keep your population in potato chips and beer for a while."

He'd spoiled the moment. The look on my face probably told him so, because he took a deep breath, pasted on his easy smile, and gave it one more try.

"So, name your price," he said.

"Mine?"

"Yours. Sure. How much you want for that splotch of land?"

"You mean, how much for selling out? The sun, moon, and stars wouldn't be enough."

The smile faded in the time it took him to look back to the motel. His was a long lock, as if he were afraid the place might run away.

Roger turned his eyes from the motel to me, scratched his nose while taking a lock-see around my face, and possibly decided my position on his deal hadn't shifted much.

His fingers returned to the laptop touchpad, but I saw it was to turn the thing off this time. He folded down the cover and slid the machine back into its canvas carrier. I searched his expression and movements for any sign of discouragement. Not a trace.

He popped the Rod-and-Gun hat back on his head, beamed his winning smile at me, then laughed his easy laugh. "Bitterroot Bob. Good name."

From an outside pocket of the canvas carrier, he fished a business card, tossed it on the table near me, and headed for the door.

I fingered the card. Roger's name, without a title, was printed in the upper right corner. The center of the card held the most ink: The Greater America River and Canal Development Project. Below that line were a Pasadena, California, address and a set of phone numbers. Whether any number would reach Roger Stegman was open to speculation. My guess, he was a don't call us, we'll call you kind of guy.

Outside, he'd walked by his Land Rover toward the motel. Like a good city kid, he stopped and looked both ways before crossing the silent, deserted highway. Not one vehicle had passed in all the time we'd been talking.

Watching him kick up dust once he gained the other side, I found myself hoping for a rattlesnake that didn't work to type.

Because, minus the rattler, that son-of-a-gun was not going away.

3

Sitting in the Saloon after Roger trotted off to the motel, I batted around evil thoughts about him and his spiel.

He was a walking advertisement for the warning that love of money was the root of evil. Roger Stegman played into the growing conviction that a pile of money creates happiness. Still, his default assumption that everyone he met, including me, agreed with his point of view wasn't what had driven me to Purgatory. I recognized the greed for and the appeal to fast money that had always been in the world. I would have to look deeper and longer for what had changed and made my country unfamiliar.

I watered that bleak thought with the last of my beer.

Having exhausted this train of thought, I expanded my idea that if Woody knew about the Nez Perce and probably also knew about their horses, there were good odds that he knew something about the woman who'd watched me from the bluff. And if not about her in particular, given his reluctance to pry, I reasoned, then at least he might know where she had ridden in *from* and whether that could be where she lived.

I said as much when I slid my empty glass across the bar to him.

He dunked it in sudsy dishwater and scrubbed like he would drown it. "Took all this time to work that out, did it?"

"Do you? Know where she hangs that western hat of hers, for instance?"

From there, our conversation went about as expected. After toying with me, his cat's-spool-on-a-string, he finally coughed up something useful. She lived on the other side of the bluff where I'd seen her on the horse.

I resolved to make a drive-by, do a little snooping of my own. But not now, not after a couple of beers had softened my head and Roger's sales talk had stirred me up. Tomorrow would be soon enough, directly after I returned the rented post driver to Burns.

Before daylight the next day, Sunrise Valley dropped away behind me as I pushed up the eastern slope of Steens Mountain. I was in a losing race with an advancing dawn to catch night's trailing tail. If the darkness acted like a skedaddling cat, then the Ranchero's headlights were fading ghosts, now stretching, now shrinking on the asphalt unreeling before me, the beams most compact and apparent when the pickup nosed into a dip, flitting and lost altogether when the truck topped any slight rise.

The lane division stripes flew past like tracer bullets. Traffic was so intermittent as to approach nonexistent. Filled to running over with metaphors, I turned off the headlamps.

Before the summit pass, I pulled off onto a shoulder on the downslope side. The sun was just cresting Saddle Butte some thirty miles away. Crystal light raked clumps of sagebrush and rock outcroppings and etched long shadows all across the valley floor. The aching blue over all seemed to reach the last disappeared star.

Wanting the moment to remain forever, I realized I'd been holding my breath, bracing against the earth's revolution.

Surely my waking reverie of the past half hour had it backward. Wasn't I hoping to catch the light, not night? Wasn't I running *from* darkness, not after it? Or maybe the fantasy was a warning not to be too cocksure about what I thought I was chasing or what I would catch.

The trip from Purgatory to Burns was roughly a hundred miles. If I wanted to make the bigger part of the drive to return the post driver to A-1 Equipment Rentals before things got too hot, I needed to get a move on.

I also wanted enough of the day left to take care of that other matter: my planned snooping. Getting shut of Roger Stegman hadn't gone as cleanly as intended. If I could turn this horsewoman away with little fuss, it would reduce my crowd—and my popularity hereabouts—by one. The sooner I could get back to figuring out what happened to my country and how I could go about living in it, the better.

I crossed the summit pass, the Ranchero humming, before I'd finished the thought.

Later, in that mid-afternoon's sun, the road's uneven asphalt simmered, creating a rippling effect in the water mirage lying always just a few miles distant. The age-scarred county road snaked along the backside of the bluff that overlooked Purgatory on the other side. To the left, a small, ranch-style frame house of faded white under a stand of trees. No fence lines to speak of except around one field next to the house. I found the Appaloosa backed into tree shade in one corner of the enclosed area, standing head down in the afternoon heat, tail taking an occasional swish. No sign of other activity.

I'd come just to have a look, but my urge to get this over with grew with every revolution of the Ranchero's wheels.

On impulse, I turned onto the newly graveled road leading to the place. Slowed immediately to reduce the dust cloud kicked up behind me. Rolling over the gravel made a racket.

By the time I pulled up before the house, she was standing on its wide front porch. No western hat now but otherwise looking pretty much the same. Black hair pulled back, loose behind her shoulders, not braided or tied that I could see. Denim shirt and pants.

I cut the engine. Got out. Closed the distance between us. She was taller somehow than I'd imagined, but then, she was up a couple of steps on the porch.

She hadn't moved. Dark, broad arches of eyebrows. Sun-warmed obsidian eyes.

"Well?" she said. Mature voice, but her face was unlined.

"Indeed." I'd hoped to make it sound like a return question.

She didn't bite.

I'm used to laconic westerners, but her collected bearing was another matter and unsettling. "That your horse? Under the trees. The Appaloosa?"

She nodded. "Yes, you've found the right person."

"How do you know who I'm looking for?"

She glanced at the Ranchero. "The truck." Then at me. "No hat. Nobody else around here would match up."

I'd forgotten I had the pickup parked by me yesterday. I managed what felt like a rueful smile.

She went on. "I thought you might show up. But I also thought it might take you longer."

It was my turn to bide my time.

That was okay with her. She added, "And I wasn't sure what to expect when you did. Or if I'd like it."

"Why on earth not?"

She came forward to the edge of the porch topping the stairs, slanted herself against the roof post. "This side of the Cascades," her eyes lifted to sweep all she could see before settling again on me, "and, for that matter, east of the Sierra, the territory has long been known as the land of little rain. It wasn't the kind of place that attracted folks who were not known through kinship or tribal relationships."

She paused, maybe to see if I was still listening. I was. She continued.

"Of course, the few people here traded with distant tribes, sometimes fought them. And the local tribes had heard stories about the trappers who had decimated their fur-bearing animals like beaver. They knew of other strangers who were moving in to the west, north and east of them. White. That was different. That and their face hair. But not long ago, say about one hundred and fifty years back, the Northern Paiutes got word from other bands to the east about a group of these people traveling through the land of little rain. The Paiutes decided to go see for themselves, find out, offer traditional hospitality. Sharing in an ungenerous land as was their way."

She stopped, cocked her head, and asked, "Do you have time for this?"

"All day," I said. She seemed accustomed to being up in front, talking.

"Nothing much happened. The Paiutes found the travelers but stayed off at a distance. They got no response to their signs of friendly invitation to come closer, nor did they receive any in return. So, they hung back but stayed around, moving on parallel trajectories until late in the day. Then they went off some distance and made camp for the night."

"Sounds a bit like you coming to have a look at me," I said. "And then going on."

She nodded.

I frowned. "Then why did you say you were unsure? Why'd you think you might not—"

Her raised hand stopped me. "Story's not over. That night around their own campfire, the white travelers talked each other into deciding that those Indians had come to murder and rob them. Early next morning they tracked down the Paiutes' camp, surprised them, shot them up, killed one or two before the rest escaped."

Now it seemed the story was done. "I see," I said.

"Maybe you do."

"I can imagine."

"Probably not. Memory lingers around here. Also, folks have learned that beliefs dangerous to us can continue across generations. You never know who you're dealing with." She looked me up and down as if considering something. "There's another California man roaming around lately, younger than you, big green SUV, looking to buy up property." She transferred her gaze to the vast acres of sage, the rolling sunburned hills. She tilted her chin in their direction. "Ownership of the likes of this." she said. "That's one of those beliefs that brings danger out here."

She straightened from the roof post. "You asked." She smiled. I hadn't noticed her wide, generous mouth, but now I did. She turned and opened the screen door and beckoned to me. "I didn't mean to stop the conversation by wondering if you and him are up to the same thing. I can see you're not armed. And you've been standing out there in the sun with no hat. You could use a drink of water."

Her and Woody, all about the no-hat business. I followed her into the welcome cool of her living room. As soon as I crossed the threshold, something in me shifted.

The sound of running water came from the kitchen along with her voice raised in question over it. That is, I registered the running water, her inflected voice and words, but not her question.

When I had entered the room, I was aware of a worn leather couch and several chairs gathered before a cold fireplace. On the wall at the other end of the long room hung a small woven rug, maybe of Navajo design, but I wouldn't know. I'd been drawn that direction by a large dining table covered with books and papers.

She found me there, slowly circling the table, when she returned from the kitchen with two glasses of water. She waited for me to look up from my scanning the books and documents, sepia-tinted photographs, and yellow note tablets centered, as everything was, toward the armchair pushed back from one end. The cover of a laptop computer was closed, or I might well have been reading the screen. Finally, I looked up from my snooping.

She didn't appear put off. She came around the table and extended one glass to me. Sharing resources in an ungenerous land?

I took it, and I took my time with several swallows of the water. It was cold and clean, artesian, I guessed. Digging or drilling the well for that represented time and expense by someone.

I wiped my mouth with the back of my hand. "Thank you. You were right. I did need that."

She took a sip of her own water. Maybe she nodded. Maybe not.

She picked up one of the one black and white photographs. I had already seen that it was of a seated, very pretty young woman, dressed in bead-decorated clothing. I'd also noticed the caption: Mourning Dove.

"I've been wondering," I said, "if you're Native American?"

Slightly frowning, she studied the photo, as if looking for something. "Always a question, in its way: What does a Native American look like? As for the personal question of identifying as a Native. That's likely more complicated than you imagine."

That felt like a challenging way not to answer my question. But I let it slide for now.

She replaced the photo. As her fingers guided it to a slightly different position on the table from before, my gaze wandered from the Mourning Dove photo across others on the table of men and women, single and in groups, posed like the young woman or engaged in some activity, all of whom I'd place in the same category. I could see, too, even without my glasses, larger-font headings on books and documents that included names of many western Native Nations. Other pages written—by her own hand?—in what could be notation for one of their languages. Then there was also the maybe-Navajo design wall hanging. And that Appaloosa outside under the trees, flicking flies and looking dozy. Although, on second thought, the handwritten pages could have been of Sanskrit for all I knew, or really, didn't know. My eyes came back to hers, now raised and waiting.

"I withdraw the question," I said. "It was ill-considered."

"As was my comment earlier, wondering whether you were a land buyer."

"Your story, though, about the two groups and their tragically misunderstood encounter resulting from assumptions based on too little. I thought your tale might be about recognizing the danger in not knowing who you're dealing with. The saying—excuse my bluntness, I'm not doing this well, bumbling through." I took a breath. "Your aphorism—you never know who you're dealing with—seemed trite." I made a futile gesture

"You 'thought,'" she said. "'It seemed.' Past tenses. And now?"

"Yes, well now, as our encounter, yours and mine, evolves, I wonder whether, in fact, you were telling the story to illustrate the danger—although it could be the fascination, I suppose—" I stopped. "See? I'm still fumbling for words. Let me start over."

"Good idea."

"Maybe you were saying, from the Paiutes' point of view in light of what happened to them, the greater danger is that you never know what strangers think they're dealing with in you."

"Was I? Telling a cautionary tale or just reciting history, I wonder. But it does bring me back to the question I asked from the kitchen that you didn't answer."

"Oh. Sorry. I heard, but not really. Got preoccupied."

"I saw that when I came back in here. I'd asked, Do you think we can find out what we can learn from each other?"

I was aware again of the shift I'd felt when I'd entered her house. I'd come here intending to discourage her interest in me, to drive her off if necessary. Now I was less sure.

"I think we'd better try," I said. "Don't you?"

4

We sat on the shaded porch, which ran the length of the front of the house and allowed a breeze to cool us, leaving the sagebrush to bake.

She'd asked me to tote a chair out while she returned to the kitchen to fill a pitcher with water. This she placed on a small table that stood between a weathered bentwood armchair already in place and the one I'd added.

In pretty short order she'd returned to her earlier wondering—ill-considered or not—about whether I intended to buy up local property.

"After all, you did erect a sign," she said. "That could be seen as a romanticized act of staking a land claim."

"No need," I said, right after thinking I hadn't been the only one making wrong guesses yesterday. "The place is already mine."

Her eyes widened in surprise. "I wasn't aware it had been sold. Or been offered for sale, for that matter."

"Gift, by way of inheritance."

I told her about my grandfather, around the turn of the twentieth century, waiting overlong in Colorado before trying to get in on the settlement rush into the Payette and Boise River valleys. Most of the good land was already gone. But soon, he'd gotten roped into a scheme of the big ranchers further to the southwest to establish a homestead along the trail routes used by cattlemen on their way to the Central Pacific railhead at Winnemucca. The ranchers lured him with the plan to control access to water and charge for it while making the improvements on the property needed to validate the homestead claim. But the big ranchers' primary scheme—unknown by my grandfather—was for him to resell his homesteaded land to them for cheap prices for their own grazing land.

"Scheme, sham, scam," she said, "based on one's perspective." She didn't smile at her wordplay. Her eyes were hard. "Could be a declension of the ranchers' intentions. At least your grandfather made real improvements, assuming that's his house standing there now. Many didn't bother. Just got those ranchers to testify to nonexistent improvements, sold them the land quickly, and got out. But now you're there. Do you own the original one hundred and sixty acres—or three twenty—depending on how he did it?"

In my mind's eye, I saw again her table covered in papers and documents. She was well informed. But then again, folks out here tended to pay attention to land, water rights, acres, ownership. And who looked like a land buyer, with or minus a tricked-out SUV. I wouldn't be surprised to learn that she knew, or knew about, Roger Stegman's Mr. Peterson.

I shook my head and explained that my grandfather had sold off most of the original homestead but kept fifty acres. One of his three sons, my uncle Jim, took it over. He had made a go at raising and breaking quarter horses. That business didn't last long. He tried to cash in on berries up in the Willamette Valley. Got squeezed by mega agribusiness groups. Finally, he'd gone off to run cattle in Honduras. The place here stood empty for decades. It was just a few years ago that my cousin had been glad to deed it to me. But the first time I came here was only a few weeks back.

"Your family sure fits the strike-it-rich-quick dreamers who washed into the West and swirled around for decades." She shifted her gaze to somewhere beyond my left shoulder, seeming to look more into time past than into the distance. "Why shouldn't I think you're here to continue their great American rugged individualism?"

A slight change of note in her voice touched the final words. She was working on something, but I hadn't figured out what. "No. I don't believe in that myth. My Uncle Jim believed in it, but he got beat out by gangs of those who didn't. My mother remained with her family in the Payette Valley of Idaho and earned her keep the old-fashioned way, as a school teacher. About the time I appeared on the scene, the family relocated to Boise."

"Okay," she said, "but you're here for some reason."

"Escape," I said.

"To Purgatory?" There was as much surprise as question in her words. But how did she know the name on my sign?

Maybe my unspoken wonder registered. Her eyes shifted to the porch railing nearest her. I followed her gaze to the saddle astride it and to the pair of binoculars hung by its strap from the saddle horn. She said, "I was on the bluff for a bit before you looked up."

"Binoculars but no camera?" I said, pursuing a suspicion.

She shook her head. "I don't use—or even own—a camera."

That solved two small mysteries: that she was not the photographer for the picture of my place that Stegman had on his computer and, second, how she had managed to read my sign from a distance. This left unanswered, however, the question of why she'd been studying me from a distance in the first place? Again, I let the question slide.

"Purgatory," I said, "A place for purging, for purification, for cooking the uglies out of you."

"You want to set up some kind of spa for escapees from cities?"

I shook my head.

"Or one of those residential drug-treatment facilities? Maybe for teenagers? Perhaps with a few horses so the kids can hang around large creatures with a slower heart rate."

"No."

"Why not? Both have been tried around here by several ranchers whose struggles weren't enough to make it on cattle or crops. Even ones with thousands of acres. Like that big spread over west of the Interstate." She studied me. "Not for you, huh?"

"To me, those ideas sound as rarefied as raising quarter horses. And about as likely to succeed."

She nodded at that. "So, it's about *you*, then. *Your* uglies, as you call them. Still sounds a lot like rehab. Have you checked yourself in out here, instead of into a mental hospital?"

I could see her point, which made me smile. "I think of it more as a getting away *from* than a running *to*. Picture those travelers to Canterbury in the fourteenth century, setting out from a tavern by London Bridge to escape the plague."

"And here I was thinking we had most of our plagues under control for the moment."

"Not the kind that destroys our language and kills thinking."

Her eyes glimmered at that. "It's been said, lose a language, lose a way of life." She paused, then added, "Many languages are endangered and go extinct every year. One about every two weeks, according to some estimates." She didn't sound sympathetic to my plague idea.

It was my turn to stare across the folds of sage. Light was shifting on the spectrum, reds toward blues. The weight of heat eased as our spot on the planet turned away from the sun. I imagined the tops of sage and grasses lifting in relief.

"I don't have in mind a language eclipsed by one of a more dominate population," I said. "This is about a dominate group warping, neutering its own language to the point that it no longer functions as a useful tool."

"Hasn't language always been a rather blunt tool in most hands?" she asked, using the same dry, unsympathetic tone as before. "It seems to me that through the ages it's been a slippery creation at best."

"True. That's why people devised safeguards. Rules of philosophy and logic. Principles of rhetoric. Even parallel languages of geometry proofs and mathematics. A scientific method evolved. Statistics. All set in place to keep us from getting tripped up in the fog of words."

"Such as lies, damn lies, and statistics?"

"My point, exactly. Even though you're trying to derail it." I hoped she didn't hear my exasperation. "Sure, twisted statistics become part of the fog. Madison Avenue built careers and an industry on purposely inverting or manipulating those rules of logic, of statistics, and the like. And the judicial system is rife with violations, and politicians do it as easily as—or maybe instead of—sleeping, and—look, we can chase this around for days. I'm only saying that it seems to me that for a long time folks could kind of roll with—even joke about—advertisers and politicians and all the other snake-oil grifters messing with their heads. But in the last few years of this plague I'm talking about, people stopped the jokes, stopped laughing about getting played. This disease set neighbors or strangers against each other, adult children and parents to shouting at each other, sent husbands and wives to separately walled silences."

"And you have a solution." She sounded more curious than skeptical, but it wasn't a question.

"I have? No, I don't. I'm not going to try to sell something I haven't even figured out for myself. I don't even know what my so-called plague is. All those people in each other's faces are only symptoms. Nobody seems to know the underlying disease. The Black Death pilgrims didn't know either. They could talk about symptoms, they could see the skin eruptions, and count piles of bodies. They had no idea what caused them. One of the best guesses of the time was a miasma that blew up the Thames on hot summer winds. We're about as far along figuring out this plague. Does this sound like I have a solution?"

"No," she said, with a slow shake of her head. I had a brief moment to reflect that she'd been admirably patient while absorbing my blabbing. "But something has me puzzled."

"Only puzzled? What's that?"

"Well, as you said a while ago, lots of this has been going on for quite some time. You said people have laughed it off, rolled with it. Symptoms, symptoms everywhere, but all your imagined pilgrims stayed home. Not even you jumped ship until now. Did the bodies start piling up to scare you out of town?"

I thought about that and found myself nodding. She'd pushed my imagined metaphor further than I had. "I think there'd been a body or two over the years," I said, "but we could just step over them and go on without thinking."

"What changed?"

"A while back—for some it now feels like yesterday, for others if feels like a hundred years ago. How long ago doesn't matter. Anyway, the country had an election that didn't turn out as most people expected. Some liked the result, some didn't, but either way, few had expected the outcome. It's as if all of them had not known who they were dealing with and got surprised."

"And you?"

"The world I thought I had been living in turned out to be a world I didn't recognize," I said. "Some of it was the overheated emotions on either side of arguments along with the politics and people involved. The election result was only another symptom, but suddenly the bodies had piled up. And I wondered, why?"

"So, you tacked up your horse," she said, "as long as we're dealing in images. But you didn't ride down to the tavern by London Bridge to join up with other pilgrims."

I said, "My turn to tell a story."

I described meeting a friend over coffee within days of the election I'd mentioned. He was as shocked as everyone by it. His idea of how the world worked hadn't included this possibility. His knowledge base had a deep crater. He told me he wanted to make a trip—maybe his version of a pilgrimage—to make a trip across the states to find out why people believed they needed what they had gotten. He wanted to fill that crater. His plan sounded to me like another *Travels with Charlie*, only with a more pointed purpose. I told him so. He said he didn't have a dog. We drank our coffee and talked about other things. As we were getting up to leave, he revealed that for his travels he thought he'd get a tee-shirt. Have it printed.

He ran a finger across his chest and said, "Printed front and back. 'I don't know anything. Talk to me.'"

On her porch, watching shadows start to overlap and the sage just begin to purple, she was in no hurry to fill the silence after I stopped talking. A horned toad climbed up one end the porch's bottom step, skittered along it, and disappeared off the other end without a sound.

"But Purgatory," she said, keeping her face turned away, maybe not wanting to make a greater challenge than implied in 'but,' "with a name like that, your place doesn't come across as the Welcome Wagon. You don't seem to want folks to come talk to you. Why not?"

"Talk? Are you kidding? There's the question I should have asked my friend. How can anyone talk? We can't agree on a meaning or definition of the words we once used to discuss our world and ideas. Even the value and validity of those safeguards I mentioned—everything from logic to the science—had been questioned, denied. More symptoms."

"Your friend sounds willing to try," she said.

"My friend has an abiding belief in dialogue that far exceeds mine."

I stopped and drew a deep breath. There was more to my setting up in Purgatory than a distrust of talking. I'd heard and read too many words. Didn't want any more. I felt drowned in words. A lot of them empty. It was getting harder every day to distinguish the empty from others that weren't. Besides, what use are the words in play, when cynics bend them to refute any attempt to live ethically?

"I need silence," I said. "I have to find my own words. I don't trust a world created from other peoples' words not to turn on me."

Now her eyes came around to mine. "The way you say that, your mistrust didn't start recently."

She was a good listener. I'd give her that.

The water level in the glass pitcher had sunk while we'd talked. She poured herself half a glass.

"Another story," I offered.

This one's about a nightmare, I told her. A childhood nightmare. Only one, but over the course of years, it came back many nights.

I don't remember when it started, how old I was. But I remember many times of waking up, crying, on the rollaway bed under the slanted roof of a second-story bedroom, usually with my mother sitting on the cot's edge, pushing the hair around on my head, saying, "It's okay. It's okay." So maybe I was four? Five? But had it started, the nightmare, at three, possibly? And I just don't remember waking up, or where?

What's more important: how young I'd been when it started, or how old before it stopped? I was at least eight or ten. By then, I'd come awake in a different bedroom, another slant to the ceiling, without a face tear-wet or a mother there. Just come awake with a hammering pulse, feeling creepy, and often not able to go back to sleep for some time.

"The nightmare's what's important," she said, reorienting my drifting tale. "Your story is about a nightmare that returns again and again. What did you see, experience?"

It was wordless, I told her, and colorless. Or rather, drained of all colors but two shades of sepia. Objects and people were darker, the space around them lighter, but the edges separating thing from non-thing varied in degrees of brown fuzziness, as if viewed through overlapping, drifting smoke puffs. Does that make three shades of sepia? Or more? I hadn't counted.

People in the dream were strangely thin and lumpy. Years later, when I first saw Giacometti sculpture of "Walking Man," the child still resident in my young adult self felt a buzz of instant recognition and wondered what might have populated the artist's dreams. Another tingle came seeing animated film characters where the body was line drawn with squiggles and crosshatching that shifted and lurched as the frames sped past the aperture. The second recognition was kindred to the first because the darker forms of the nightmare were always in continual, swimming motion.

None of that's what truly terrified me as a child. Not the vague sepia tones, the lack of words, the strange and morphing forms, the elastic motion. None of that. I was frightened by the contradiction between my visual and tactile senses. A telephone pole when grasped in the dream felt as thin as a pencil. A taken-up pencil was as fat as a tree trunk. The skinny leg of a Giacometti-man peddling by on a deformed bicycle was experienced even at a distance as huge bolder. What felt solid would separate into thin porridge or squirming cross-hatching and be seen clear through. The sequence of contradictions would accelerate in the dream in a smothering crescendo.

"You get the idea," I said to her. "Nothing was as it seemed."

Listening to the story, she hadn't taken a drink of water or so much as raised a hand from the bare-wood arm of her chair. Nor had she taken her eyes off me. "You said the nightmare stopped."

I nodded. "I'd had one during an afternoon nap. I woke up, shook it off, and started downstairs. There was a dowel handrail. When I took hold of it, it felt like a telephone pole. I recoiled like a scalded cat. After a minute, heart no longer pounding, I cautiously reached to touch it again. Normal. I caressed it all the way down the stairs. The nightmare never returned."

"Interesting," she said. "Not the dream. That's a different realm. Your sensory experience seems an interesting form of synesthesia."

"Not really. When I was older, I realized I'd come up in a house full of secrets—or maybe just one or two big ones such as being told my father was dead when he wasn't—and a lot of pretended realities, mostly about our family's station in society. Growing up, I'd had trouble making a coherent world. And in the nightmare, what I did synthesize from my waking experience and what I had been told about it was frightening."

Then she did move, to slide one hand across a smile before it got well started. "That seems a reasonable interpretation. But by synesthesia I meant the experiencing of one sense through another. Some people read or hear a word or number as a particular color. That's something of a classic example. A note of music might be sensed as a lemon scent. Your overlap of sight and touch could be a kind of synesthesia. With a twist."

"Oh, I heard synthesis." My throat was dry due to more sustained talking than I'd done in weeks. "You're probably right about the synesthesia." I decided on a drink of water.

We were coming into twilight now, shadows deepest under the porch roof. Against the lighter sagebrush stretching from us, she'd become a silhouette.

"We'd been talking about your Purgatory," she prompted so quietly I barely caught her words. "About why you came back here. I got two stories instead of one answer. I'm guessing they suggest a direction?"

My throat was no longer dry, but the back was stiff. I straightened and put down my empty glass. We'd drained the pitcher. I let out a long breath, cleared my pipes.

"It has returned," I said, "my nightmare. And now, sometimes even when I'm awake."

"And you think that's because, once again, you can't make heads or tails of the world—the hows and whys of its mechanism?"

I nodded. "I think my nightmare is another symptom of the gathering strength of what I called a plague. I think coming to Purgatory is my best bet to survive the disease eating away our language and reasoning tools. At the very least, I need to figure out how to live in that world without becoming infected."

She was silent and shifted her gaze to the diming outline of hills. I checked my watch but could barely make out the hands.

"I've taken up a lot of your time," I said, standing up. I gestured at where I'd been sitting. "Can I carry the chair back in for you?"

"Leave it," she said, coming to her feet. "I hope you'll fill it again. I can get the other things myself."

I started toward the steps but stopped in front of her. "I don't know your name."

"Judith Clearwater."

My laugh popped out before I could stifle it. "Sorry. I don't mean any disrespect. But your water was very clear and sure did hit the spot. Thank you." She seemed slightly amused more than put off, but she held her peace. I added, "I *would* like to come back."

She held out her hand. "You'll be welcome."

I took the hand, held it, and let go before I wanted to. Attraction wasn't what made me want to keep hold. I didn't want to break the feeling of connection.

"But don't get me wrong," I said. "I came here to find out about you. So far, I know only your name. Your turn next."

That gave her a chuckle. "Still wonder if I'm *Native American*?" She gave the tag a little twist.

"You do have a lot of information about them on the table in there," I said, pointing past the screen door. "There are those pictures, maybe it's your writing in there of what might be a Native language, maybe not. There's your Appaloosa out back and your story about the Paiutes."

"It that all?"

I'd felt sure of myself up to then. Sure enough to spill all that. But she'd brought me up short.

"No, it's not all," I said, "and whether or not you're Native is not all that makes me curious about you. No one thing has me wondering. There's a whole tangle of them." I paused to see if she'd comment. She didn't. I continued. "I have no idea who I'm dealing with in you, let alone what you think you're dealing with in me. But you listen. And that's another thing. It beats me what someone like you could learn from me. But I want a shot at finding out what I can learn from you."

I turned and went on down the steps and over to the Ranchero. Before I opened its door, I looked back. She was standing at the edge of the porch as she had earlier, leaning against the roof support post, arms now crossed, watching me through the deepening twilight.

"You've talked more," she said, "and, I'd guess, probably thought more, about your nightmare and plague than you have about that boy on his staircase."

"What about him?"

"What was his secret? What did he do to escape the nightmare's spell?"

"What are you suggesting?"

The slit of twilight along the western ridges closed, and the night's seep became a flood. Overhead, stars popped out and gave a steely sheen to the space around us but left the porch in blackness. I heard her voice more than saw her.

"Outside of your Purgatory," she said, "in the hills around here, there are many trails. Maybe you should go out there. Look around for that young boy."

That rocked me back. "Where out there? What trails?"

"Ask Woody," she said.

Terrific! I thought as I climbed into the pickup and fired up the engine. Just what I needed. I flicked the headlights on and off in farewell, turned the truck back down the drive.

I come here looking for the whats and whys of my world. Now I'd been sent on a personal quest through territory infested with snakes and threats of sunstroke. All in search of a child long gone.

5

Woody didn't even glance my way when I clomped into his saloon shortly before noon the next day. I'd slept in fits and starts, was cranky as all get out, wasn't there to drink, and was further put out by what I took to be his disregard of me or, at least, of my noisy approach. Still, I gentled the strike of my heels on the worn planks for my final half-dozen steps to the barstool.

As I sat, he raised one hand, palm toward me. I understood it wasn't a greeting and managed to keep my mouth shut. The dish of peanuts that was close by my hand he pulled off the bar and slid under the counter. He rounded up two glass ashtrays from the surface, held one up to the light and then dropped it into his soapy sink water. The other he lowered out of sight to the vicinity of the peanut dish. Ditto a maverick saltshaker.

"Just getting the breakables to safer ground," he said and leveled his appraising gaze on me.

I should learn that when Woody didn't seem to be paying attention, he was. Someday I might stop underestimating him.

"You know more about that woman than you pretended," I said.

"That woman would be Judith Clearwater?" I felt he'd tried to make it sound like he was making a wild guess among alternatives.

"You know damn well that's who I mean."

He wasn't ruffled by my vehemence. "I never pretend," he said. "Of course, I might leave this or that out. I know her last name is the same as a river's that shapes one of the boundaries of the Nez Perce reservation up north. Is that what you have in mind?"

"That's interesting," I allowed. I felt the grip on my petulance slipping. It gave me all the rewards of punching a marshmallow. "And no, it's not what I have in mind."

36

Woody leaned back against the counter under the saloon's huge mirror. With studied care, he folded the towel that had been hanging over one shoulder into smaller and smaller rectangles. I swear his eyes, half hidden by his lowered eyelids, twinkled.

"She tell you her story about the Paiutes' first encounter with the white settlers coming into this territory?"

"Yes," I said with a sinking heart. "What about it?"

The neatly squared towel got placed on the bar. Woody straightened the edge of cloth nearest him to a perfect parallel with that of the edge. "Nothing about it. She likes that story," he said.

"See? That right there—your knowing what stories she's got—that's what I have in mind."

He shook his head. "I'm pretty sure you have something else in mind." He made a micro adjustment to the alignment of the folded towel. "But maybe I got that wrong."

"You're pretty sure." I loaded that up with as much derision as I could muster, tired as I was. It was also all I could muster. Other than heap up silence. So, I built a wall of it—one of those tall looming walls that implies it will fall on the other person if he or she doesn't speak to end the quiet.

He couldn't seem to get the towel's position to his satisfaction. He spoke to the towel. "No shave, hair barely slathered into place." Words came slowly, as if he was working it out as he went. "The noisy walk of a pissed-off cat, sitting one leg up on that stool and half off it like you're itching to pounce."

Finally, he looked up at me. "What'd I miss?" He wanted to know.

"The dark circles under my eyes," I said. "Maybe."

He fussed more at the towel. "You look like you spent most of the night wrestling with yourself. Come in here this morning thinking to spread the fight around. I just don't believe I'm the main event, that's all I'm saying."

I pulled up my foot and put it on another of the stool's rungs, squared up to the bar, and leaned on both elbows. How is it, I wondered, that people who seem to have the least going on, so often have the most going on?

I decided to give it up. All my storming didn't seem right. Angry as I'd been all night, I hadn't felt this hopeful in I didn't know how long. My grievance, I guess, was that rather than my own efforts, Judith Clearwater seemed to have caused it.

Find the kid on the stairs.

That kind of cryptic statement usually left me skeptical. Yet all night long, I kept returning to the idea. And feeling foolish. But hopeful—different from optimism—nevertheless.

"That woman," I said, "she wound me up like a dime toy. I went to find out about her, and she pumped me instead."

"Sounds about right," Woody said.

I wasn't done complaining. "Stuff came out of me like sand from a cut sack."

"She's got the knack."

"I didn't even mind. Not 'til later."

"I've seen that from time to time." Woody was back to fingering the folded towel on the bar. "Men, especially. They open up. Feel exposed. Get resentful. Pick a fight, sometimes with fists, other times with something worse."

"How'd she do that?"

He shrugged. "Don't know her that well, do I?"

"Don't give me that. Or we'll be back where we started."

Woody glanced around, apparently for other breakables. "Ain't it great when someone right off proves your point for you?"

"You can mess me around all day, Woody. I'm not letting go." I thought I saw one of his fleeting eye-twinkles. "After hanging around here enough, watching you operate, I believe you don't need to know her all that well to peg her." He scratched his nose and arched an eyebrow in my direction. Maybe that was supposed to be surprise or denial. But he knew Judith Clearwater a whole lot better than *not-that-well*. "How'd she do it, Woody?"

"She listens," he said. "Maybe you noticed."

"Not good enough. Other people listen. You, for one. I don't roll out events of my life like used carpets."

Woody nodded as if that idea might be worth taking for a walk. "Sounds like you were working a backstreet *souk*."

What'd he mean by that? And what'd he know about *souks*, anyway?

Before I could react, he'd slipped the towel from the bar and snapped it out. "My guess," he said, "Judith listens between words, around the corners of sentences." He flapped the fabric open onto the bar. "She notices repetitions, shifting rhythms, changing tones in your telling." Starting from one edge, he rolled up the towel and folded the result in two. Wringing nonexistent extra moisture from the cloth into the sink, he added,

"She listens to where you were most exposed." The drops stopped falling. He was done. He looked over at me. "But maybe I got that wrong."

A quiet came hard on the heels of his last word, broken here and there by a clink or thump as he replaced the ashtrays, the bowl of peanuts, the saltshaker along with its pepper mate. I tried to imagine what Judith Clearwater could hear in all those inbetweeny places he'd listed, but I couldn't come up with any words to wrap around non-words.

"What else?" Woody asked.

"What else?" I snapped back. "What do you mean, what else? You're the one talking. You tell me."

"And you're the one who went all silent. It wasn't only her listening that got under your skin. What else?"

I sighed and considered ordering a beer after all. "I'm supposed to go hiking out there." I jerked a thumb over my shoulder in the general direction of everything beyond the saloon door.

"Where, out there?"

"I don't know. I'm new here. She said to ask you."

"Did she now?" Woody busied himself straightening the shelved glasses, readjusting the placement of the ashtrays and salt shaker, putting his eyes everywhere I couldn't quite see them. "Why'd she do that, do you suppose?"

"I'd guess it'd have something to do with your *not* being new here."

He nodded as if I'd put deep thought into that. His eyes got a distant look as if he were wondering about something. I thought I heard him grumble under his breath, "What's she playing at?" He came over closer to me. "She mention a direction I ought to send you in?"

I shook my head. "Not really. Kind of took me by surprise. I'd been talking about figuring out for myself how the world works and . . . other stuff."

He made a snort that was neither here nor there and gave me one of those sideways looks that had me thinking he was accustomed to sorting half-truths from the real *stuff*. Maybe he was turning something over in his mind.

Woody cleared his throat. "A long time ago there was this scientist-guy who said the first step to understanding everything—including your-self—was to understand the physical world, figuring out how it works and why."

"And my roaming around the countryside is supposed to make that happen?"

"You'll need a hat," he said. Squinting past my shoulder into the sun-lit outdoors, he added, "Oh, look, here comes your sidekick."

I twisted on my stool to look through the open door. Roger Steg-man, loping across the highway in our direction, was not a welcome sight.

"He's no sidekick of mine," I said.

"Tell *him* that." Woody pulled out a narrow drawer from his side of the bar and set it on top near me. His fingers rummaged through string ends, assorted washers, scotch tape dispenser, screwdriver, and the other of life's oddities that hold court in your standard junk drawer.

How it works and *why*, Woody had said. It felt like an echo of me talking to Judith. "Who is he?" I asked.

"You know him. He's the fella interested in all the real estate hereabouts."

"Not Stegman, dammit! Your old-timey scientist."

"Oh, him." Woody extracted a pencil stub and scrap of paper from the drawer. "Aristotle."

"Hey, Bitterroot Bob," Roger Stegman called from the door. I spun around. He'd come to a panting halt with a big grin on his face. "I was coming out from talking with Fred and Doris in the General Store and saw your truck. I've got something to show you." He motioned for me to join him at the window table.

"Beer?" Woody asked from behind my back.

I considered his offer. "Better make it water." I rose and started to-ward Roger. I managed less than six steps before I pivoted back to Woody. Leaning over the bar at him, I said, "We're not done, you and me," hoping it sounded threatening.

He smoothed his paper scrap on the bar. "I know," he said. "I'll fix up some kind of map and directions." He tapped his pencil on the paper.

"That's not the half of it, Woody." I drew another breath. "Judith Clearwater? Now Aristotle? You're piling it up."

I resumed my journey across the floor. "And *souks*, for Christ's sake," I added under my breath.

Over at the window table, Roger was setting up his laptop with the silky motions of a magician laying out his red cloth, top hat, and white-tipped wand.

6

Roger had tossed his Rod and Gun cap on top of his empty computer satchel. He still wore no socks between himself and his running shoes. *Please, Rattlesnakes, pay attention.* But he'd changed his blue tee-shirt for a red one. Couldn't tell if the cargo shorts were fresh. Maybe it's the only kind of clothing he packs. That would be one way to get more items into less space.

Roger started talking before I'd finished pulling out my chair.

"Last time we spoke, you didn't seem much interested hearing my initial offer for your place."

"No," I said. "And if you're going to start in again, we're wasting our time here. I'm not selling."

"Oh, you'll sell," he said, taking up his argument where he'd left off the first time. There was a sharp edge in his voice I hadn't noticed before. "You strike me as one of our Left Coast types, serious about progressive issues. I'm thinking money doesn't much interest you, but you like to be on the right side of progress."

Again, I shook my head. "I'm not a big fan of progress. Especially as it relates to territory west of the Continental Divide."

The last raised old Roger's eyebrows. "Really?"

"Excepting indoor plumbing. And hot water on demand, if I'm pressed."

"Everything west of the Continental Divide is a big chunk of land."

"Also, Public Health," I added. "Like understanding we shouldn't pollute our natural water supply."

"That's a great lot of land," he tried again.

"It is." I shrugged. "Also, I'm glad vaccines have pretty well knocked out polio and so forth."

His eyes were getting a faraway look. He brought the laptop screen to life and pulled up a map of the northwest American continent, from Canada's western provinces to the Rio Grande River dividing Texas and Mexico. State and province borders were sketched in dotted lines. A network of bolder markings coursing over all of them meant nothing to me.

"Fire," I said.

"Okay. Have a look at progress," Roger said, as if I'd been agreeing with him all along.

"I didn't mean, *fire away*," I said. "I meant, fire, you know, that burning stuff."

"Fire?" Roger face twitched. Whether his struggle was to control it or me, I wasn't sure.

"Sure. People learning about fire, how to start it, control it as a tool, cook with it, was maybe the biggest bit of progress ever. If you think about it."

He seemed to wrench his face into stillness and staple it in place with a hard line of compressed lips. "And *I* meant, take a look at the future." He pointed at his computer screen.

I fished glasses out of my shirt pocket and put them on. I scooted my chair closer to him for a better look at his computer. But I sat back, removed my glasses, and pursed my lips.

"And also, there's thread," I said.

"Thread?" The squeaky higher pitch in his voice warmed my heart.

"You have to admit, the woman who thought to twist strands into thread really gave the world something to hold things together."

Roger's blinking rate tripled. Looking beyond his shoulder, I saw Woody, a cloth and glass in his hands, had stopped polishing. Like the turntable on an old Victrola that slowly resumed turning as someone cranked it back to life, he went back to polishing. I replaced the glasses on my face.

Leaning toward Roger's screen, I made out two networks of lines, one of darker blue than the other. The lighter blue set I guessed were the major and minor rivers. The darker ones remained a puzzle. But one of the dark blue lines, I couldn't help notice, ran through the territory up around Rome and Jordan Valley, lately mentioned by Roger. And it sure looked like the line continued south, right through Purgatory and Woody's saloon.

What was that about? I stopped myself from glancing Woody's way. Did he know? Had Roger offered to buy the saloon, too? Had Woody accepted an *initial offer*?

I figured if this snake-in-the-grass was going to insist on invading my life and had run his blue line through my Purgatory, I'd better stop teasing him and find out more about what he was up to. My mood shifted, shading from light blue to dark blue to black.

Roger slipped a ballpoint pen from a pocket of his cargo shorts. With that movement, he went from loose and easy to excited animation. He pointed the tip of his pen to a light blue line separating Oregon and Washington on the map. "This you recognize, I'm sure."

"I assume it's the Columbia River," I said.

Roger couldn't have looked more pleased with that than if I were his bright sixth grade student. "Fourth biggest river in the country. And do you know, every couple of days enough water flows from its mouth—wasted into the Pacific Ocean—to meet the needs of the Los Angeles basin for a year?"

I didn't answer. He'd set my mind to replaying dimly remembered arguments from my childhood for diverting the Snake and Columbia River waters to California. Back then, a couple of bright senators, Henry Jackson and Frank Church, had outsmarted the promoters and ended their plans. Over the years since, I'd read hints of others trying to revive the scheme or some remnant of it. I now had a feeling that one of the schemers—or their henchman—had newly arrived in Fast Buck: this honey-tongued salesman of sudden wealth for no work other than the accident of being in the right place at an opportune time. Except, now, he was no longer selling my getting a bunch of money, he was selling his idea of progress. A curious shift.

"People say we're in the middle of a drought," Roger said.

"People tend to be partial to the obvious," I said. "The majority of people."

"Actually, we're just at the beginning of one that will probably last our lifetime," he went on like an upbeat undertaker, "maybe centuries, maybe longer."

"Only an amendment to your original observation."

"But we don't have to die of thirst," Roger chirped, swishing his pen like a magic wand. All he needed was that cape, top hat, and one of the local jack rabbits. "We can have progress."

He made his pen tip dance above the laptop screen. In British Columbia, he conjured dams on every sizable river between Vancouver and the Yukon. He pointed them out on the Fraser and on the upper Columbia River where it began not far below the ice fields of the Canadian Rockies. His pen tapped where more dams were proposed on all the rivers in between.

He wants to buy, not sell, I reminded myself. Yet his spiel had the cadences of a well-oiled performance. That'd be snake-oil. Why work so hard selling folks like me to take his money? It felt backwards. Or like a warning glimpsed from the corner of my eye.

"But installing dams will be just a start." His voice urged my attention back to his screen.

From one reservoir to another, and from one river to another, his pen traced the dark-blue lines. They represented, he told me, interconnected aqueduct and tunnel systems to divert the captured water into Klamath and Shasta Lakes in Oregon and California, then on to points south.

Absorbing the web of lines over the Pacific Northwest, I realized Roger wanted to buy my land, in fact, buy all of the land under those lines, not for resale at a higher price. He wanted to drown every acre of it. He and his Greater America River and Canal Development Project needed the land for the rights-of-way necessary to dam, store, and move all that water without outside objections from the likes of senators similar to Jackson and Church and those they represented. Roger and Company wanted to remove the land from private and public holdings and drown it. What could I possibly find either progressive or positive in such an idea?

"Think of the endless of miles of kayaking and river canoeing from California all the way north into Canada," he said. "It would create hundreds of jobs just to fill the demand for canoes and kayaks. Think of all the restored water-sports resorts. And of the thousands of jobs—jobs that have dried up from the drought—that would return to be able to service the sportspeople. Imagine the many new resorts and riverside parks that would be built. Jobs and more jobs."

About here I stopped hearing his promises for employing two-thirds of the Pacific Northwest. Jobs, jobs, jobs, I thought. Every grifting politician's and Chamber of Commerce booster's favorite pixie dust. They sprinkled it over whatever they were promoting to transform it into whatever the suckers imagined it to be. I wished Judith Clearwater could hear this demonstration of a world created by other peoples' words. More and more these days, smoke and mirrors.

And yet—I broke my own stream of thought—and yet, smoke and mirrors to distort or conceal just what, exactly?

"One glass of water," Woody called from his side of the bar. For a moment, I thought he had been listening and was being satirical. Then I remembered that I'd asked for the water.

Excusing myself, I went to fetch it. After Roger's spiel, the walk over had a dreamlike quality. I was back to what I'd tried to describe for Judith Clearwater. I saw an ongoing attempt to confuse, and I registered the generalized anger and upset that resulted. But I was still not able to name the source of this pernicious force, which had seemed to come out of nowhere and now was everywhere. For me, the mismatch between words about everyday reality and my experience of it were probably the cause of my reoccurring nightmare, both dreaming and awake.

At the bar, I reached toward the glass but stopped just short of grasping it and took a deep breath. Would this be one of those waking times when what I felt would grotesquely distort what I saw? I wrapped my fingers, one by one, around the object. It didn't feel like a barrel. It felt like a glass. Not a cask. Just a regular water glass. I exhaled. I noticed Woody watching, so I took a couple of gulps of liquid, hoping to look casual.

He moved over to wipe up the damp spot on the bar left by the water glass. "He do that to you?" He asked so quietly I almost didn't hear.

I shook my head once. "I do it to myself." I started back toward Roger, wishing it was that easy, that my nightmare, whether I was awake or asleep, could be connected to an immediate source. If it could, I wouldn't have needed to come to Purgatory.

I also wished I could shake free of Roger, get that map Woody was supposed to be drawing for me, hike out on the trails, look for my lost child as Judith Clearwater had suggested, and find out if in doing so I'd learn anything relevant to my nightmare.

Roger repositioned his computer screen to improve my ease of viewing. Apparently, he had decided to stop with the *jobs* pixie dust. It is possible, he burbled, to avoid most of those pesky Oregon mountains like the Siskiyou—his magic pen hinted their location—by grabbing the Pend Oreille waters.

"Most people never heard of the Pend Oreille River," Roger said, again breaking from his sales spiel. His pen traced a light blue line from the Idaho panhandle into Washington near the Canadian border. "It runs more water than the Hudson or Wabash or Sacramento rivers."

"It looks like what you're doing—"

But he was off again. More aqueducts-tunnels-catch basins to move the water south. Dark-blue lines intersected—and obliterated, in places—the upper Owyhee River in Oregon, the confluence into it of our Rattlesnake and Crooked Creek Rivers, and if I saw it right, exactly where we sat in this saloon. More lines crossed into Nevada, connected to the Humboldt River and Lake, miraculously augured thirty miles under the White Mountains on California's border, emptied into the Owens Valley and, from there, flowed on to slake the thirst of every person, animal, or plant from Los Angeles to San Diego.

"Imagine a green Mojave Desert!" Roger's voice carried the élan of a magician's *ta-da!*

I tried again. "It looks like—"

"Imagine all the water-rich farmland," he insisted. "All this desert"— he gestured to the Great Basin unfolding away from Fast Buck—"not brown and dry, but green, green, green."

Perhaps it was the repetition, the drum beat rhythm of green, but a sense came at me from nowhere: Roger wanted me to think about color, about water sports, farms of busy people—*he* wanted to concentrate on them—because, taking all that wide-open terrain as it is, the gaping immensity of it would suspend him in thin air. That, I suspected, troubled him deeply.

Or maybe not. I had no way of knowing what troubled him deeply. My idea amounted to surface description, hardly analysis. Speculation based on fleeting impressions, on a repeated word. If I wanted a world of my own words, I reminded myself, I had to avoid my personal smoke and mirrors.

"You're making water run uphill," I got in finally. "Most of those lines anyway. Can't say about all of them. But the places where I do know, that's water going uphill."

Roger shook his head and looked disappointed. His star pupil had failed him this time. "As it does now most everywhere in the western United States. From the Colorado River into New Mexico and Arizona. It's been done. From central California to the San Fernando Valley. We do it every day. It works. We're just thinking a little bigger here. A little more modern."

"This is the progress you mentioned? Your future?"

"This project will sensibly rebalance over- and underabundance of water among regions. It will solve all the West's water problems. It will generate tens of thousands of megawatts of surplus power—clean hydro-electric power."

He paused for breath or maybe to evaluate the look on my face, which, from the inside, felt baleful. I didn't bother to ask how many hundreds of thousands of those megawatts would be required for the pumps needed to pull all that weight uphill. The thing about pixie dust, the more you blow away, the more gets sprinkled.

"Water's the basic resource that all civilizations need to grow." he said.

I watched him blink at the dull thud of that appeal and gather himself for another try.

"Many people are enthusiastic about the project," he said. Was this his invocation to my herd instinct? A tribal appeal? "Citizens of Washington and Oregon like the hydropower and irrigation water. Even Canadians like all the money they'd get selling their water to Uncle Sam."

I stayed silent, tabulating this magician's sleights of hand. *Water, community, power, money* So far, this time, no *jobs.*

"Not to mention jobs." I saw him rein in his temptation to beat out, Jobs, jobs, jobs.

He also looked like he was drowning.

That my subconscious had delivered *drowning* to mind somehow pleased me. I thought I'd throw old Roger an anvil. "For every one of your boosters, I can imagine dozens of other people detailing how your project would cause the greatest ecological disasters of all times."

"You still haven't asked about my initial offer," Roger said.

"Not likely to." It was on the tip of my tongue to add suggestions for what he could do with his initial offer, but that seemed a waste of air, so I didn't.

I scanned again his dead-serious countenance. Seeing him as a magician had been wrong. His was not the work of silk cape and top hat. This was a pulpit calling. He believed. He wasn't the high priest by any stretch, but certainly a dedicated disciple. He worked for salvation. Not of souls, but of this vast space opening away from us. The longing I'd seen on his face the other day had come from a desire to transform the western landscape, to tame it, to transmute what was not comprehensible, controllable, or merciful to something that was.

Roger was another of the infected, not the disease. But he was a believer, and that made him as dangerous as any zealot.

And I'd glimpsed something else. As he'd cycled from one image to another on his computer, I'd seen flash by a larger map of the United State and Canada, from north of the Great Lakes, through the Mississippi and Ohio river basins, to the Gulf of Mexico. Overlaid on the map was a similar maze of lines. I was stunned by the staggering amount of real estate involved. Whoever was behind the Greater America River and Canal Development Project had bales of money available to pay for it. At least some of those investors would be very powerful people. Powerful and possibly not to be trusted.

Here with their business card was Roger, their representative. His magician's glove might not be velvet. Could well be chain mail. My anger at him, my hatred, dispersed as quickly as it had come. A chill ran down my back.

Perhaps my face betrayed this change of heart. He scooted his chair closer and leaned in toward me. He glanced from me to his computer's map and back to me. "Maybe you're grasping the scale of what's imagined here. You can see this project will be one of our technology's most powerful solutions to global warming."

"You expect—" I blurted and stopped, blinking hard, trying to believe what I'd just heard. "You actually expect to counteract the climate shift of our entire planet with a handful of dams and ditches?"

I had catapulted my exclamation into his face, and a shadow fell across it. He shrank back. His hands went all busy powering down and closing his laptop, stowing it in its canvas shoulder bag. He pulled his Rod and Gun cap firmly on his head, deepening the shadow across his eyes, except for the knife glint I saw at their centers. He stood.

"You'll sell," he said. "You can think about what I've shown you. Or forget progress. Forget about the money as well. I don't care. But consider your options. I suggest you weigh *our* options, too. Our initial offer is the most pleasant. For you."

Roger didn't expect a response and stalked out the door.

I took my half-empty glass back to Woody. As I put it on the bar, my hand was shaking.

He pushed his scrap of paper with his sketched map and written directions across the bar to me. I folded and stuffed it in my shirt pocket along with my glasses. My "Thanks" was as much nodded as spoken.

It felt like a long walk to the saloon door.

Outside, I scanned the terrain past Fast Buck's scatter of buildings. It looked like an even longer walk into the range after range of hills that rose toward the distant horizon. Where would the map in my pocket lead? And into what?

7

Early the next morning before striking out on one of Woody's trails, I was in the General Store, pushing money across the counter to Fred. My old water bottle had gone missing. I resisted, obstinate cuss that I am, Woody's insistence on a hat.

Fred revolved the new bottle I'd handed him so he could read the price sticker. "I'll give it to you half off."

When I entered, both he and Doris had seemed in bouncier moods than other times I'd been in.

"What'd I do to deserve the price break?"

It turned out I hadn't done anything. He and Doris had. Or more accurately, Roger Stegman had turned the trick.

First time Roger had come into their store, according to Fred, they didn't make much of him other than his sawed-off pants with all the pockets, but he was quiet-spoken and polite as all get out, tipping his cap to Doris and all. He'd been after a sack of ice so he could keep his rum and Cokes cool while he sipped them in his motel room. He asked how their business was doing. Seemed real sympathetic, listening to their estimation that business wasn't doing too much, barely enough to get by, to be honest.

As Fred related this last to me, I thought I saw a defiant look harden his eyes and narrow their corners. His brows lifted momentarily, as if to demand understanding. *It isn't us. It's the times. It's the place. We've done what we—I—could. Don't dismiss us.*

The attitudes in our country toward wearisome work for meager income that left him defensive like this saddened me. If that really was defiance I saw deep in his eyes, resentment was liable to hide behind it.

"Sounds tough," I said, hoping to sound understanding.

As for Roger, he had said it was a shame and gone off with his bag of chipped ice from the freezer against the back wall, shaking his head and saying that there ought to be something that could be done.

Doris and Fred had thought that was the end of it, and they wouldn't see the nice young man in the cap again until he needed a bag of Cheetos or Corn Nuts.

"For the salt," Doris said, returning from the back with my water bottle that she'd offered to fill. "You know, salt to fight the sweet of his rum and Coke."

I nodded to acknowledge this profound understanding of men's habits of trash food and drink. At the same time, I aimed a smile of camaraderie in Fred's direction. She's caught us out.

While Doris concentrated on wiping stray water drops from the bottle's surface with her apron, Fred shot me a wink that Doris couldn't see. Bros in solidarity. Even though I'd talked with them only a couple of times during the few weeks I'd been here, I now felt disloyal to Doris and bogus to Fred at the same time.

"But you asked about Mr. Stegman," Fred said.

Had I? No matter. He was already well into telling me that they had missed the mark on Roger Stegman. Fred related that he and Doris had gone back to what they'd been doing when Roger walked in again, which was tallying up their inventory, listing the items Fred needed to pick up on his next supply trip over to Burns. This General Store was hardly a Safeway or Albertson's, you know. They couldn't afford any of those eighteen-wheelers pulling into their cargo bay with their monthly order.

"Cargo bay," Doris laughed. "Listen to you. Maybe we should get one built."

I took a deep breath and let it out slowly to suppress a sigh. Although I was itching to hit the road or trail or whatever, I could tell this was going to take a while. It seemed like any information shared in these parts expanded well past a stark transfer of the basic facts. The listener got the whole provenance surrounding any fact with which the telling of it had been baited. It wasn't meant as a rhetorical trick. It was a way of life. I'd do better leaning into, rather than away. Come to that, a life built around storytelling must have its plusses, I reminded myself, seeing as how parables do a lot of societies' heavy lifting.

"Anyway," Fred was saying, "He'd come back, Roger had. He said we could call him Roger."

I'll just bet he did. My soul crisped and shriveled at the edges from the heat of dislike I was developing for Roger Stegman.

"He came back okay," Fred said, "but not for Corn Nuts or Cheetos."

Even before Fred told me, I guessed Roger had come back about real estate, about property, about Doris and Fred's General Store, specifically, and the land that bounded it. Sure enough.

"Roger had said he'd been thinking about our . . ." Fred stopped and squinted at the ceiling.

"He said he'd been thinking about our . . . our . . . what was it, Doris? What's the fancy word in your bodice rippers that means, you know, a hard situation?"

"Plight," Doris said. "He said he'd been thinking about our plight."

"Plight." Fred nodded. "That's it. Not your everyday word you hear often in conversation, is it? He could have said predicament. That's an everyday word. I would have remembered that one."

"Could have said pickle," Doris murmured under her breath to me. "But Fred would have pointed him to the produce."

Fred was plowing on. Roger had told them he just might know someone who maybe, just maybe, mind you, could be persuaded to consider buying their General Store. He couldn't guarantee it, of course. Nor could he promise a big sale price, seeing as how business wasn't booming. But this someone liked to dabble in things, kind of like a hobby. Roger thought he could talk up the General Store. If that someone got interested, would Doris and Fred think about selling? Once he got the ball rolling, Roger would be more than happy, of course, to help them dicker about the price.

Listening to Fred, I had to hand it to Roger. He might not be an angler. At least a few things he'd said had to be true. But he sure could drop different lines in different pools, play the river bank or midstream ripples, depending on what he was after. No promises of jobs or progress for these good folks. No greening deserts. No initial offer. Just the hint of simple exit from their tedious grind, maybe a little extra to see them on their way. My soul-crisping heat ticked up.

"Saves our bacon, so to speak," Fred said. "When it works out. We might be gone before you know it. So, you get the bottle half price. We need to lower inventory, not restock."

"*If* it works out, Fred," Doris said. "If, my dear." She gave his shoulder a loving rub while her cool eyes sought his.

In vain. He wasn't ready for a dose of reality from his wife, even if she sugar-coated it with affection. I thought this town wasn't named Fast Buck without reason.

"You said you were going for a hike," Fred said to me. "Which way you headed?"

"Don't know exactly," I said. "Some trail a little south and east of here. I'm following a map that Woody, over at the saloon, sketched for me."

"Ah," Fred ran his finger down a tax table, looking for the amount to add to the half-price of the bottle. "If anybody knows where to go out there, it'd be that Indian."

"Now, Fred." Doris's voice carried an edge. Their turn in conversation brought my ears up.

"Well, he is," Fred said. "Can't pretend he's not."

I thought I saw Doris straighten as she turned to face her husband. "Woody did his military, just like you. And he wasn't working a commissary supply group stateside, either, like some. His boots were in combat on those godforsaken deserts over there. He's American as you and me."

"He's still . . . strange." Fred's tight mouth had a stubborn look. He leaned on his fists over the counter to make his appeal to me. "I once asked Woody if those deserts were much different from what's around here." Fred went silent. Kept leaning my direction. Stayed silent.

"And?" I said, trying a minimum to prime the pump.

"Didn't say. Exactly like me, now. He gave me a look. Walked back down among the shelves there." Fred's head nodded a vague direction into his store. "Came back with something he'd forgot. Package of Uncle Ben's converted, I think. Gave me another look and said, 'Their deserts make ours seem lush.' Clammed up and started pulling bills out of his pocket to pay."

Fred rocked back off his fists and crossed his arms, as if to ask, What do you make of that?

"I see." I made it as noncommittal as I could manage.

"Well, I didn't," Fred said. "'That's it?'" I asked him. "Seemed a simple question, but he stayed mum, counting out his dollars. So, I put it to him straight. 'That's all?' But I didn't raise my voice like just now. I paid out his change. He gathered everything up. Went over there to the door before he stopped. Didn't look back, though. 'Here,' he says, looking to out yonder, 'Here, there's fewer airborne bullets,' and the screen door was swinging shut behind him before I could say hi, boo, or kiss my caboose."

I glanced Doris's way. She shrugged. "What he says he's seen sounds reasonable to me," she said.

"Not very sociable, though, was he?" Fred still had his arms crossed.

"Still . . ." Doris wasn't backing down.

Fred unwound and deflated a little. "Ah, nuts. You got a soft spot for him."

She laughed, and her hand swatted something invisible from the air. "Fred's talking ancient history."

"Last year," he said.

"Or more like two, Silly. You want to know what he's talking about?" she asked me.

Did I? I wasn't sure. But listening sure beat walking into the heat outside. I admitted to being curious about Woody, and this gossip had already solved the mystery of how he knew about *souks*. Maybe I'd learn more. In any case, Doris hadn't needed an answer to her question.

"Here's what hatched Fred's little green-eyed dragon."

She told me that when Woody first showed up as the new owner of the saloon, they'd managed to worm out of him that he didn't have any local family.

"I'd asked him," Fred said, "if he was from around here. He said his people—his *people*, mind you—were over further west of us. Didn't take us long to put two and two together. That's the direction of the Fort Bidwell reservation." Fred raised his chin at Doris, as if to imply that he'd made his case.

She gave him one of those pointed, coded looks that couples send each other.

He stepped back and said, "But it's your story, Doris."

She and Fred could see Woody was alone, she went on, tending the saloon, and in off-hours, keeping to the rooms in the second story at the back where owners lived. So, when he caught sick—it was at least a couple of winters ago—he kind of disappeared into those rooms. The saloon was dark, doors closed. No sign of Woody. They'd got concerned.

"*You* got concerned," Fred said.

"Fred!" Doris bit her lower lip. "I think I've got the hang of telling it on my own here." She turned back to me and got on with her story.

One evening there'd been a bit of snow falling. Those real tiny, you know, light flakes that just float down? Almost seem to hang in the air when there's no wind. While she described the snowfall, her eyes looked right through me to watch again the lazily drifting crystals.

Doris had prepared a double recipe of chicken soup and ladled half into her casserole dish with a lid, the blue one she usually used for her mac and tuna. Wrapped it up in a couple of clean dishtowels to keep it piping and carted it over. Place was dark, so she didn't even try the front door, but went around and saw a lighted window. Went up the steps at back. Knocked. Had to do it twice before any answer came. Or whatever passed for an answer that she took to mean come on in. So, in she went.

There was Woody in bed against the wall, sitting up with a book and blankets pulled up to his chin. He started to get up but got told, Stay put.

I imagined Doris could probably freeze a tiger at sixty feet with the same two words. Even though the idea tickled me, I managed a straight face.

She'd unwrapped the soup dish in the little kitchenette at the back corner and scolded herself for not bringing her ladle. She wasn't sure he had one. Or a bowl either, at least a clean one. To be honest, she'd more than half-expected to have to wash a sink full of dirty dishes before she could get started, but both sink and counters were clear of everything but the air over them. Found a bowl neatly stacked with two others in a cupboard. Soup spoon and ladle were shining in utensil drawers. She was having trouble keeping her face blank and not running her mouth with something she'd regret. Something like, "Who washed your dishes?"

But while she busied her hands with the soup, she let her eyes drift every now and then. On the walk over to the saloon, she had practiced ways of saying *never mind* to his apologies for the mess the place was in. Wasted effort on her part. Here was not the usual male den of clothes and towels and newspapers scattered about. All that was in sight, other than furniture, were his shoes side by side under the chair by his bed. Everything was so tidy she'd felt light-headed carrying the bowl of soup over to him.

He'd croaked a Thanks, and she got to trot out her Never mind, after all. Told him he could return her casserole dish when he felt better. No hurry. And she was out the door.

"Now I ask you," Doris said, "any of that strike you as something that should set a torch to Fred's imagination?"

Lucky for me, while I hesitated, Fred answered. "You didn't tell how your empty soup dish came back."

Doris didn't seem the type to blush, but a light pink warmed her neck and cheeks. Her gentle smile could have opened the gates of heaven.

"It was filled with chocolate truffles," she said. "Woody knows I love my chocolate. He must have driven all the way over to Burns and back, to the See's shop there." Despite her smile, her eyes sparked to warn me and Fred not to make more of it.

"I only said you got a soft spot for him."

"It was just a nice way of saying thank you," she said. "And you didn't mind eating more than one, either." Fred pursed his lips and nodded.

Despite their back and forth, or perhaps on display within it, maybe it was a sense of gentleness that ran through all, but it was obvious that these two adored each other. Why or how? I wasn't about to try to figure out.

Doris turned back to me. "There was one thing I noticed that evening."

"There's more?" I had plenty to think about as it was. Like why had it never occurred to me that Woody might be Native? Did his camo hat mislead me? Short cropped hair? The OCD behavior? He wasn't white, but maybe I was so used to seeing Hispanics or Middle Eastern folks running stores that I'd placed him in one of those groups without thinking. I hadn't thought about it one way or another, that was sure, and I wasn't going to have time to now.

"Hold on to your socks," Doris said with a firm nod. "Woody's a male, living alone, right? Along with my other assumings, I'd expected to find piles of those glossy magazines laying around, if you catch my meaning."

She paused. I nodded once and braced.

Shaking her head, Doris said, "Thinking those kinds of thoughts didn't do me any good, either. No magazines, only two books on his bedside table, in addition to the one he'd been reading. Oh, and there was a couple of three-shelf bookcases on one wall, both stocked with books. But here's the kicker. I got a glimpse of the cover of what he was reading, just before he caught me staring and turned it over onto his blanket so I couldn't see."

She'd paused again, so I said, "Yes? Was it racy?"

"Racy!" She snorted. "My Aunt Fannie. It was Aristotle."

"Aristotle?"

"You know, the philosopher way back when. I spotted others in the bookcases on my way out. Imagine, Woody reading about a philosopher. What do you think of that?"

"I never know how to figure why people read what they read," I said. But now Woody has even more explaining to do.

"I don't care what he reads." Fred had his stubborn look back. "He's not really one of us."

Doris's spread hands asked, What's a person to do?

I wondered if what Fred had going on wasn't so much jealousy as his resentment looking for something safe to be outraged about.

"This has been interesting," I said. "But I must get going before I bake out there."

"How about a hat?" Fred pointed to a rack of them near the door.

"Not this time," I said, collecting my water bottle and change from the counter. "But many thanks for the price break. And for the water." I made a drink-toasting salute with the bottle, first to Fred and then Doris and high-tailed it for the door while I had the chance.

I made a show of hustling myself into the pickup in case Fred or Doris were watching.

The heat already collecting inside the cab was real enough, even with the windows down. Even the steering wheel had heated to the touch. Ordinarily, I would plan to get out by six or seven o'clock at the latest to take advantage of the night's cooling. In past years, I would have wanted to be on the trail by then, but these days that was asking too much of my old lazy bones. And my scrabbling around for my misplaced water bottle slowed things up. Now I was going to pay and cursed myself for dawdling in the store.

As captivated as I just had been in learning about Woody, I was eager to get out and walking. I still chafed from my attempt last night to write something—anything—that might begin to restore my peace of mind or sense of security. The page stayed blank, or I tore up paragraphs of nonsense that I stuffed into the trash. I wasn't any further in regaining some capacity for collected thought or useful action. My country's lurch in direction that had driven me to Purgatory remained, in my mind, too extraordinary to believe. The events *must* be extraordinary, in the sense of unusual, or outside of ordinary rules. The whole thing was an accident, simply a random collision of unknowns.

I'd given up, turned off the lights, and slid into bed.

Now, starting up the Ranchero, I felt another turning over, one deep inside myself. I remembered something had insinuated itself between my thoughts and feelings just like the way I had slid between my sheets. A nagging suspicion whispered that I hung onto disbelieving the country's turn of direction to protect myself. That stubborn disbelief allowed me not to confront the underlying wreckage of my basic concepts, of all those abstract ideas used to define myself and, for that matter, my country. Not knowing what and how much had been wrecked and how badly was what had unsettled my mind and emotions in the first place.

Contemplating the wreckage for the first time, although as if from a distance, and while feeling an urge to go closer for a better look, yet reluctant to take a first step in that direction, left me fighting for sleep, which had eluded me long into the night.

And now, sitting on the hot vinyl of the Ranchero, I didn't like feeling that Fred's resentment had fed his intolerance of Woody's differentness. Something about the resentment and intolerance had resurfaced the memory of my last night's tossing and turning. Something about it felt very like the specters that had troubled my sleep.

I gunned the pickup onto the highway and headed south. Only a few isolated clouds cut the sun. I was more than ready to see if there was anything to Judith Clearwater's idea about finding my lost child—or would I dismiss it as nonsense?

$$=== 8 ===$$

Behind me, from the bed of the pickup an annoying *clackity-clank* sounded in response to road bumps. I guessed the metal bed was getting knocked by the working end of the ax or shovel or both I'd tossed onto a folded canvas tarp before driving out. A collapsed canvas bucket rode under all of it. I wasn't likely to take on a range fire today, but growing up with rules about travel in primitive areas makes old habits die hard. Besides, I had no idea where Woody was sending me. I'd also checked the air in my spare tire when I filled up the Ranchero's tank at Millie's.

The highway south had unreeled peacefully for the past half hour. My only company were a single hawk sitting on a power pole and a couple of magpies dining on roadkill. Sighting the highway mileage marker named on Woody's map, I slowed and located the road running off to the left. The ride was about to get slower and rougher. If I did this again, I'd have the sense to fold those tools inside the tarp.

The pickup swayed crossing the uneven seam at the intersection, and I headed east. My tools clattered.

The road looked graded and maintained pretty well, maybe for the big stock trucks used to move White Face cattle out here for summer grazing. At least Woody hadn't sent me into untracked wilderness.

The sweep of sagebrush in every direction was unremarkable Now at a slower speed, the pickup's motor established a low harmonic with the rumble of tires over the dirt road's rippled surface. No doubt that would turn to heavy washboard after a thunderstorm. The hum, coupled with an even vibration of the steering wheel and seat back, deepened my already drowsy state. My mind drifted back to Woody behind his bar, asking about what Judith Clearwater had said to me, then refusing to meet my eye, and under his breath, wondering what she was playing at. I had wanted to ask, "What possibilities are you considering?"

But I hadn't asked, and there was no use to my being back there, then, when I could be out here, now. I pushed the question aside, thinking later would be soon enough to ask Woody.

Although I could see signs that a fire had burned through this range some years past, the expanse of passing sagebrush continued in its sameness. It reminded me of decades earlier, when as a child peering out our car window while we sped along southern Idaho's mind-numbing desert, I had joined thousands of other similarly car-bound children and their parents eager to spot a billboard that read, *Boring Ain't it?* Everyone had agreed. Me, too.

Yet as always, watching a desert panorama slide by for hours, I was content. It was easy to remember why. At a summer's midday, the landscape can be as stark and unforgiving as a thunderbolt, or at dawn and dusk, as subtle and gentle as a mother's touch. Sunlight tints it according to the time of day. Shadows pattern it, cast by overhead barges of cumulous clouds, the darkness of their flat bottoms indicating the quantity of moisture within their white-wrapped loads. Well, not this day so far, but there, in the long distance a pale flotilla was taking shape. Which reminded me: rain. The scent of newly wet sage beats that of any incense or perfume in the world. But I wouldn't smell it today.

The engine's pitch dropped. The pickup bucked as the motor lugged. Snatched back from romanticizing, I downshifted and brought the revs back up to cope with the steepened road grade. When it eased a bit, I shifted up again and increased my speed and quickly realized my mistake. On this incline, the washboard was deeper. The tools in back clattered along with my teeth. I downshifted again, slowed, and exhaled. No sense rushing something that didn't want to be rushed, and the roadbed of loose shale wasn't about to be rushed. I concentrated on finding the least corrugated line and avoiding rocks that could cause a blowout. The summit didn't look far off.

At the top, I coasted to a stop without pulling onto the shoulder and cut the engine. Silence settled around me at a pace that matched the languid dust lifting from my wake and drifting apart.

When I got out and swung the door shut, the *bang* in the quiet sounded like a collision. The rustle and bump as I restowed my ax and shovel entirely inside folds of tarp also seemed a wildly loud activity and made me feel self-conscious. The crunch of my boots on shale accompanied me and my curiosity around to the passenger side of the pickup. After retrieving a map from the glove compartment, I left the door standing open and was about to open the map on the simmering hood of the truck but just in time thought better of it. I walked to the back, dropped the tailgate, and opened the map on the bed.

As near as I could tell, I was crossing a flank of the southern end of the Strawberry Mountains. *Strawberries? Here?* Maybe somebody had found some wild along a nearby stream or river bottom. This pass was probably around six thousand feet. Folding the map, I turned a slow circle. My personal dimension shrank against the ever-receding expanse.

Like rollers from an ocean, wave after wave of mountain ranges as far as I could see. As always when faced with similar vistas, I imagined the dropping hearts of those who had walked this landscape with wagons and animals and children. Top a rise after hours, perhaps days of struggle, only to confront another height lying ahead. And see more further on. And keep walking.

Other than dogged determination to put one foot ahead of another, I couldn't guess what they thought or felt. They'd had no idea about this continent. Nothing in their lives had prepared them. So rather than no idea, they held a wrong idea. I recalled latter-day indulgent accounts that related how their concept of land dimensions had fooled them. I tried to see this terrain through their misled eyes. A mountain range as high, say, as the one to my left must be only a half-day on. And three days later, they were still trudging toward it. They didn't know folds in the earth came that big. Or that the folds could range onward from sunrise to sunset for weeks on end.

I took a deep breath, and the air came hot and dry into my throat and lungs. My lips were dry, tending to stick together, but I wasn't about to lick them. I had an aversion to Chapstick, lip balm, whatever. The stuff has a way of melting in a hot pocket and making a slick mess. Don't lick your lips, I recited, they don't crack.

And a hundred and fifty years ago, I wondered, did they know that, those colonists, those people who had not established themselves in a place where they were not indigenous? Or did they resort to plastering their lips with butter, animal fat, or axle grease? It had not occurred to me before this moment that those people had never encountered air as dry this. Nor known anyone who had. Except for those from Spain or northwestern Mexico, most had come from east of the Mississippi, east of the Alleghenies, east of the Atlantic Ocean, from places where rain fell regularly and humidity stayed at least three times the level I felt standing next to the pickup.

For the first time in my life, I visualized what they could not have realized they were *not* able to see. Humidity. Airborne water particles. Those invisible refractors and dispersers of sunlight that create a gauzy haze between the observer and far-off sights. The same white haze that Renaissance painters had learned to add in increasing density to give the impression of ever further distances. The water particles and haze that are absent in the West's Great Basin. Everywhere I looked, I saw crisp outlines of the landscape features.

The colonists' perceptions of distance were distorted not only by the mountains being bigger and higher than anything they'd ever encountered but also by the lack of moisture in the air. How many other of their markers for living were distorted for this new world without their knowing it? I shook my head for the benefit of any passing jackrabbit. They really had been strangers on a strange land with only a hope of reaching their goal to sustain them.

I recalled the Paiutes of Judith Clearwater's story and Woody's "people," as Fred had called them. For thousands of years, they have lived here, have not been *on* but *in* it, not straining to reach a distant goal but already home, not foreigners to alien landscape but participants within familiar spaces. No wonder they did not view the newcomers as pioneers or settlers or even colonists. Those very alien ideas they were taught later. At first the newcomers were just a curiosity, but soon after they were seen as invaders.

And those two groups, the Already Here and the Newly Come, crossed paths.

What words had we exchanged, Judith and I? *You never know who you're dealing with. You never know what someone else thinks they are dealing with in you.*

And I'd accused her of being trite. My skin now crawled with embarrassment. I slammed shut the tailgate and fastened the latches, hoping to shake off the feeling. It only got worse. It hadn't occurred to me that she might have been thinking about two totally different perspectives, two mindsets, worlds apart, crossing paths back then.

I worked on getting my mind around the idea while I put the map back in the glove compartment, closed the passenger door, and climbed in behind the wheel. Then the memory of Fred's intolerance of Woody's *people* jolted me further, and I felt doubly stupid.

Our paths are crossing still.

The remainder of the drive to the trailhead marked on Woody's map went faster than the climb up the Strawberry Mountains. I had found the well-marked intersection of dirt roads and had driven more directly south for about forty minutes before squeezing into a small parking space not far from a damp stream bed.

I hadn't seen another soul since leaving the main highway. Did Woody think that my trying to understand for myself how the world works would best be done in a landscape of solitude?

A note scrawled on his map said, "follow streambed," with an arrow pointing to a line on the paper. Seemed easy enough, so I hopped out of the Ranchero, grabbed my daypack, pushed my arms through its shoulder straps, and went off between willow thickets.

Except for having to bob and weave around, under, and through the willows, the walking was easy enough. For the most part I stuck to dry gravel channels, but now and then I'd have to step from rock to rock or even ford the stream to a more passable way on the other side. The fords were shallow but sometimes wide, so it wasn't long before my boots and lower legs were wet. The cooling effect was welcome. As long as I didn't keep at this too long—and I didn't intend to, lost child or not—I thought I'd not get blisters.

The way was uphill just enough to be noticed. Still, I was enjoying myself, getting back in the swing of rock hopping and picking a route of least resistance. Here and there I glimpsed a flitting wing or tail feathers or heard the calls of redwing blackbirds and western meadowlarks.

I also heard my breathing increase and felt my heart rate rise. While the thickets provided some shade when they arched over my path, they also trapped the heat. My cotton shirt was soon as soaking wet as my pants cuffs. Reminding myself that I was further north from being thirty-nine years old than Woody might suspect, that cell phone reception out here was probably zero, and that I was alone. I guessed some kiting turkey buzzards would find me before any help he might dispatch from his saloon. I slowed to a more sensible pace.

Going slower, I could look around more widely. While concentrating on picking a path and minding where to step, I hadn't noticed the canyon walls rising on either side. They were now higher than when I started out.

I remembered being often surprised by how the western desert plateaus often disguise or hide these deep gouges in the earth's crust. I recalled seeing them from an airplane window at thirty thousand feet and thinking of claw marks by a gigantic mythic cat.

A large knot of willow thicket blocked my way. Maybe Judith Clearwater thought my lost boy, like Sleeping Beauty, lay behind tangled growth.

There was nothing for it but scramble upslope and boulder-hop around the tangle. I used to like this sort of exercise. At least the elevation above the creekside willows gave me a look up the canyon. The pallet of soft green against pink and grey rock against blue sky was satisfying. And now higher, I could traverse the slope above the willows.

Or not.

I hadn't gone far before a tall abutment of rock blocked the slope. I saw no slot to clamber through or safe path to edge around it. Back down I went, thinking *staircase*, thinking *maybe the kid will show up here.*

Daring myself to see this oversized landscape as anthills in sepia browns, I paused my descent and looked around. On either side rose heavy shoulders of cliffs and rounded outcrops that went up at least two to four hundred feet above me, their grey rhyolite stone tinged pink where the sun touched it just right. Not a sepia tone in sight. Nor any sign of my waking nightmare.

I regained the streambed and grabbed the largest willow shoot nearby, willing it to feel as huge as a giant redwood in my hand. It didn't. I grabbed a twig. How about only as large as a telephone pole? Still no dice.

Everything I touched felt as it should, everything I saw looked normal. No shapes with fuzzy outlines. No haze of sepia tones. No fidgety squiggly lines. And no sign anywhere of a lost boy.

I couldn't force the waking nightmare any more than I could force the appearance of Clearwater's lost child. I reminded myself that the nightmare—when asleep or awake—was especially terrifying precisely because I *couldn't* control it.

To be fair, she probably hadn't meant that I should force the child's appearance. I decided to see out this so-called trail of Woody's and call it a day.

A little further on, another canyon branched away to the west. A huge rock tower rose from a gravel bar, tall enough to cast a welcome shadow. I started around it, but on the south side found an opening to a cave. The inside looked invitingly cool.

Rattlesnakes would like it, too, I reminded myself with a tinge of having dodged a bullet purely by luck. Today I'd been careless about where I stuck my hands and placed my feet. I edged closer to the cave mouth and peered in. No movement. No hiss or rattle. Seeing nothing on the floor but sand and gravel, I crept in.

It was bigger inside than the cave mouth suggested. The floor was dry. I slipped off my daypack and sat, grateful to take weight off my legs and escape the sun.

Doris and Fred's bottle that I pulled from my pack still felt cool, and the water went down in gulps. I decided this was a perfect lunch café. Before settling in, however, I removed my boots, shed my socks, and stuck the latter onto a hot, rough rock surface just outside in the sun.

Inside the cave, I sat back against the cold wall and sighed. I wiggled my bare toes. A brief rummage in the dark daypack found the PB&J sandwich I'd assembled in the Airstream. Munching, I reflected that the morning seemed long past.

Slowly, my eyes adjusted to the dim light inside the cave. Something about the far wall looked out of place. I finished the sandwich, pushed the plastic bag into my pack, and moved over for a closer look.

On the rocks were a spiral line, two others parallel, one more that was wavy, a couple of other shapes that could be symbols or depictions of objects. One did seem to have four legs and one end different from the other. I couldn't tell if they were meant to be in a related series to tell a story or make a statement or were just a collection of random symbols. Any meaning was lost to me.

They appeared to be more painted on the rock surface than chipped into it, but in the dim light I couldn't be sure. I reached fingers to touch but stopped myself. Why contribute to their disappearance? Whether they were pictographs or petroglyphs didn't matter. Whichever, I was late to the party by more than a thousand years.

Making another dive into my daypack, I found the small spiral notebook and pen I always traveled with. I hoped the sketches I made would be enough for Judith Clearwater to tell me what they said. Or Woody, although he did not have a dining room table littered with pages of what could be a Native language.

My drawings didn't take long to complete, but the originals were a reminder that I had been long interested in Native place names in particular and descriptions of western landscape along with its creatures and plants in general. One or the other of them might know something about such things. Already I wondered what I'd learn by asking.

Outside again, with nearly dried socks and boots on once more, I pushed to my feet and set out. And groaned. I had sat still and cooled too long. My leg muscles telegraphed nasty messages about my lack of youth and conditioning. I told myself to be more sensible about attacking the rest of this trail.

Trail? It didn't feel like I'd traveled much distance beyond the cave before the canyon was blocked by a sizeable water pool between vertical cliffs.

I went searching for Woody's map in my shirt pocket. He had diligently indicated the pool on his sketch. "Pond," it said, an arrow pointed at a circle on the paper. Perhaps he knew this water obstacle was created by beaver. A second line on the map led my eye to another minute scrawl: "Try left side."

Try what, I wondered? Swim or wade? The left side, near rocks and willows, looked shallow as far out as I could see, although rolling up my pants legs would be a waste of time. I opted for wading and stepped in. I was slowed when the water reached my thighs but pushed on and soon climbed out dripping. Not bad. It was worse realizing I'd have to ford that again on the way back. I squelched on.

More gravel stream bed, more willow thickets, other beaver ponds to wade or dry hillsides to scramble up to get around them. This section of Woody's map felt a lot more difficult than the one before my pause. It was a matter of terrain more than my flagging body.

One thing was definitely missing. Any suggestion of a trail. Pausing for breath on a dusty slope, I again consulted the map. A single arrow pointing, which I now realized indicated not a path but a direction. No clues about a trail or landmarks.

"What the hell, Woody?" I said out loud toward the nearest boulder. Looking ahead, I had the distinct feeling that I could continue walking until I dropped. Not a good idea. Turning around, I scanned the way I'd come. Best that could be said about it was that going that way would be generally downhill.

A gliding form caught my eye and disappeared against a distant cliff. About half way up the canyon wall, I made out several stick nests. Aeries of Golden Eagles. I wished I could fly home, a fantasy that made me even more aware of my fatigue.

The sky remained clear, but my watch told me that there weren't many remaining daylight hours. Prudence insisted I should start back. I didn't want to be on the secondary roads after dusk, and if I got going now, I should just about make the Airstream by dark.

On the trek back, I regretted not stumbling across anything resembling a lost boy, my own or any other. But I was reluctant to give up Clearwater's suggestion, a feeling that surprised me. That feeling, I realized, plus the experience of being one of the Newly Come among the Already Here, the less pleasant one of recognizing Fred's intolerance of Woody's *people*, a collection of petroglyphs or pictographs, and a reminder that I wanted to learn some Native place names and landscape descriptors— this hike had delivered much to think about.

Assuming I would make it back without mishap.

I unfolded Woody's map, gave it one last look, and shook my head. As he had about Judith Clearwater, *I* now wondered what *he* was playing at.

9

The day after my canyon walk, the luminous sky felt lower and wider than usual, thanks to hundreds of passing stacks of cumulous clouds in blinding white. When I walked into Woody's Saloon, the early afternoon light filled the place like clear liquid from ceiling to floor.

He looked me over before I'd cleared the open doorway and ran a tall glass of water. He placed that on the bar just as I'd made it to the stool and sat. He tossed a Snack-Pak of chips after it.

"Best cure for dehydration," he said. "The water, I mean."

Drumming the fingers of one hand on the bar, I watched him pull my usual.

"Judith Clearwater told me to ask you about local hiking trails," I said.

I emptied the water glass, feeling slightly like the child eating his vegetables to be allowed what he really wants. Woody arrived with my beer.

"Yes," he said, "you told me about Clearwater and you." He scanned the bar's spotless surface, squinting a bit against the bright light glancing from it. Instead of reaching for his towel, he opted to refill my water glass. His movements were languid as a hunter's when stalking prey, only the glitter of his eyes betrayed interest in where I would go with this.

"Hiking *trails*," I said.

He nodded. "Got that."

"You call what you sent me to a trail?" I heard my words come out as about half question and half accusation.

He set the refilled water glass in front of me.

"You expected something different, I take it." He remained wooden-faced. But those eyes.

"The notion of trails brings to my mind something resembling a beaten track," I said. "Maybe with a trail marker. A blaze now and then. A stack of three rocks to assist the hapless traveler when a path goes vague. Anything that's more than nothing."

"Hapless traveler?" Woody scratched his ear. "You said, *hapless?*"

I spread his map on the bar, turned it his direction and thumped my finger on it. "Where's the trail?"

He squared the bottom of the paper with the bar's edge. Lowered his head as if to get a closer look. He ran his hand over the page to smooth the creases, all the while making a faint humming noise that seemed to come from deep in his chest rather than his throat.

"Maybe I should have suggested down-canyon." He slid his index finger in the opposite direction from the arrows on his sketch.

"There's a trail that way?"

"Higher cliffs. Longer runs of dry streambed. Less bushwhacking through willows or jumping boulder to boulder."

"Trail?"

"About the same. Going north, though, after the canyon joins the Owyhee River, you could probably hike into Idaho if you wanted."

"That's not the point, Woody."

He turned the piece of paper over as if to see if there was something he'd scrawled on the reverse side. "I thought you said the point was you wanted to figure out for yourself how the world works. But maybe I got that wrong."

"What's that got to do with my trail question?"

"I thought you were serious about the *figure out for yourself* part," Woody said.

"I was—am," I said, "even though that part was really about my finding my own words for describing the world, maybe explaining it."

"*For yourself,*" he said.

"Yes," I said. "And?"

"So, you want to find out for yourself how the world works, but when you go out into the physical world, now you want beaten tracks and trail markers for when the trail goes vague? Don't all those things come from people who are *not* yourself?"

I took a long look at Woody's straight face and his gimlet eyes managing to be friendly. He stood there, not a muscle twitching, waiting for me, his cornered quarry.

I shook my head, sat back, and said, "You are one clever fox, you are."

He thought about that for a hot second. "Probably more coyotes than foxes around here."

I sipped my beer to buy time. Setting down the glass on the bar top, I saw a straw to grasp. I grabbed Woody's paper, flipped it over to his sketch and directions, and slapped it down.

"But you *did* give me a map!" I did a poor job of suppressing a note of triumph.

Woody's nod didn't give me confidence. "A map is not the territory," he said.

"That fact did come to my attention," I said. "And why does what you just said sound familiar?"

"The idea's been around almost a hundred years. General Semantics got started with it."

I was shaking my head again. "Semantics? How does semantics end up on a hike with me?"

He shrugged away my suggestion of outrage. "*General* semantics," he corrected. "Korzybski, the man who started talking about *a map is not the territory*, was reminding us that a map is only an abstraction of the terrain."

"Big deal," I said, unable to filter the scorn from my voice. "Sounds like a lawyer's boilerplate disclaimer for a cartographer's product. You know, *this map may cause confusion, loss of direction, or climbing a mountain you hadn't expected. Use at your own risk.*"

Woody didn't look amused. "It wasn't a disclaimer for maps. It was a warning about words."

"Now we're back to those items I'm interested in?"

"We are. He was. Korzybski wanted to make the point that words—one alone, or a bunch taken together—are also abstractions about the world, the territory. Those abstractions, he said, were often misleading."

He pushed his map a few inches across the sunlit bar in my direction. "Words . . . Map," he tilted his head to one side, then the other, "sort of fits your situation."

That made me laugh. Had to. A laugh of recognition. "I never heard of your Korzybski guy but, boy, he would be in pig heaven today. You'd be his star pupil."

"You, more likely. You tested the idea, hiked it."

I chased my laugh with several swallows of beer. "You know, I get the feeling you could follow all this with a spiel from your Aristotle books."

Woody reached ever so slowly for the map paper. He folded it up more neatly than I'd done and handed it to me.

"You've been talking to Doris," he said.

It never pays to be off balance and run your mouth at the same time, I reminded myself. It wasn't the way I'd wanted to come around to the subject, but it seemed best to come clean.

I confessed that Doris found his reading material a surprise when she had delivered soup on the evening he'd been down with a cold or the flu.

He nodded. "Probably helped me get better. It was thoughtful of her."

I was eager to shift the line of conversation away from this subject that could turn ticklish if it shaded into Fred's intolerance of Woody's being *different*.

"But here's what I found interesting when I talked with them, her and Fred," I said and related Doris and Fred's whole encounter with Roger Stegman. "So, he's hoping to buy their store, too. Not just my acres."

Woody didn't look surprised. "My guess, he wants it all."

"All? All what?"

He swung his hand in a wide arc. "Everything around here. Couple of days ago, he offered to buy the saloon."

"You going to sell?"

"No."

"How'd he take that?"

"Kept pushing, like you'd expect."

I made a thing of looking around the empty saloon. "Appears he went away. How'd you manage to get that accomplished."

Woody considered both of the glasses in front of me. They were more than half full. Bringing his eyes back to mine, he said, "I told him it wasn't mine to sell."

"Really?" I asked. "Fred and Doris are under the impression you bought the saloon from the previous owners."

He nodded. "That's accurate. But then I deeded it to the Paiute-Shoshoni Nations Land Trust."

I sat back on the bar stool.

"That other impression they have, Fred and Doris," he said, "is accurate, too. My people are the Prairie Dog Eaters. Fort Bidwell rez," with a tilt of his head to the east. "Some say Groundhog Eaters."

"About those impressions, particularly the second one? Doris says you're just as American as Fred, you serving in the military and all." I wasn't sure why I thought I needed to defend her.

Woody nodded and looked out the window. A long look. He nodded again. "Doris is a good woman. But I didn't sign up to become American. Me, my family, been here since before it got that name. Military wasn't for citizenship. It was a way off the rez and to save some money."

My turn to nod. All this coming at once had me reeling. Cool glass in my hand and beer going down were both welcome diversions.

"Makes sense though, doesn't it?" Woody asked.

"What's that?"

"Stegman going after the General Store."

"What's sensible? He wants to buy up everything between the Canadian and Mexican borders. Nothing about his project is sensible."

In Woody's faint smile and raised eyebrows I read his reassessment that I was only minimally functional in his world, the real world.

"Buy the General Store. Close it. Everyone around here would have to travel to Jordan Valley or Burns to get supplies. Next to go would be Milly's café and gas pump. If you have to drive to Burns for groceries, why not buy the cheaper gas while you're there?"

"I get it," I said. "Besides just being plain inconvenient, all that driving around would push up the cost of hanging on here. Stegman's figuring to dry up resources in order to force folks around here to sell out to him or starve to death. Quick of you to catch on."

He didn't look impressed by my compliment. "Traditional tactic in these parts," Woody said.

"It is?"

"Worked for the U.S. Cavalry in the 1800s. Starved resisting bands of Natives into submission more often than defeated them in battle."

"I've read about senseless massacres, but this siege tactic is new to me," I said.

"Sometimes they just starved the helpless women and children to bring the warriors to heel. Later on, they kept food and resources from families if they didn't surrender their children to missionary boarding schools."

From somewhere he'd gotten hold of a towel and wadded it up. He now tossed it somewhere under the counter. He pulled out a drawer. From a neat stack inside, he selected a replacement and slid the drawer shut.

"Stegman may not be aware of his history," Woody added "but his impulse for killing to possess and dominate is pretty well hardwired into his culture."

Generous of him to label it *his*—Stegman's—history and culture. Woody and I knew that I shared both. His not mentioning me in the same breath didn't make the implication sting any less.

I could think of nothing to say. But his comment lit a match in my dark thoughts. Turning over what I found in there, I finished my beer.

Woody busied himself restocking the refrigerator's supply of bottled beer. I didn't see any green ones.

After leaving the cost of the drink and pack of chips next to the empty glass on the bar, I headed for the saloon door.

Woody looked up. "Late for an appointment?"

"In a way. Sorry, I forgot my manners and didn't say good-by."

He nodded. "See you later."

Thinking I owed him a little more, I added, "You set me thinking. I may not be able to stop this siege, but I've got an idea that might slow up Roger Stegman."

Doris replaced her smile with widened eyes when I asked if Fred was nearby so I could have a word or two with them. She rounded him up quickly enough with a solid Hey, Fred.

I let them know I'd been thinking about our conversation when I'd bought the water bottle. The two listened to me from behind their counter, curiosity and a touch of mistrust in their pinched faces and crossed arms reminding me that I was not truly from around here.

"Here's something to consider, if you're of a mind to," I said, "and have the time. About that idea Roger Stegman mentioned of buying this place."

"Shoot," Fred said. "And I sure hope he doesn't take too much time getting back to us."

"I suspect he'll return quicker than you might imagine," I said. "I'm suggesting you might think twice before jumping at what he first says he'll give you for it. His 'initial offer' he'll call it."

"He made it sound like it'd be a squeaker to get his friend interested at all," Doris said. "If that person comes across, why shouldn't we jump?"

"Do you know a Mr. Peterson, a rancher or farmer up around Rome, Jordan Valley?" I asked.

"Peterson?" Fred and Doris looked at each other. "Peterson?"

The name didn't ring a bell. I let them know about Roger buying the Petersons' acres and Roger's hinting to me that his offered price was sizeable enough to excite their attention. I suggested Fred or Doris do some checking around with folks they knew up that way.

"You're likely to form the idea that Roger has a lot more money than he pretends to have for buying up property around here. And a burning desire to do it."

I waved good-by to the surprised looks they exchanged.

Chuckling to myself, I thought maybe this Fast Buck mentality could work against Roger as effectively as for him.

But my chuckling faded when I remembered his threats about options. His options particularly, his and those of whomever he worked for. What price would I pay for this game I'd joined?

Back in my Airstream, I pulled my laptop from the cabinet under a wall seat. Feeling both optimistic and anxious about whether anything would come from this effort, I sat staring at the unopened machine.

For me, writing had been my way of finding out, and I was determined to find a glimmer of sense in some fragment of my recent experiences, starting with yesterday's hike, map or no map, even with any lost boy still lost.

Outside the propped open door, evening was cooling. But inside, my ears still burned from Woody's characterization of the instinct to starve out women and children being lodged in Stegman's culture. And mine. *Killing to possess and dominate.*

Just sharing any idea or instinct with ol' Roger made me queasy, but I had to admit the scheme did seem like the way of the world. History said so. Histories written in words by people other than me, Woody would remind me. Did—do—those words distort my perception of how the world works? Are those word maps *not* the territory? Are they more than simply poor descriptions, like Woody's map? Or are they misleading, maybe false?

And had Woody thought I'd find a different way of the world when he sent me into unfamiliar, unmarked territory with his "map"? If so, different how? His kind of different? Or mine?

I opened my laptop, switched it on, put fingers to the keys and typed a question.

What if I had gone out there or stumbled on the place without Woody's sketch and cryptic notes?

The clicking of laptop keys stopped. I felt my face stretch a grim smile of recognition. What I would do? I'd reach for another map.

Hadn't I pulled out a roadmap when I stopped at the pass over Strawberry Mountain? It reassures me somehow to use maps to anchor myself, kind of settle myself into a location. Reassures me about what?

My fingers floated, poised over letters, waiting for words to order the letters into sentences.

I imagined myself in the pass without the roadmap. Would I have seen anything different? Wouldn't I have been just as aware of the expanse of mountain ridges marching away in every direction? Most likely, I would have seen the endless land, the sky, the clouds. Been aware of the silence, the drifting dust from my tires. I might have even recalled the stories of the colonists trudging across it with exhausted children, half-starved animals.

Seen, yes, but what would I have *felt* without that roadmap in my hand? Or more to the point, without Woody's map in the depths of the canyon I hiked.

Then words came, filling the screen. My fingers tapped again on the laptop keys.

I let both maps fly away on the wind of my imagination. I relived yesterday's hike and my being a long way from help if I were disabled by a rattlesnake or exhaustion from dehydration or a broken leg, a hip. Alone and scared and mapless. Fear filled me from the toes up. It seemed that dread of the vast reach of distance and of my solitary, isolated existence in it was held off only by a thin membrane. Maps—or words, in other situations—are the membrane.

I imagined waking up in that canyon, without Woody's map or any memory of it. In which direction would I decide to bet on my rejoining other people? Downstream, as all Boy Scouts learn? Woody had said I could walk all the way into Idaho that direction. How long would that take? Would I meet anyone along the way? This seemed a very little traveled corner of western landscape. Which way lay safety and how would I recognize it if I stumbled onto it? The greater comfort of maps, I realized, comes not from pointing a way into the unknown but from showing the way home.

Again, my fingers paused, the laptop keys fell silent. Something niggled from another corner of memory.

I knew that lonely, isolated, lost feeling from sometime less recent. Then I was in it, reliving my growing dread.

The laptop keys went *clickity-click,* words flowed into the laptop, across the screen.

In the hours, days, and weeks immediately after the country's change of direction, I had also felt like I was walking in unknown, unrecognizable territory without a map, without words to describe what had happened, was happening, was liable to happen as the days passed.

Or more accurately, I had *misleading* words. Words that no longer accurately described my world. Nowhere lay a handy map that gave a useful picture of the territory.

Everybody, winner or loser, grasped for explanations, for words. But they found old words, other people's words, any words from history, ancient or last century. Politics, psychology, philosophy, religion or speculative fiction. But none fit, or fit poorly, incompletely, or worse, the words—the maps—that had once seemed helpful, accurate abstractions about my world, had become inadequate. Like Woody's map of the canyon, the word maps were not the territory. The result left people reeling, some in a nightmare, some reveling in their new political and social age.

There was talk of a division between two camps, some thought it a chasm. To most, it felt less like a rift in the landscape than like the camps were in separate worlds. The word map of one group did not match that of the other.

So, wake up in unfamiliar territory without a map, no recognizable trail markers, no indication of others having passed this way . . . lost, scared, solitary, a heavy sense that things might not end well . . . how do you map yourself out of that?

I stopped poking at the laptop keys.

Were the pictographs or petroglyphs in the cave someone's attempt to do just that? Figure it out and leave an indication of the lay of the land, maybe even a direction or destination?

Perhaps my coming to Purgatory was lucky. I had met Judith Clearwater.

Of course, the idea that she was the right person to talk to was based on an abstraction in my own imagination, another map, not of lines on paper or of words this time. More like a map of symbols: her long hair braid, her Appaloosa, a Navajo rug, the table littered with writings in a language unknown to me and that collection of pictures. She had said nothing to verify my assumption. I felt my own rueful smile. I had been surprised to learn Woody was a Native. Would I be surprised to find out she was not? I could find out soon enough.

Well, I'd now written something.

But what to do with it?

There remained Woody's accusation about *killing to possess and dominate.* Those five words hadn't been on my world map in the way he had placed them. I wasn't sure how to integrate them into my personal map or if I should draw a new one. For instance, were we, Roger and I, now, the same as those who had done that? Once fleeing unfairness, injustice, oppression and outrage elsewhere, had they—and now we—become authors of our own oppression and outrage against others? Had we brought that disease, that open wound with us along with our biological infections? Are we inflicting it still? Must it fester forever?

My fatigue was shutting down mental synapses by the millions. I'd run any line of thought as far as I could for the time.

But I was beginning to appreciate the advice of Woody's ancient buddy, Aristotle: if you want to learn how to live in the world, first understand how the physical world works. Given maps that are not the territory and words being similar abstractions, my whole enterprise now seemed more difficult than I'd imagined.

For now, the best thing to do was to save the file, turn off the computer, and try for a night's sleep.

I intended on an early start at Judith Clearwater before she rode out on her Appaloosa.

TIME

═══ *10* ═══

Early morning. The air was cool. I drove through crystal clear light to Judith Clearwater's place. She met me on her porch, probably having heard my pickup's approach as she had on my first visit. Calling ahead seemed so out of date. And why would I text or she answer? Would I even ask for her phone number from Woody? Would he give it?

My good morning barely cleared my lips before she spoke.

"I didn't think you'd show up again this soon," she said. Her warm voice kept her words from sounding like a challenge. I continued toward the porch.

"Remember when I was last here?" I asked.

"I invited you back."

"And I said my next visit, it would be to find out about *you*."

"I remember. I suspect you have a starting place in mind."

I lifted my chin toward her house and said, "Maybe with what's on your work table in there."

She turned back to the screen door, swung it open, and held it for me to enter.

Inside, golden patches on the wall announced the day's heat to come. We ended our transition to stand by her document-covered table.

"Is this what you're wondering about?" she asked, pulling toward us a three-ring binder that lay open to a page of handwriting I guessed was hers. She turned one after another of the pages to show others similarly marked.

"I think so," I said. "What is it?"

"A lesson plan."

I looked closer at one page. Only because of indentations, varying spacing between blocks of printing, what looked like headings and other formatting was I able to see some logic shaping a presentation. But most all of it was not in a language I recognized. The letters were Roman alphabet. But they ordered to form a sound I might guess at but even the sound would not be familiar.

"A lesson plan about what?"

"Paviotso. Or Numu, depending on your naming preference. I'm using the Wycliffe spellings"

I shook my head. "I can guarantee you I don't know enough to have any preference. Should I have?"

"Wouldn't know why. Both are names of the Northern Paiute language. It's a regional dialect of the Uto-Aztecan that was once spoken from Oregon to Panama."

So, her handwriting was in a Native language. My hesitation about asking her my questions dissolved. I'd come to the right person.

"Coffee?" she said.

We returned outside with mugs of strong coffee and the day warming fast. We put our coffee mugs on the small table between two chairs. After a little prompting, she told me that she was a linguist by training and a professor at one of the few remaining Ethnic Studies Programs at U.S. universities. She taught Native Literature, if that detail mattered to me. Currently, she was using a six-month sabbatical to give a writing class as well as speaking Paviotso at the reservation school south of us, near the Oregon-Nevada border.

"I think I mentioned before," she said, "people warn us, lose a language, lose a way of life. We're trying to slow both losses through a larger effort to save and revitalize Native languages."

That shed some light on what she'd called her lesson plan. But many of her other pictures and documents looked like they were intended for something else.

"Your sabbatical seems a bit of a busman's holiday, taking a break from teaching to do more teaching, if you see what I mean."

"You mean, what about all the other material spread out on my work table?" She smiled and looked down at her hands folded in her lap. "I'm also hoping to find a way to write something that's not academic

. . . something of my own, from me, that imagines another world about Native way of life without any comparison to concepts of nationalism . . ." Her voice trailed off. "But I don't talk about it much."

I sympathized with her hesitation.

We had a go at our coffee and let a silence grow. Each of us, I suspected, followed our own thoughts about looking for another world away from anybody's nationalism. Wasn't that concept, nationalism, another of those ideas that I was trying to ignore in hopes of finding a satisfactory way of life outside other people's words? I was both excited by and wary of her personal writing impulse that seemed to parallel to mine.

"I'd like to show you something," I said, "to ask you about it."

I pulled out my sketches of the petroglyphs or pictographs. "I found these on a cave wall during the hike Woody sent me on."

She took the drawing from me. She smiled again and fluttered the paper in my direction. "No cell phone pictures? Was your battery not charged?"

"I guess I'm a bigger Luddite than I thought. It never occurred to me to take pictures. But if it had, I wouldn't have wanted to use the flash anyway."

"Why not?"

"These days, art museums usually prohibit the use of camera flashes. Degrades the art. I didn't want to touch those pictographs for the same reason."

She seemed to take a second look at me. "Thank you for respecting—I won't say the art in our museum—more like the art on the wall of a home."

I pointed to my sketches. "What do they say? What's their meaning?"

She looked at them again, a tinge of sadness or regret in her eyes, I thought. "There's a lot of speculation," she said. "But nobody knows for sure. They're likely over a thousand years old, and their meaning is lost in time. A part of the language that's disappeared forever."

She handed the sketches back to me.

"I'm sorry to hear that," I said.

"You're not alone. But why your interest? It seems more than simple curiosity."

I shifted my gaze to the raw miles of uninterrupted sage and dried grasses under the wide, blue sky. I slid back in time. The differences between this vista and the ones around where I'd grown up were mainly differences of contours in the terrain.

I was aware of her picking up my coffee mug. "I'll warm this up," she said.

It didn't take her long to reheat more coffee and refill the mugs, but it was enough time for me to collect my thoughts about another time-zone, year-wise. I began talking soon after she'd set down our mugs and sat herself.

Listening to myself was an odd experience, my words sounded to me as if filtered through layers of volcanic rock.

I told her of my careful education by teachers and textbooks of grade-school history, which informed me that my childhood-state's name, Idaho, was derived from the Shoshoni word, "ee-da-how," meaning "behold, the sun-coming-down-the-mountain." Local booster information and literature said so, too. I told her about a local radio program, probably of the late 'forties or early 'fifties, which presented the state's history. Each show began with beating tom-toms and a drawn-out chant of "Eeee-daaaa-hoooow," additionally tarted out with plenty of reverb. I didn't know about reverb at the time and only later imagined the overall effect was much like the version of the once-popular song, "Indian Love Call," which Yosemite Park officials used to broadcast over outside loud-speakers each dusk back when they still staged the fire-falls from a cliff above the valley.

"For me," I said, that business of the sun-coming-down-the-moun-tain fit what I saw every day. And the radio's romanticized chant of ee-da-how—no doubt, cheesy as all get out—I thought it was cool."

Relating all this, I'd gone perversely slow, watching her increas-ingly pained expression as her lips tightened and the corners of her eyes narrowed.

"You can imagine," I went on, "how disappointed I was to learn years later that none of what I'd been taught was true. The real origin of Idaho's name is unknown. Some guy made up the Shoshoni ee-da-how business for reasons of his own that remain obscure."

Judith Clearwater's face relaxed. I assumed she was relieved not to have to break the bad news to me.

"I guess it would have been too easy for someone to have asked us," she said.

"Us?"

She smiled. "Shoshoni. Now you know."

Woody, you old fox, I thought. You misled me with that Appaloosa horse and the Nez Perce business.

"That's great," I said. "Because I'm hoping you can help me out."

Right off I admitted to her that I might have been warped at an early age by my ee-da-how experience. Be that as it may be, through my later years, the people I read about in books, saw in plays, in movies, their lives, their emotional preoccupations always seemed foreign.

"Is what you're talking about any different from what social scientists tell us," she asked, "that everyone feels out of place in their culture, in their own family? We all feel we've been adopted by aliens. They say it's a kind of emotional estrangement that's everyone's natural condition."

I'd read some of that, too, but I told her I also felt out of place in the settings of those literary and dramatic stories. Their locations. The characters lived in apartments and flats, in crowded buildings, in big cities with tangled streets. The characters in stories set in urban places commuted to work on trains, spent their time in factories or in offices of white shirts, polished shoes and high heels. They relaxed at backyard barbecues and pools.

"No one worked with or around animals," I said, "or wrecked their hands with blisters, splinters or cuts, worried about what disaster this year's bad weather might bring to the family's income. Nobody lost a finger or thumb because they missed a roping dally or got their arm destroyed in a baling machine."

"You identified with the country mouse, not the city mouse."

I nodded. "At least in the sense that I felt like the country mouse trying to survive in the country using the city mouse's methods. The myths I was learning didn't fit my experience in my own backyard."

"Like what?" she asked.

"Well, for instance that myth about rugged individualism we talked about last time. Our books and movies—especially the westerns—project the idea of a single person, usually male, although the women who accompany them are painted with the same brush, who go it alone to win against great odds and build the Great American West. It doesn't matter whether the opposing odds are the elements or overly armed mobs, the singular hero always comes out on top. John Wayne built a career around the character."

She nodded. "I recognize both the type-casting and the role. Why didn't it *fit* your world?"

"Because my other received story about building the West was about my grandparents. You might remember that I mentioned they arrived early on in the development of a small town in the Payette Valley."

She nodded. I went on to tell her that according to my grandmother, after the first dust had settled a bit, all the folks who'd come there thought it was time to put up a church. Like every other house or barn raising, it was going to be a project shared by the community, not built by a lone rugged individual. The problem was that the community was not of a single religion. There were many. So, what kind of a church should they put up? They took a census of the religions. They learned that all denominations were represented. Except one, either Unitarian or Congregationalist. So as a community, they raised the roof for that one, and they attended it as a community for many years. I got the impression they never caught sight of a rugged individualist.

When I paused here, her quiet attention invited me to stitch it all together. I gave it a shot, saying that what was now going on in my country made the whole place feel foreign to me, not just my backyard. But given that I'd always felt somewhat estranged, I wondered if I needed to understand those old feelings before trying to figure out how to live comfortably in this more recent situation. In fact, I thought that if I had grown up knowing the meanings of Native words for my surroundings, the *real* ee-da-how's for white-water rivers and sun-struck mountains, for sage-covered hills and sunbaked plateaus, for mesquite and sand and rock and bunch grass, maybe I would have felt more at home in that backyard.

"Recently, I've been wondering if I learned those meanings now, whether I'd feel less out of place here, in my own back yard. Then maybe I could more easily figure out what's making me feel that the rest of the country has become a foreign place. And maybe then, how to live in it."

"That's a lot of maybes," she said. "But it sounds to me like you'd hoped to begin with learning the meaning of your pictographs." She gestured to the paper with the sketches still in my hands.

"Maybe start with basics," I said. "Seemed practical. But I'm even more late to the party than I'd imagined." I put the sketches back in my pocket, but I was far from defeated. "Of course, I might start with the words you're teaching in your classes, maybe with those words I saw on your teaching plan."

She sipped her coffee and looked out at the sage. Her eyes shifted from something out there to something else and back again as if she were deciding which to choose. "I thought you were going to start out there,"— she gestured toward most everything beyond her porch railing—"walking Woody's trails."

"I didn't find the child who vanquished my nightmare, though," I said.

She shook her head. "How about red rock? Find any of that?"

"Red rock?"

"You know, like boulders, cliffs, rock shelves, mesas. Red-colored. See any red stones during your day?"

"Sure," I said, "lots, particularly if the light's right. Some places more than others." I frowned. "And?"

"*Atsa koodakwa*," she said.

"Sorry, I . . . uh, wha-?"

"*Atsa koodakwa*," she repeated. "Paviotso for red mountain or peak."

"I couldn't begin to pronounce that."

"You could learn."

"Maybe with practice I could say it," I agreed.

"I'm sure you could. And now that you've heard it and know its meaning, do you feel more connected to the land? Are you more at home with those red rocks and buttes out there?"

I paused and tried to. I really worked at it, but I couldn't force a greater or different feeling of connection to a pile of red rocks any more than I could re-create my nightmare at will or call up that lost child.

"I only just now heard the word," I said, feeling myself squirm and hoping it didn't show. "Maybe with some time, I'll get the hang of it."

"By all means, take your time," she said. "Take a few hours, take a day, take a week of days. How long would you suppose would be about right? A month of weeks? A year of months?"

The heat coming my direction wasn't only from the sun-hammered sand and sagebrush. This was a new side of Judith Clearwater. I took a closer look. She saw my reaction immediately.

"I apologize," she said. "You didn't deserve that."

"No, really, my fault. I was flip with something I don't know anything about. Sometimes I'm not careful as I should be in unfamiliar territory. I step on toes, feelings that I should know are there. I should be . . . I'm the sorry one here."

"Possibly it was your mention of time that stirred me."

"Time?"

"Or maybe your overly casual use of time," she said. "Tossed out, unthinking."

"I don't get—"

"Because you're right about time being necessary to comprehend the meaning of *atsa koodakwa*. But it's not clock time or calendar time you need. At least not for comprehending it as the *Atsa koodakwa tubewabe*, the Red Mountain Dwellers, understand the word. Even thinking to *comprehend* its meaning misses the point. It's too mental. *Absorb* all its meanings would be closer. Absorb the meaning into your nerves and dreams."

I was listening, but I knew I was frowning. I could tell my quip had missed the mark by a country mile and more. How much more extended over the horizon. Did the miss have an end point?

She seemed to measure whatever she saw on my face because her own softened a little, relented. She rose and walked toward the south end of her porch, saying, "Maybe this will help."

She eased her backside against the south railing, pointed past her shoulder with her thumb, and told me that not far in that direction toward the Santa Rosa Mountains were other red mountains, the territory of the *Atsa koodakwa tubewabe*. We, she and I, should pay attention to their name because their name designation is geographical. Most Paiute bands are known by their traditional food source, by what they eat rather than by where they live.

"You mean like Woody's people being the Ground Hog Eaters?" I guessed.

She looked a little surprised, but she nodded. "Yes, the *Kedu Tukadu*. That's the more usual way of clan naming, like the Pine Nut Eaters or Camas Root Eaters, say, or further south around Mono Lake, the Larva Eaters."

A name doesn't indicate a group's sole diet, she went on. The bands moved around as necessary to hunt and gather what was available. Still, in most cases each group's identity was tied to a particular food. Yet, for some reason, the Red Mountain Dwellers identify with a particular geography. That element, like the traditional food source of other bands, is part of their particular creation story and woven into who they are and how they live. A lifetime of study will not grant comprehension of what that means for them.

"You look skeptical," she said.

"Well, you seem to have a pretty good understanding. Are you trying to say that's because you're Native?"

She came away from the porch rail, shaking her head. "I'm talking *about* it. I am not a Red Mountain Dweller. I didn't grow up hearing traditional stories and chants about the Red Mountains, about how they were formed, where to find food and water sources. I haven't listened to the changes of voices in good times and bad. I haven't taken part in the telling and retelling of my peoples' origin and passage through past millennia, of how the Red Peaks shaped us and how we should act among them. I didn't hear how my father shaped the stories, or how my grandfather had passed them down, or how my grandfather's father heard and retold them. That shared history is not within me. I didn't have the growing years absorbing my place among and within my people. I have my own identity and place within another part of the land. My knowing the vocabulary of the Red Mountain Dwellers will not give me their identity and place. Everything that's imbedded in *Atsa koodakwa,* I could absorb in my lifetime only if I had been born a Red Mountain Dweller."

She fell into a silence. I said nothing. She picked up our coffee mugs and disappeared through the door.

I stood, arched my back, and went down the steps into the direct sunlight and raised my nose into the breeze moving across the land. Sage. Dry cheat grass. Hot gritty soil. Three separate scents mingled on the air currents buffeting my ears.

Judith Clearwater had made it clear that I was without a long history here. Not anywhere in the Great Basin. Not in Idaho. Probably not anywhere in America. I lacked a territorial pedigree. Seen from the perspective she'd laid out, a few hundred years wasn't enough to evolve from being a colonist. I was still the animal established in a place where it is not indigenous.

And yet, *I am here.*

Stooping, I grasped a fistful of dry soil, scraping it from the rim of the globe. I straightened, held my fist at eye level, and let the grains stream to float with the breeze. Their plume disappeared in an ever-lightening haze.

Here *I am.*

I clapped my hands free of dust and turned toward the house to see her watching me from her chair on the porch. She had replaced our coffee mugs with glasses of water. It seemed a sign she was willing to take more time away from whatever she had been doing before I'd appeared.

After going far enough up the stairs to rest one foot on the top step, I leaned against a roof-support post. I'd been sitting long enough to stiffen and needed some time vertical.

"My intention wasn't to invalidate your past or connection to this part of the world," she said, as if our conversation hadn't had a gap. "Yours is just different."

"I got the different part," I said. "But it felt to me like my connection comes up short compared to what's been *absorbed*, to use your word, by the Red Mountain folks."

"More like it comes up from different times and places." She took a deep breath and exhaled, half sigh, half exasperation, it seemed. "But I'll admit there are many who think that those different times and places leave you lacking. Or misdirected. Or dangerous." She thought a second. "Or all three."

"Whatever distinction you're making, it's lost on me."

She pointed northwest. "See that mountain range in the distance?"

I looked and made a guess based on my drives over to Burns. "The Steens Range?"

"For centuries and longer, it was known as the home of the *Tsoso'odo tubewabe,* the Cold Dwellers. One of the few other people not named by a food source. Granted, the temperatures above six thousand feet might rivet your attention more than what food sources there might be. But about a hundred and sixty years ago, U.S. Army Major Steen broke the last of the Paiute resistance in a battle up there and forced out the Cold Dwellers. Now *you* know the place as Steens Mountain. Your maps and connection to the territory come up in a different time frame than those of the *Tsoso'odo tubewabe.*"

"Seems a naming mistake to me," I heard the grumble in my voice. "I find the likes of War Chief Joseph are more admirable than the several unsuccessful Army Captains and Majors and their cavalries. They had to chased him and his band and their women and children and Appaloosa horses over the Lolo Pass through the Bitterroot Mountains. And even then, they only narrowly captured them in the end."

She smiled "Your sentiments for the Nez Perce are appreciated."

"But," I said, once again feeling I was about to grasp at smoke, "wasn't Steens Mountain also called Snowy Mountain? A name like Snowy must have roots back more than a couple of hundred years."

Shaking her head, she said, "You miss my point. It's not about the quantity of time embedded in a word or a name."

"It's not?"

"No. Think about Rome. No, not that one—another Rome. That town north of here on Highway 95. Forget any Native names for the area.

The town got its current name of Rome because the first colonialists on their way to western Oregon saw the rock cliffs that are near there. Those palisades put them in mind of the ancient temples of Rome."

"At least the temples were a couple of thousand years back."

"But it was a different couple of thousands of years," she said.

"What do you mean? A thousand years is a thousand years."

"We share an illusion that we're all on the one train riding a single time track from the past to the present and into the future. But it seems to me there are many tracks, many trains."

"You're not going to go all Einstein on me, are you?"

She shrugged. "I couldn't say. I'm a linguist, not a physicist. But I don't think so."

Good, I thought. Woody talking Aristotle to me is more than enough.

"Although, maybe there are parallels," she added. "The way I see it, there are at least two time tracks through here. One brought a train that had previously stopped at ancient Rome—the one in Italy—another had previously stopped at Red Mountains. Also, the tracks of the Red Mountain train extended further back to the origins of the *Atsa Koodakwa Tubewabe* among the red peaks. The tracks of the Rome train ran from the Garden of Eden."

I shifted, feeling uneasy. "I bet your trains and tracks are headed toward different destinations, too."

Her laugh was kind when she was moved to let it out.

"Remember my story when we met," she said, "about the first contact of the early settlers and Paiutes? The story goes on. Stories never end, really, do they? That one, too. It's not over."

My blank look was enough to get her to continue.

"It also starts earlier than where I started telling it." She gestured toward everything past the porch railing. "Out there. Hostile place. Forever unpredictable. The Paiutes' story had always been about surviving their territory's uncertainty. It emphasized hospitality to remote kinsmen and unknown visitors. Be friendly. Another band's pine nut harvest fails, you allow them to have some of your crop in your territory."

Sharing in an ungenerous land, as I recalled her words.

"Okay," I said. "But what has this to do with your time tracks and different trains rolling through centuries?"

"That Paiute story," she said, "began, of course, in myths and creation stories. The people retold them through the centuries because they were guides for how to survive in an uncertain, hostile world. Then there's the—what would it be?—the chapter of it that I told you. And the story continues to the present. It's still not over. But always the story was told for listening. Not reading. There was no written language until very recently when a few linguistic anthropologists began inventing a notation system for Native languages."

"You're talking about an oral history," I said.

"Yes." She nodded. "You see what I'm getting at?"

"Not really," I said. "You hear a story and retell it. Maybe you're saying you grew up in that oral tradition. But how's that make any difference to the story itself from you or me reading it?"

"Written and read, the story is not the same. The told story includes a different way of understanding the world and how to survive."

I shook my head. "I don't see it, a difference. Seems little more than nuance or emphasis to me."

"You don't *see*. Exactly. Because you're looking for written words. That's your train, running on your track from the Garden of Eden. There's another train."

"I can certainly *hear* your frustration with me."

"There you go," she said. "That's a different story from what you might get from only *reading* my words. Yes?"

"If I say, could be, or even, yes, different trains, different tracks, different stories, that gets us exactly where?"

She nodded, very slowly. "I think you'll recognize the place."

She redirected her gaze from me and scanned what lay beyond her porch from horizon to horizon. "Look around. A culture survives out here for four thousand plus years with an oral philosophy to cope with uncertainty by means of group sharing and living as a part of nature. Into this comes another culture that survived where it came from for over four thousand years with a written philosophy for coping with uncertainty by means of private possession and dominating every aspect of nature. The second culture conquers the first and forces the subdued people to live their lives according to the conquerors' philosophy. The subdued folks say, Whoa, Nellie. That's not our idea of how the world works. We're being forced to break rules that govern the universe. This isn't going to end well."

My ears pricked up. *Not my idea of how the world works.* That had an uncanny echo of what my friend had said soon after our country had changed unexpectedly. Her entire description, for that matter, was eerily similar to what I'd tried to relate to her about what had caused me to look for solitude out here, namely that my country now felt like a foreign place.

"And so?" I asked.

"And so, what?"

"Sounds like a prediction to me. Defy the world's reality and it's not going to end well. Yet here we are, the subdued and the conqueror. If I look at that idea from the subdueds's perspective, their situation begins to feel a lot like mine in Purgatory."

A smile twitched the corners of her mouth. "Purgatory. A name you brought here and posted on your sign. You nailed it on a post and stuck the post into a patch of land surrounded by territories of the *Atsa kooda-kwa,* the *Tsoso'odo tubewabe,* and the *Tagotoka,* the Tuber Eaters."

I got the point and nodded.

"But see," she said, "where that gets us? You *do* recognize the place."

"Oh, yes, it's the place where both of us, the Red Mountain Dwellers and I, must learn to live while dominated by beliefs at odds with our own."

11

*A*ll roads lead to Rome.

Most likely, I figured, cruising along in the Ranchero, the cliché was a literal exaggeration even back when it was a metaphor for Imperial Rome.

Nevertheless, in my world, U.S. Interstate 95 does veer toward Rome just north of the Burns Junction. At that point the highway curves east, reaching toward Idaho, and just across the border, as if having abrupt second thoughts about its trajectory, it swerves directly north again to run up inside the western border of the state to Canada.

My getting to Rome would be a fraction of that total distance.

Grateful, I steered past the Burns Junction and through the arc directing me toward Rome. I was unsure of what I'd find or even what I was looking for. But it seemed important to look.

What did they do? I had wanted to ask Judith Clearwater about those Paiutes when they realized they'd been overwhelmed by a way of thinking and a philosophy of life they didn't agree with.

My question was self-centered, I acknowledged to myself. More and more, I realized that my sense of being a foreigner in my own country was because I felt—like the Paiutes—that I had been overwhelmed by a thinking and philosophy I didn't agree with. To find that understanding was part of why I'd come here and staked out my Purgatory in the first place. At least that's progress, I told myself. But there remained the question of how to live in a country that's acting on a philosophy counter to mine.

What did they do? But I had checked my question before asked.

In the first place, her story had made me uncomfortable as a fellow traveler on the same time train as those first colonists whose philosophy had overwhelmed the Paiutes. I was disconcerted by feeling overwhelmed myself and being one of those who has overwhelmed others. I was eager to find out how I would react to those rock palisades near the town called Rome. My desire mixed unpleasantly with sensing a vain hope that a different reaction would get me off the colonists' train.

And the second reason I hadn't asked my question was that Judith Clearwater had already given up her morning to talking with me.

The odometer rolled over to eight miles past the Burns Junction. I should get to Rome in a few miles. I slowed the pickup to take another glance at the map sketched, once again, by Woody. He'd told me the road to the Pillars of Rome wasn't well marked. Maybe not marked at all. Smart of me, he'd said, to check directions with him.

"As long as any map you give me has some vague relationship to the territory." I hadn't included a smile with my words.

"Can't promise," he'd said. "Been a few years since I've been out that way. Best to keep your wits active. In all things, maps or no maps" He hadn't been a beacon of smiles either. "Many times, a compass is more useful than a map."

"More wisdom from Aristotle?"

"I have to think on that." Woody had found another scrap of paper in his junk drawer and, at last, a stub of pencil. Applying the second to the first with two strokes, he'd shaped a large "Y" and added "BJ" at the intersection of lines. I awarded myself no points for understanding the lines as highways and the initials as Burns Junction.

Not the territory, alright, but hopefully, his drawing would be a useful overlay.

Woody repositioned the paper but looked up from his handicraft before proceeding. "Although Aristotle made it pretty clear any idea of his was a work in progress. He revised his theories throughout his life." He made a short mark beside the right arm of the Y. "But maybe I got that wrong."

His casual comment hadn't been about the tick he'd made beside the Y. Next to the tick he'd noted, *Rome,* and the distance between it and BJ as about twelve miles. At what might be a couple of miles before that, he'd scribbled some curlicues on the north side of the highway. The curlicues, he explained, were a copse and some buildings. Hard after that, another line swung left. He labeled that the Rome Road Cutoff.

And sure enough, as my Ranchero's odometer ticked over to ten miles, there, up to the left was a stand of trees.

I let the pickup coast and slow to under fifty. A yellow diamond CAUTION sign on my side of the road drifted past.

"There may still be a gravel storage against a couple of plywood sheets where the Rome Road Cutoff angles away from the highway," Woody had said.

Just past a hard-used barn and house under the trees and beyond some kind of parked or abandoned machinery were two piles of gravel and the plywood, as predicted. A third short billboard looked kneecapped and sagged from the one good upright. Whatever it had advertised was no longer legible. A dirt road angled past the gravel dump turnaround and headed north. Woody was right again. Absolutely nothing marked the track as the Rome Road Cutoff.

"Ah, what the heck," I muttered and accelerated. Woody had told me that if I missed the cutoff, there was another road I could take from Rome itself. He'd marked that on the map, too. I'd driven this far, why should I deny myself the pleasures of seeing the urban wonders of these parts?

In a gust of wind, the damaged sign swayed, as if waving a forlorn good-by as I passed.

I'd barely regained sixty miles per hour when I took my foot off the gas again. What I took to be Rome rose like a blister on the right side of the highway ahead. I coasted onto the paved apron by the first buildings and had to brake to keep from coasting right on out the other end of town.

My dust thinned and settled when the air let it. Leaving the pickup idling, I got out to stretch my legs and snatch a look around.

Rome was a spare collection of buildings, one of which appeared to be a café plus office for an overnight trailer park that sprawled a little further off the highway. Rising above the parking area were tall poles capped with what would be vicious floodlights. Around the office/café, not a geranium or so much as a flowerpot was anywhere in sight. In fact, I didn't see much to distinguish Rome from Fast Buck and the many other places like it other than here, no metropolis expansion had spilled to the opposite side of the highway.

Across the road from Rome was another dusty expanse. Another dirt and gravel road ran dead away into the desert. From Woody's map-that-wasn't-the-territory, I guessed the rutted trace to be the Rome Road proper. Once again, not a road marker in sight.

No sense hanging around.

I kicked my front tire just to make me feel good, climbed back in, turned and crossed the highway, bumping off the far side.

Watching Rome grow smaller in my rear-view mirror, I marveled again at the difference of western towns from those where rain fell in greater quantity. Ordering nature in a Japanese garden, on a bluegrass estate, or an Ohio farm looks fine. Order imposed on the landscape west of the Rockies tends to look forlorn. Seen from a distance, especially from the air, there is something about western towns of any size, when they are positioned against the endless landscape, that strikes me as spare, even mean. The whole enterprise can look temporary and particularly with all shadows flattened by a hard noontime sun, despairing. Closer on, the places often feel not life-affirming, as if the residents are not working at it. They are, but maybe it's hard to make headway lacking enough water. Even the big coastal cities look like huddled outposts against the onslaught of untamed land just beyond a protective mountain range.

Maybe my feeling was an instinctive recognition of optimistic attempts to dominate a wilderness with permanent buildings rather than organizing nomadic camps that could easily move on as necessary. Even while they were being overwhelmed by a way of life based on dominance and possession, the Paiutes must have been puzzled, confused, and frightened by its impractical approach to living.

The pickup jolted across a pothole I hadn't seen coming. Or maybe, I thought, my disparaging evaluation was more a reflection of my feeling so completely severed from my country and the people I've loved. Because, although many more people leave the Romes and Fast Bucks than stay, those who remain are the strain of people who match the harsh landscape and are as much the sinew, bone, and muscle of the nation as those living in flashier places.

Rome disappeared in the dust cloud billowing from my tires. I shifted my attention forward.

After a short bit, a second dirt road ran in from my left and joined the one I was on. Because this was approximately where the Rome Road Cutoff might reach the Rome Road, I stopped a little past where they came together. Only God—and maybe Woody—knew how many tracks there were out here and where they crisscrossed. I got out and looked back the way I'd come, trying to identify landmarks to find the cutoff so that I could take it on my return home. There wasn't much.

After extracting the ax from the tarp in the pickup bed, I lopped off a branch of nearby sagebrush that was big enough not to blow away and set it with the cut exposed to sight, opposite where the road split. Even if it was dark on my way back, my headlights should find the marker. With the ax back in the folds of tarp and me climbing into the Ranchero, I told myself I was getting to be a Nervous Nellie.

For the most part, the road was more or less well maintained. Two miles on, the right turn and then the left noted on Woody's map were easily located and taken. I slipped his sketch under the visor and looked about for the Pillars of Rome.

Woody had said they wouldn't be hard to find. The rock formations had been a landmark for the ford of the Owyhee River for travelers on that particular leg of the Oregon Trail.

Sure enough, as the road began a gradual decline along a hill's flank, a line of rock abutments on the far side of a shallow valley rose higher as I drove nearer. The road was straight, no dust rose to indicate an approaching vehicle. I could take in the formations instead of paying attention to steering and was only half aware of my speed slowing by degrees.

Suspended in time. My feeling registered as I thought the words. There are many places where the timeless immensity of western landscape simply stills the mind.

Five miles long, Woody had told me while he described what to look for, about two miles wide, and around a hundred feet high. Seeing them, I found the formations less like temple pillars than a defensive wall. Across geographical features similar to these, the Roman Hadrian had chosen to build his wall to keep back the Picts.

I was not amused to notice from whence my time-train had run. A couple of thousand years back, true, but onto the moors of Northumberland—or the lowlands of Scotland, depending on your perspective—and not into the wilderness forests or deserts of North America.

At the bottom of the grade, I let the pickup roll to a stop as close to the edge of the road as possible. I turned it off and got out.

The only sound was intermittent buffeting of wind in my ears. It wasn't far across the valley floor to the base of the cliffs.

Off I went.

The rhythm of my steady pace, the brush of sage against my Levi's, took me back to another hill at the outer edge of the Boise city limits where I used to take my dog just to get away. We'd sit at the top, her with nose to the breeze, me looking across the valley to watch the sunset stretch to the Owyhee range at the distant horizon. I'd often imagine walking in the opposite direction, up the hills rising behind me. It awed me to think I could ascend the foothills into the mountains, into the primitive area further north, and keep going north all the way into Canada. Assuming I had the ways and means to survive, I might not see any trace of people save those on the few sparsely driven highways I'd have to cross along the way.

Now, approaching the Pillars of Rome, that childhood fantasy did make me smile. Maybe I, too, had a time track that ran into the forests of North America. *And from there*, I imagined Judith Clearwater insisting, *on to the Garden of Eden*. I shook my head. It seemed there was no escaping my own heritage. My feeling overwhelmed by a philosophy I didn't agree with was not because I valued sharing over possession. I was too much part of a possession culture to feel alienated by it.

The cliff, one hundred feet up, if it was that from where I stood, was imposing when seen from its base. I stretched out my hand and rested it flat against the sheared rock, as if to find a heartbeat.

None, I thought.

And thought again.

Perhaps its pulse is too slow to register while I stand here. How far back was the previous beat?

The next one could come after I was gone. Or in a decade. Or after I was dead. Maybe in the eon after people go extinct. I found myself somewhere in Judith Clearwater's geologic time, beyond clocks and calendars.

I lowered my hand, turned, leaned my back against the rock, and looked back the way I'd come.

Dwarfed by the flank of the hill opposite, my waiting pickup looked like a discarded toy. Some would call that Ranchero a classic, I thought. If that's a classic, I'm what—a relic? For either of us, it seemed like too brief a time span to earn such a title. An inappropriate measuring stick applied, less than that of a person's lifespan.

I realized that I, too, being habitually enveloped within a wash of people, had difficulty registering passing time in units bigger than a season. Decades were hazier, and the outlines of generations were downright confusing. A single century was but an abstraction. Yet here I was leaning against another timepiece. A fractional tick from its internal gears would surpass hundreds of decades and thousands of centuries.

The rise and fall of seas from one ice age to the next, though slow, nonetheless sweep much away. The shallow cup I'd just crossed from my pickup to the cliffs probably once held the remnant of an inland lake left by ice-melt of a thousand-foot glacier. The formation rising behind me had, on and off, been seabed.

I turned and walked beside the rockface, running my hand along it at eye level.

Striations in several colors ran the length of the cliff, thicker here, thinned-to-vanishing there. They reminded me of the timelines in a history atlas. I ran my finger along the streaks, up and down the lattice. Maybe this grain of volcanic rock dates from when land creatures no longer needed gills, and here a fleck of mica from about the time someone learned to relate to horses as sentient beings. Does the distance that separates the first from the second measure a thousand years or a few million? Does anyone know for sure? What is the time scale of this surface five miles long and one hundred feet high? Maybe when a pebble near the top was laid to rest, Cleopatra got bit by her asp. Are the fragments of fossilized seashells under my feet from the last little ice age or from one of the bigger ones that came millions of years before?

By continuing to follow the irregular contours of the bluffs for the next quarter to half an hour, I walked myself around several bends, which long since had turned me away from where I could see the pickup. A rising slope ahead offered me one last perspective of the line of cliffs before I started back.

About half way up the steepening trail, I saw a dried sage branch lying on the sand move and change shape.

Two thoughts elbowed for attention.

First, an inanimate object had become animate: my nightmare was back.

Second, perhaps the young boy who'd first had the nightmare—the one Judith Clearwater said I should seek in these hills—maybe he was close at hand.

The branch continued moving. It coiled, rose. I heard the dry rattle before I registered its wedge-shaped head.

Rattlesnake.

I stopped, one foot ahead of the other.

Not a nightmare, only a real-time threat. From its higher position beside the trail, would the rattler be more likely to strike at my arm than leg? Or my neck?

Slowly, I inched my forward foot back.

The rattling sped up. The snake reset its coil, tongue flicking to catch my scent.

A gunshot made me jump—sideways—to avoid the flying snake, before I realized it had jolted backwards. Headless.

$=12=$

I stared at the reptile's writhing body and tried to sort out which had startled me more, report of the gun or the jerk of the snake.

For a moment, I could search only with my eyes for the source of the shot.

Nothing—or more accurately—no one.

Finally, I managed to turn my body and look down trail behind me.

Roger Stegman, rifle held at his waist, climbed the rise toward me. By the time he closed to a dozen steps from me, I had time to take a deep breath. I used it like a hatchet.

"What the hell? You dumb . . . !"

My words stopped him in his tracks. "You're welcome," he said, a smirk flitting across his mouth.

"That was no thank-you. I only had to keep backing up, and the rattler would have crawled away."

He pushed back his Rod and Gun cap and shrugged. "One less snake is a good thing."

"Wrong snake, in my opinion," I said under my breath. I thought.

One of his eyebrows rose, then the other one. "A sanctimonious insult?"

"I forgot how far words can travel when not masked by urban noise."

"And that's an explanation without an apology." He nodded. "Which fits your type pretty well."

"My *type*?"

"The type always whining about global warming, ecological disaster, bad men making everything worse. The type that thinks they're better than the people they call bad who are only taking sensible steps to fix a problem. Like killing a snake that's going to strike."

"Highly likely your fixers are more interested in making a buck than their half-baked fix. You expect a dollar for the bullet you spent?"

"See? Sanctimonious. Thinks anybody who's rich is bad."

"Like you and your kind think somebody's bad if they're a tad short of cash."

He shifted his weight. The way he was standing got me to notice his rifle was still leveled in my direction. He left it there.

"You and your kind always believe help is on the way," he said. "Especially, if they just back off and are nice." His laugh was a harsh, agitated bark. "And the help that's coming? They always think it's help for them."

I struggled with that for a moment. "If I need help, why *wouldn't* I imagine any help that's on the way is coming to help me?"

"Oh, man! And your type calls my kind of folks arrogant." He shook his head to emphasize his disbelief. The gun muzzle dropped a couple of notches toward the ground. He brought it right back up. "Because, Bitterroot Baby, any coming help is just as likely to be on the way to reinforce your opponent to help wipe you out."

Struck by the absurdity of grown men surrounded by a wilderness of sagebrush calling each other names, I curbed my tongue.

He raised his head to scan the cliff face rising above us. "All those pretty lines of mineral deposits. Inch by foot by yard, each band of sediment adds weight on those below. Flattens them."

I didn't know which was more disturbing, his sudden interest in geology or his gun aimed at my chest. The second was black steel and looked ugly mean. Judith Clearwater's words ran through my head. *You never know who you're dealing with.*

"Notice all the lines are horizontal," he said.

He brought his eyes back to me to check if I was looking at the cliff. I wasn't. His hard stare gained force from that slight sneer lifting his upper lip. "Show me up there, in any line," he dripped each word cold, "the arc of moral history bending toward justice."

"You're talking rock, not people," I said, despite the dark muzzle I faced.

"This rock is the world's message to people, your type especially. You might say it's a monument for you."

A chill dropped down my spine. *Monument for you.* I could only see a tombstone.

Maybe he noticed I'd flinched. His sneer reverted to thin suggestion of smile. "In stone, the world is telling you that whatever you see at this moment is what you will have for a lifetime."

"So says the cynic," I said.

"Says the realist. Any bend of moral history's arc is so slow you can give up hope that you'll see some difference you believed in become permanent. The mineral content of those layers changes, but they repeat cycles with little variation. Changing content didn't alter the process. All that mattered in every era was to have weight, the most power."

"Power wielded solely for more power is just an aspiration. It's self-centered opportunism, always shifting. It's a favorite tool—or crutch—for people without ethics."

Why, I wondered, was I continuing to bait him? I thought myself a fool.

He cast his gaze past me and across all the landscape not in my neighborhood. The rifle muzzle didn't budge an inch.

"A lot of empty around here," he said, "a big place to be alone in. A person could die from a fall before help showed up."

I nodded, trying to project a serious appreciation for the obvious. "I'm not much of a faller. And disinclined to jump."

He'd cocked his head like he was working to understand. I decided to complete the thought.

"Bullet hole, though, could look suspicious in an unarmed person. Might suggest an agent other than accident."

"But that agent" he said, "could drag the body off, shove it under a stand of sage way out there, sweep away any marks leading that direction. In the off chance anyone paid attention to circling buzzards, all the carrion eaters would have destroyed any trace of a shot by the time anybody got a closer look. Particularly if the bullet—or bullets—went through soft tissue."

Again, I nodded. This time my appreciation was real. "You've put some thought into this."

He seemed as intent on convincing me about his doing away with me as he had about moral lessons taught by geology. Still, I wasn't sure whether arguing or agreeing with him was more likely to keep me alive. Would he really shoot me? *You never know who you're dealing with.* And in theory, a murderer lurks in all of us. But if he was having doubts, I didn't want to help him overcome them.

"So," I said, "first you're only a roving property buyer, then a geologist, a philosopher? Now you're an assassin?"

"The only person I've told about my buying Mr. Peterson's ranch was you." His voice had an absent quality that left me thinking he had other things in mind.

"Ah. Doris and Fred." I shifted a tad to show him more side of me than front, just as his eyes came back to me.

"You made things a lot more difficult." he added, taking a sideways step and a half that realigned his rifle approximately with my full-on midsection. "It upsets me when people put their noses where they don't belong."

He took a single step that put him in firing stance. Roger took his time, slowly raising the rifle to his shoulder. *He's trying to scare me,* I thought, immediately recognizing wishful thinking.

His finger slid off the guard, onto the trigger. A vision of the flying rattler flared in my imagination.

"Hey, what's up?" Woody's call was startlingly close.

I saw he'd just rounded a cliff bend below us. I had been so intent on Roger, I'd not heard or sensed Woody's approach.

Neither had Roger. He stiffened and turned toward Woody. Although he lowered the rifle to his waist again, I could almost feel him calculating the odds of suspicion if two bodies were found out under the sagebrush.

And then there was the consideration of the rifle that Woody carried in the crook of his arm.

He didn't break stride until he was a few lengths from Roger. "Who woulda thought?" Woody said. "All of us meeting in this small spot in such a wide-open place?" He cocked his head, cool eyes on Roger. "I did think I heard a shot. But maybe I got that wrong."

"No," I said, more than glad to be helpful. "Roger blew the head off a rattlesnake."

"Isn't Mr. Stegman just full of surprises?" Woody, again asking questions that weren't questions. His eyes flicked to me and narrowed, then back to Roger. "About thirty yards. Not bad." Roger barely shrugged. "Also," Woody went on, "good invitation to ricochet. All these rocks. But maybe you don't care."

"I don't miss," Roger said. "So, no ricochet."

Woody's gaze hadn't moved from Roger. "All the same, I figure you've maybe nine rounds left in that 10/20 Ruger. I'd sure feel better about the marksmanship if you'd reset the safety on your weapon."

Roger's finger drifted away from the trigger, and I breathed easier. He brought his left hand up to the stock by the trigger guard. I heard the safety catch click.

"You claimed not to be a hunter," I said to Roger. I hoped to ease the tense silence gripping the three of us.

"Always liked target shooting, though," Roger said. "Develops accuracy."

"You think you could do it again? On another snake? Or was that first shot beginner's luck?"

He shifted his rifle. At the movement, Woody's came up a tic, then he relaxed. The reflex wasn't lost on Roger. He nodded at Woody, then me.

"See? Power. Anywhere. Any time."

More slowly than his previous movements, Roger shifted his rifle to the crook of his elbow. It looked like a struggle against less rational thoughts. "It's been a pleasant hike, but time's wasting. I should be off." He started down the path, saying, "Glad to have done you the favor." After he'd passed Woody, he stopped, turned, and added to me, "I'm good to at least fifty yards without a scope. That wasn't the first snake I've shot."

After Roger left, silence hung around. Woody and I stared after the vanished figure. It was like we half-expected him to double back. Only an erratic breeze rippled around corners of the bluff and into our faces.

Eventually, Woody leaned back against the cliff face. He looked down at his weapon and flicked the safety on. He cleared a round from the breach and disappeared it into his pocket.

I went down the path to him. "Woody, how did you know . . ." I started, "Why . . . ?" I let my upturned hands ask the question.

"Right after you got your map and took off," Woody said, "I saw Roger come storming out of the General Store."

I nodded. "I suspect he'd been dickering with Doris and Fred. Or trying to."

Woody considered me coolly while I told him of my seducing Fred and Doris into holding out for more than Stegman's initial offer.

Woody nodded. "That would explain the look on his face when I saw him."

"What look?"

"The look I used to see in the squad after a routine operation went sideways. Your story would also explain why Roger trotted from the store over to his motel room and came right back out with that rifle of his and hopped into his SUV and moved out briskly in the direction you'd taken."

Woody turned to go back the way we'd come. I hopped after him.

"And?" I asked.

He shrugged and kept walking. "And it seemed like a good idea to follow the both of you."

"Must have taken you a bit to get collected, shut the saloon and all that. How in the world did you find us out here?"

Our path widened, and I caught up to walk beside him. He gave me one of those corner-of-the-eye-looks parents give kids asking questions about the obvious.

"I'd given you directions, for one. And found where he parked behind your pickup, for another."

"Yeah but," I jabbered, "it's three-sixty from the road. Into a big landscape, as you mentioned."

He sighed. "It's not like it's hard to track you two or that either of you move very fast."

"We spent a bit of time in philosophical discussion."

He kept his eyes front, but the raised eyebrows could have meant he thought I was kidding. Or it may have been that my words had come out sounding breathless, because I was short of air from trying to keep up with him. At any rate, he pulled up in a shady patch by the cliff face, dropped to a squat so that his back was braced by the rock.

"Philosophy, huh?" he said.

I slid down beside him and gave him a taste of the back and forth, Roger's and mine, about whether the arc of moral history was fact or phantom, straight line or curve.

While Woody listened, he pulled a red bandana from his back pocket and used it to wipe dust from the barrel and metal work of his rifle. I mentioned Roger's skeptical vote on the arc.

"Moral history, huh," Woody said. "My people say that the animals gave Togokwa, the rattlesnake, much power, and it turned to poison and went to his head. He's dumb and dangerous and a powerful enemy. Togokwa must be handled properly to maintain balance in the world."

"*One less snake is a good thing*," I said, remembering the headless rattler snapping backward onto the sand. "That's what Roger said after shooting it."

"No one should kill Togokwa."

"What? No Old Testament curse that man shall crush the snake's head?" In my head, an image of Judith Clearwater's two trains wound from separate origins. Roger rode the one from the Garden of Eden. But my remark, *wrong snake,* put me right there with him on the same train.

Woody gave a final rub, possibly to some fingerprint only he could see, and stuffed the bandana back in his pocket. He plucked a dried stem of bunchgrass and alternately chewed on or twirled it between a thumb and forefinger. I thought he was done with the subject. Once again, I was wrong.

"My old people believe one should capture Snake and return him to his home among the brush and rocks."

Definitely a different train, I thought. Certainly different etiquettes and morals.

Woody stuck the grass stem between his teeth. "Well, that's my world. Then there's yours, where moral history does or doesn't arc over time."

He paused and stared toward the horizon.

"Aristotle now," he said past the bit of grass, "of course, he was a bit before the Old Testament. He thought we're only aware of time passing because we saw movement in our physical world. Something changes position from one moment to the next. You know, like the sun changing position or the lines in our faces getting deeper."

"Well," I said, "Roger seems to believe in the changes of progress, but he doesn't see any change in the arc of moral history—it's flatlined, according to him. As far as the arc is concerned, he sounds like time halted with man's first footsteps. He doesn't see progression, only cycles. You know, like the sun going through seasons, youth going through old age to rebirth."

Woody checked my face to see that I wasn't mocking him. I wasn't. He plucked a new stem of grass and tossed away the used one. He stopped short of sticking the fresh stem in his mouth.

"The thing about a con man is that he's good at holding up his particular picture frame in front of the world and getting you to look only at what's inside his frame."

"You think Roger's a con?" I asked.

"You don't?"

"He's buying, not selling. And he even offered to buy my place for *more* than market value."

Woody chewed on his stem before answering. "A really good con man gets you to think he's buying when, really, he's selling."

"I don't get it," I said.

"That's my point." Woody said. "It looks to me like he's trying to sell you—you, me, Fred and Doris, most likely Milly—on the idea of selling out, trying to con us into leaving the land, get out of his way, so he can do what he wants with it. His little talk with you a few days ago, about being on the side of progress? He was just trying on another con to get you to leave." Woody watched me scratch my head. "That's what got his jaw tight about your suggestion to Doris and Fred. He didn't care that he might have to pay more. Look what he offered you. It's that you kind of broke his spell with them to get out and not look back." He rose to standing and shook out one leg and then the other.

Rising to my feet with him, I said, "What's this got to do with Aristotle, anyway, and with time and change and the moral arc of history?"

"There once was a man named Zeno." Woody stopped to see if the name rang a bell.

It didn't.

"Sounds like the start of a limerick," I said.

He didn't blink. "Zeno managed to get under Aristotle's skin. Asked about an arrow in flight."

"There's a trajectory with an arc," I said, already working to keep up.

"Zeno mentioned that the arrow at rest on a table takes up exactly its own amount of space. Aristotle agreed and told him to go on. Zeno did. He said when he takes a picture of an arrow in flight with his iPhone, in the fraction of time of that picture, the arrow still takes up its own amount of space."

I thought he was pulling my leg. "Zeno had an iPhone?"

"Work with me here," Woody said. "I'm not some fancy-pants philosopher. I just read stuff and try to understand what your civilization's got going on."

"Sorry," I said. "Okay, so, arrow on table, arrow in Zeno's iPhone picture, both the same size in reality. What's he want to make of that?"

"He said that the equal sizes proved the arrow in flight is actually at rest at the instant of the picture, standing still. So, there must be something wrong with how we experience reality that makes us think the arrow is in motion."

"Seems to me, he's got a point," I said, "so to speak."

Woody shook his head. "Aristotle just came back with, there's something wrong with the way you, Zeno, experience time. It doesn't come in little packages. You can't cut it up into pieces small enough to get to where one packet is on the side of the past, and another packet is on the side of the present. There are only periods of time. Over a given period, the arrow moves. There's an arc. Zeno and Aristotle never found a way to agree."

He struck off in the direction of the road.

"What about Roger?" I called after him. "Him and his moral arc?"

Woody stopped and turned and tossed away the stem he'd chewed to next to nothing.

"Roger conned you into seeing only what was on his iPhone picture." He looked past me to scan the Pillars of Rome. "A picture of *that*. It's just a small cluster of one hundred-foot bluffs over five miles." Leveling a hard stare at me, he added, "A bit north of here," lifting his chin to aid my sense of direction, "Hells Canyon runs more than a hundred miles and is almost eight thousand feet deep. Deepest gorge in North America. Took the Snake River more than six million years to carve." He flicked his hand as if brushing away an insect. "I'd say Roger's iPhone picture, the one inside his frame, is pretty small—near vanishing, in fact. But maybe I got that wrong."

"But wouldn't Roger be just as happy to use your Hells Canyon to make his argument?"

"The Canyon rocks got shoved up when the planet's tectonic plates pushed into each other. A lot bigger even than what made the Pillars of Rome."

"You mean Roger would see rock strata curving up . . . toward justice?"

Woody just grunted and shook his head. "Not saying he would. Not saying he wouldn't. Just saying it seems more likely he might."

He set off again and didn't seem inclined to say more. I trailed him, concentrating on keeping up with his even pace, which looked relaxed as all get out, but was a lot like that steady trot of a wolf that just eats up ground.

He stopped and turned on me. "Rock faces of western mountains show many places where upward pressure by one earth plate on another was so great the strata lines run nearly vertical. I know you've seen this."

From the Sierra to the Rockies, tilted granite lines were as familiar to me as the veins on the back of my hand. "You're right," I said.

"Roger Stegman made you forget that. That's the strength of his con."

"Made me forget it, even got me not to think there might be any view other than his."

Woody nodded. "People forever underestimate the hypnotic power of a stalker." He struck off as if he hadn't stopped walking. Although caught flatfooted, I went after him as briskly as I could.

"One thing I'm curious about," I called after him.

"Yeah?" He didn't turn or stop.

"How'd you get caught up in Aristotle?"

"Because of a lieutenant of mine. Had a Ph.D. in philosophy."

"In the military?" I hadn't meant to sound incredulous.

"Said he wanted to see some real life. Stuck around. Mentioned he preferred it to university politics."

"He taught you . . . somehow?"

Woody stopped in his tracks. "He took a bullet for me."

I stopped beside him. Staying silent seemed to honor both of them more than a *sorry* to Woody. For several moments he looked past the horizon. Finally, he tilted his head toward the sun.

"I asked to pack his personals for transfer home with his body." Woody lowered his eyes, blinking, from the sun. "A book of Aristotle's Ethics was on the bunk. I kept it."

"But why?" I blurted.

Woody looked at me hard. "He offered. Once when he caught me watching him read it."

"No. I mean, why did the book interest you?"

"He'd talked about it."

"Must have been some teacher," I said.

Woody smiled a bit at that. "Not really. Words like virtue, pleasure, happiness from Aristotle didn't mean much. His talk didn't fix me."

"Then why?"

He hesitated. "Because . . ." he tilted his head to the sun again. Came back, eyes sparkling. "Because . . ." He was loud and stopped himself. "Okay," he said in his usual tone, "because, I was holding a pressure pack on him, waiting for medics, see, and I asked him, Why? With his shirt cuff, Woody rubbed a fleck of dust from his rifle barrel. "He said, 'Makes me happy.' And he was gone."

Woody flicked his eyes to the sun once more and took off at a fierce walk. I let him open a space between us before I set out after. Despite our pace, I noticed my feelings had lightened. After a bit, I caught up beside him again and cleared my throat.

"I'm glad you showed up today. Thanks."

He just kept walking like I hadn't said anything. There was only the measured crunch of our boots on the arid ground, the crackle of dried grasses when we stepped on them, the repeated rasp of sage against denim.

"He throw a scare into you?" Woody hadn't looked my direction. We didn't break stride.

"Yes," I said, without having to think it over, "you bet."

He veered around a large sage. I was afraid he'd find my reaction cowardly.

Rejoining our direction of travel, he said, "Good," with a slow nod I took to mean he thought I had some trace of sense after all. "Roger acted without thinking today. From now on, with more thought, he'll get more dangerous."

Woody clambered up the incline to the road. I labored up after him to stand, panting, next to him by the Ranchero. He took off his camo hat and dried the band.

"My people say to move Snake to a place where he can't harm folks," he said. "But respect Togokwa's power."

Woody started to walk on to his vehicle but turned back, talking as he approached me.

"You noticed Aristotle didn't win that argument with Zeno," he said.

I tried to reconstruct it, while waiting for my heart and breathing to slow, feeling my newly revived spirits also decline. "Seems like Aristotle just kind of changed the subject," I said at last.

"Because the argument is unwinnable. A great paradox. When you come down to it, any argument on either side is based on assumptions that can't be proved. Aristotle might say that if you think change can happen, you just have to make your best case for it while keeping an open mind. Meanwhile, the other person sees your choice makes you happy." He turned again toward his truck, adding, "But maybe I got that wrong."

Woody drove a Dodge Power Wagon, vintage undecipherable by me. I realized this must be the vehicle I'd spied through the cracks between the boards of the old garage in Fast Buck.

After he had U-turned it on the road, he whipped by me. Through his open driver's side window, he sketched a wave that was as spare as the landscape. He sped back toward his saloon, disappeared in a cloud of dust and a hearty Hi-yo, Silver, awa . . . Ah, nuts.

Besides, Tonto never raised his voice at Scout.

I shook my head. With Roger's threat gone, my overcharged nerves were short-circuiting.

I sat in the Ranchero for a while. Tension ebbed from my shoulders, and fatigue crawled up my legs. Shadows lengthened from the bluffs.

I started up the pickup, but before turning it around, I gave the Pillars of Rome one more look. Ol' Roger's pontificating about sediment layers and power had erased for me any ability to see the cliff faces as ruined temples or remnants of ancient fortifications. I saw now only Roger's cynical monument.

Shifting my gaze across the terrain to the hazy, distant horizon, I thought, this territory inspires hope because you really need it. And the land's endless scope makes you realize hope alone is not enough.

I threw the cliff face a final baleful look. Despite Woody's pep talk, Roger had gotten through to me. His bullet would have put an end to any consideration by me whether arcs bent in one hundred or one million years. But no bullet. That left me, according to Woody, having to make my best case for ethical living being stronger than brute power struggles. Cynic? I should have called Roger a nihilist.

The cliff face did not return my gaze. Its heart was stone cold. What argument for ethical living could I possibly find in this desert sojourn of mine for the likes of Roger?

The question made me put spurs to the Ranchero when I swung it around, and it fishtailed on the loose surface as I accelerated up the road.

Was there, or is there a Paiute word for nihilist? Did it matter, if the Pillars of Rome look the same, no matter the vocabulary? Besides, Judith Clearwater had made it crystal clear that any Paiute word once translated would have a different impact on me than on the native speaker. And in any case, even with our shared English, my calling Roger Stegman a cynic hadn't touched him.

It'd been a day. I'd come to the Pillars of Rome hoping I'd react differently than the colonists. I had. But I was still on their train from the past, rather than the Paiute one. They had been overwhelmed by a culture with a different morality: personal possession instead of sharing. It had taken good old Roger, true to his pain-in-the-ass character, to show me that I wasn't feeling like a stranger in my own land because of a different morality had taken the field. It was a nihilistic *absence* of morality that had overwhelmed me. Brute power had overwhelmed the principle of seeking a moral arc bending toward justice.

I'd come to Purgatory to figure out the nature of what had changed in my country. Maybe now I had a better idea. But I still hadn't a clue about how to live with it.

What did they do? Those Natives, after being overwhelmed by a different culture that only believed in power and possession?

It was time to ask Judith Clearwater.

13

As it turned out, she showed up before I went to her. My intention had been to make another morning trek over to her place, but my night had not gone well.

It's been said that any close-up with death alters the experience of living. Having a loaded gun poked in your face along with the threat it will be used should be one of those events.

And yet . . .

True, as I'd driven back from the Pillars of Rome, wind through my rolled-down window felt increasingly sensuous. My shirt collar flapped pleasantly at my neck and collar bone.

True, at that moment, no other sight could have been more beautiful than the sage endlessly unfolding toward the amber sunset.

And yet . . .

I was aware of seeing a world that appeared exactly as it would appear if I had *not* been looking, as if I were dead. Just as it had appeared yesterday. As it would appear tomorrow. To my survival or demise, the planet was indifferent. I was aware of my existing in the same moment as I was aware that my existence was irrelevant. And I felt completely unchanged by my perception. And running under that was disappointment, a sense I'd been cheated in my brush with death.

An unsettling feeling of observing me observing a world without me, of being here and not-here at the same time persisted into the evening. It seemed not so much an altered experience of living as an additional one. I suspect my strange dual personality skulked through my exhausted sleep.

The next morning, Judith Clearwater found me inside the shack next to my Airstream.

Standing at one end of the zinc sink attached to the far wall, I was working the arm of the water pump. No water.

And working it.

A dribble.

I had primed it a second time and worked it some more. I had a reservoir in the Airstream, of course, but this antique pump helped me extend my supply of water.

Every day it seemed to take longer to draw a full bucket. What with my frustration, the squeaking pump, and water sometimes falling into my galvanized bucket, I didn't hear her arrive.

When she came to stand in the open doorway, she blocked enough sunlight for the room to dim. I kept working the pump arm and looked around.

"Water table keeps dropping," she said. "Fact of life around here."

The bright light behind her reduced her to a silhouette. Other than being able tell she wore pants and a shirt with long sleeves and a collar, I could see no detail. That irritated me. I redirected my attention to my slowly filling bucket.

"Feels a lot like the project I came here to do in the first place," I said. "I keep pumping, get only dribbles that disappear, and the main flow of what I'm trying to get to, or draw from, gets farther and farther away."

"Maybe another fact of life around here," she said.

I nodded and waited and kept the handle going up and down.

She stepped through the doorway to lean against the inside of the doorjamb. The ambient light ticked brighter.

"What you're saying may be related to why I came by," she said.

"I'm pleased you came," I said, still without turning to her. "Just why *did* you come by?"

She didn't respond right away. I glanced across the silence to see her still leaning against the doorjamb, but now with her head cocked to one side.

"Do you have something on your mind?" she asked. "Or are you just irritated with your plumbing."

"I'm prickly on just about everything this morning, including this pump, which probably needs a valve replacement about as much as it could use another fifty feet of well pipe. I didn't mean to put a particular edge into my question, if that's why you ask, although I could see how you could think so."

"Edge or no, there seems to be some energy behind your questioning my visit." By her even tone of voice, she sounded sincerely interested.

"Ah, it's something Woody said a while back."

"Woody . . ." From the way she let the name hang in the air she didn't sound surprised.

The pump was drawing now, and the drumming of water into my bucket forestalled more words between us for the time.

When the bucket was full, I hefted it from the sink and started back to the Airstream. She let me pass by her to the outside, then she pulled the door shut behind us. When she caught up with me, I told her about Woody's comment while he was drawing my first hiking map.

"He muttered something about wondering what you were playing at." I stopped at the step up to the door of the Airstream and turned to her. "And I have to admit, during and after that first hike he sent me on, I got to wondering too."

She didn't rush to answer but stood, silent and without any change to her expression, apparently willing to hear me out, but I wasn't sure how to continue. I had one arm extended to the Airstream door handle and the other hand gripping a bucket handle. My arrested movement and speech left me feeling foolish. As with everything else since I'd come here, digging out the information I hoped to get was going to take more time than I'd anticipated.

"Look," I said, "I'm half awake and was about to make coffee to dynamite my brain. Can I offer you a mug of the stuff?"

She smiled. "Perhaps not quite that strong, if possible. But I'd welcome some, too."

While she stood just outside the open door, I went into the galley and got on with heating water, measuring and grinding coffee beans, setting a portable table just outside under the worn awning unfurled from the edge of the Airstream, and adding a couple of folding chairs. The movement allowed me time to ramble around what I felt was the touchy subject I'd broached.

"I can see that *I* might wonder what you're playing at," I said, "because I'm personally unmoored and more or less wandering around out here. Easily confused. No familiar landmarks. Thinking I'm on a track to somewhere but finding out I've gone to a place and experienced something quite unexpected. So, after that's happened, I might question whether you're messing with me. But none of that description fits Woody, does it?"

I paused what I was doing to look in her direction. She shook her head.

"So, why would *he* wonder?" I asked.

"You could put the question to him, but it might get you cryptic answers," she said. "Lacking that, I can make a guess of my own."

The coffee was ready, but I didn't reach for the mugs.

"Maybe," she said, "just maybe, he was wary that I was sending you out to play Indian."

Now I did reach for the mugs, a cover while I collected my thoughts. Her words repeated in my head on a continuous loop: *play Indian . . . play Indian . . . play Indian . . .* Coffee sloshing into the mugs broke the word cycle, but despite my brain welcoming a rising aroma, I got no closer to deciphering a meaning. Carrying the filled mugs to the table outside allowed me time to attempt resetting the question.

"I went asking Woody about local trails because I'd taken your friendly suggestion to take a hike as just that—a sympathetic guess at a way for me to master, or at least banish, my daytime nightmare I'd told you about. He didn't know why you'd suggested I go out there, I didn't tell him. But why, even before I set out or came back and told him what happened, would Woody think you might have more up your sleeve than a suggestion to me to explore the hills?"

By this time, we'd drifted over to the folding table and sat down. I pushed one of the mugs across to her.

"As I remember, you take it black," I said.

She nodded, said, "Thank you," and raised it to inhale the rising vapor.

"Play Indian?" I asked. "What's that got to do with Woody and me wrinkling our brows about your possible motives?"

"The term or idea, playing Indian, comes from a book by that title published in the nineteen-nineties by Philip Deloria. I don't know how much Woody might have read, but I bet he's absorbed enough by any other means. Of course, there's another book, *Speaking of Indians,* written some fifty years earlier. It explored many of the same thoughts. I don't know if Woody knows of it, either. With him it's hard to know what idea threads his active mind has pursued. If he's painting my motives with the thoughts expressed in those works, it could touch a nerve."

"Playing cowboy and Indians I know about," I said. "But I've never heard of either book or just playing Indian. You've got a full mug of coffee. Let's see how far you get explaining the term before you see bottom."

She glanced at the mug, as if to estimate how long she might take to empty it. "The organizing principle of both books isn't that complicated," she said. Basically, they look at many of the ways the early colonialists and the later occupiers of North America appropriated and acted out aspects of Native cultures. How they played Indian, in other words."

She paused there and took a pull of her coffee while watching me over its rim as if to assess what I'd made of her statement.

Not much.

I thought I owed it to her to say so. "I've never been good with summaries."

"You'd like examples," she said.

"Something to weigh down the generalizations helps me along. And with me, you might as well not hurry."

"I'll just plod along. Of the early colonialists, consider the men who threw shiploads of boxes into Boston Bay."

"The Boston Tea Party, you're talking about."

"Yes. Men garbed as Indians," she said.

"To disguise their identity while committing a crime, I'd guess, more than to act on some desire for playing Indian."

"They could have dressed as pirates or worn masks and been more disguised. Their identities were not hidden. They partied afterward in the same blankets, face-paint, and feathers. Besides, pirates were heroic figures to many back then."

"Maybe," I admitted, "but the Indians were possibly more notorious at the time for local folks."

She shrugged. "You might have a better chance with your arguments if dress-up and act-like behavior had ended with the Boston Tea Party."

"It didn't?"

"Later came Girl and Boy Scouts organizations and many of their promoted pastimes."

"I learned to tie a bunch of knots, which seemed as much linked to packers and sailors as Indians. Can't say much about Girl Scouts. Knew a few, but I never participated."

She didn't smile. "Maybe not you, but many of both genders hung out in tepees, they started fires without matches, the girls did a lot of beadwork on dresses and moccasins."

"Also, I learned to braid plastic bracelets and key fobs," I said, "Probably I wasn't a very good Scout, but what you named seems like kids wanting to learn basic survival skills before there were Rangers or SEALS as models."

"I don't disagree," she said. "The founders of Scouting thought the nation was going soft and looked to Mountain Men as models. Who, by the way, hung around with Natives and often married among them. I think the point is that the youth clubs weren't the Sons of Sparta or the Valkyrie Girls. Plenty of tough-guy survivalist models in the ancient western world, but American choices tended toward playing Indian."

"Choices, plural . . .?"

"The Tammany Society is another, for instance."

"A bunch of political operatives?" I scratched my head.

"Wouldn't you think they'd start out calling themselves something like Cambridge Glee Club or Athens Debate Society. But no. They named their group after a chief of the Lenni-Lanape named Tamanend. They appropriated many Native customs and words in their proceedings, including wearing war paint at their gatherings and calling their meeting hall a wigwam."

"And eventually evolved into Tammany Hall?" I guessed.

"Yes. You want more?

"Well . . ."

"There were secret fraternal orders like the Improved Order of Red Men—not the Better Viking Fathers, you notice, or Upgraded Riders of El Cid."

I looked closer at her to see if she was enjoying ribbing me. Her serous-looking gaze gave the impression she wasn't. I sensed she was on a roll and kept silent.

"Drum circles," she said. "Hippie beads and feathers and more beaded dresses. Peyote and other drugs-for-spiritual-enlightenment. All those New Agers' movements and their beliefs drawing from Native religions."

She took a pull of coffee and peered into the mug as she set it down. From where I sat, she was only half done, at best.

"Maybe you see a pattern?"

I swirled the coffee in my mug and, while watching the liquid circle, said, "I seem to recall much interest in Zen during some of those times. Also, Dharma bums, you remember? Were those folks playing Japanese or playing Tibetan? Or are we going around and around here?"

She acknowledged what I said with the briefest smile and nod. "I'm not trying to sell a proven fact. You asked, and I'm setting out ideas that are blowing in the wind."

She settled back in her chair, let her hands fall into her lap, and took a run at a fuller explanation for me.

"The authors of those books I mentioned," she said.

"About playing Indian . . ."

"Yes.

"They looked," she said, "at those groups I've mentioned, and connected the dots across the centuries."

"Sounds like reading tea leaves," I said.

"How much isn't? I hear Woody asking," she said.

"Sure, it took thousands of years and getting past a little torture and mayhem to get the earth revolving around the sun. He'd admit," I said.

"But dot-connecting did get us there," she said.

"While five hundred years on, we've still some who believe the science they're told is hooey because it doesn't match their gut feelings."

She drew a long breath. "I don't get many disbelievers or hecklers in my lectures and classrooms."

"Sure. Why would they?"

"Would they, what."

"Take a class," I said, "about what they didn't agree with."

"You mean like members of the Inquisition—"

"Rough crowd," I said.

"They wouldn't enroll in Copernicus's course of Astronomy," she said.

"I don't know the facts. It seems unlikely."

"Doesn't mean I don't recognize them," she said.

"Them, who?"

"Disbelievers or hecklers," she said.

"Even nice college kids get cranky as they age and tire," I grumbled.

"I can stop or go on. It's all the same."

I open my hand to her, half in apology, half for her to continue.

"Connecting dots, those writers saw a picture," she said. "A tableau of those later-comers to the continent wrapping themselves in the original occupants' clothing and rituals to define the newcomers' American differentness and specialness from Europeans."

"Tough case to make," I said, nodding. "Seeing as how there were plenty of Protestants—even Puritans—still in Europe and most of the colonists came from there."

"Yes, especially in the country's early years," she said. "But as time rolled on, the authors believe, playing Indian was also a way to cope with Natives who managed to survive all attempts to eradicate their territorial homes, religions, languages, cultures, and very existences. Playing Indian could include or admit the aboriginal or ancient wisdoms—preferably in a museum, archeological study, or if absolutely necessary, on a reservation—and at the same time *exclude* the present-day Natives as equal members of the dominate society or even as humans."

"Dominant society," I said. "Smacks of *white* and *oppression*. Not to be defensive, but what of our *melting pot*, our *equality* for all creeds and races?" I smothered the irony I usually added when I recited these sanctimonious beliefs. "Most would say the country hasn't been all-white, all Protestant for a long time."

Her face didn't change. "See? I wish they'd say the place hasn't been all-white since Raleigh's ship landed on Roanoke Island. Not to mention since the landing of slave ships. The writers connecting dots believe playing Indian went hand in hand with the pressures on Natives to assimilate in language, religion and customs but to accept being racially inferior. We might poll the many shades of nonwhite people here today whether they feel similar pressure."

Her voice had taken on a speculative tone, supplanting her sometimes academic delivery that, I supposed, were born of many hours of delivering information she'd covered many times. With the hint of speculation, however, came another note, perhaps one of wishing that playing Indian *had* ended with the Boston Tea Party, or maybe, of her sadly recognizing a human trait that dictated it continue. If the last, it seemed blended with another voice from somewhere within her that added an anguished *Why? Why the trait? Why must it seek domination?*

Or perhaps some or all of those competing voices I thought I heard from her were actually mine.

She had stopped and looked at me, as if to assess whether I had any idea what she was talking about.

"This is about the place in my lectures where I pause," she said, "and ask, 'Some examples?' I scan my students and nail the sleepy-eyed one toward the back: Bitterroot Bob, please, from your own experience?"

I shifted in my chair, no doubt as her sleepy-eyed pupil might do, tried to buy some time with a pull at my own coffee. Was she being high-handed? A bit. But I also thought she'd earned it. Among her several voices I heard below her words, I'd also sensed notes of anger.

"All this," I said, "sounds like our love and promotion of, say, jazz as a *uniquely American* creation while at the same time refusing African Americans through the front door and ignoring their many contributions in medicine, science, literature or just plain living in everyday society."

She nodded.

"And again," I said, "as long as I've brought up music, I suppose it's like pointing to country music as especially *American* while at the same time shunning anyone with a southern drawl or twang or wearing any hat resembling a Stetson."

"You've grasped the idea," she said. "Many think playing Indian salves the internal conflicts, the ambivalence about personal identity in all those situations."

"You'll have to help me," I admitted, feeling not only sleepy-eyed but also like one of her slower students. "Why would they think that?"

"Because everywhere there's a tension between beliefs of equality and inequality—among Americans and within individuals. That tension sends people searching for what it means to be American, both as personal identity and as a nation. Playing Indian or dancing to jazz or country is all part of the search."

It might have been her use of the word *search* that derailed me, or at least diverted me from her lecture and set me thinking of my own search in this high desert. Searching for *my own words*, I'd told myself. Lately also for a *lost child*. And just yesterday, for the *arc of moral history*, thank you very much, Roger Stegman.

Before I'd made my self-important exodus from the social noises of the mainstream world, it had seemed the previous months had been filled by so many searching for an explanation or multiple explanations for the nation's turn. They found themselves hard put to shape a *why*. Why the turn, was one issue, but the greater one seemed to be, Why the grievance and interpersonal rancor? Why hate as reflex? Whether counting themselves among the winners or the losers, anyone thinking about it seemed to feel that something had been lost, a way of thinking about people and things, maybe. A familiar approach to living had been—what?—marred? As if a favorite car of many years, still serviceable, kept clean and waxed despite the color slightly fading, had been discovered one morning keyed from head to tail light: front fender, doors, rear panel.

Now there was a metaphor on wheels. But it left the basic questions unanswered. Just what lost? What marred? Or was the feeling not so much of loss as it was a recognition that something darkly ugly had been lately rediscovered and newly burnished?

It wasn't the loss of polished fender. It was the act of keying that upset. What I had thought submerged, those emotions that had not been acceptable to express, had become something to shout about, to act on. Again, it wasn't the shouting of those emotions that disturbed me, it was their resurgence, the strength of that resurgence that shocked. What I'd thought was merely intolerance revealed itself as hate.

But why was I shocked? Isn't the strength of those emotions a danger to be guarded against? Always? Everywhere? Otherwise, why have a Commandment against coveting, which is only a fancy word for envy? Why have another against bearing false witness? Why a parable about the hated foreigner, the Samaritan? Why the Great Commandment to love thy neighbor?

Shocked? I had been fairly and loudly warned.

And in any case, was people searching for a *why* part of what Judith Clearwater was describing? Was the looking for *why* just the continuing attempt to define a personal or national identity? Was this search one more way of playing Indian or listening to jazz?

"Okay, yes," I said, simultaneously admiring her silent attentiveness while she waited out my slow-turning mental gears, "so the matter of personal identity—of national identity—gets tricky. But—"

"Yes. Sometimes more than others," she added. "I've left out that our dot-connecting writers thought the rise of playing Indian movements corresponded with times of great social change."

"Like times of impending revolutions?" I said.

"And financial recessions, shifts of international balance, massive migrations…"

"Okay, or unexpected election results," I said. "Or when confronted with the presence and strength of unacceptable emotions in our society. And, full disclosure, I like jazz and country. But we seem to have gotten sidetracked. Assuming you're right about this playing Indian business, what would lead Woody to wondering what you were up to?"

"He might think I was encouraging you to play Indian."

Her simple words jolted me. "Just where does Woody get off thinking you were sending me, or even could send me out to play Indian?

"Because I was?"

She waited to see if I had more to say.

I didn't.

She shrugged. "Or at least it could look like I was. There are many traditions of Natives walking off alone to find greater understanding of their place in the world. That wasn't exactly what I'd suggested for you, but it wasn't exactly not, either. Given the ambivalences within playing Indian that I mentioned, Woody could be uneasy about being part of sending you into the hills."

"Oh, for crying in a bucket!" I stopped short of slamming my mug onto the table. "Quest fables are in many cultures, from walkabouts to odysseys, from hunting for a magic flute to going at windmills with tin lances. I went for a couple of hikes. The first time, I admit, had something to do with chasing down a ghost of my childhood self, but yesterday I went as much to see what you'd told me about as to look for anything else. In either case, or when I trot off again, nobody should make a big deal out of it."

"Okay," she said. "Maybe Woody won't notice that when you wanted solitude to find whatever you're looking for, you did not go to a remote Pacific Island. You did not ask to join a silent monastery. You did not check in to a Zen center. Like that Bay Area one, where is it?

"Marin County," I said.

"That would have been closer to home," she said. "Or your fabled Wine Country. Land of many spas, which, I understand, offer many forms of navel-gazing. But, no. You came out to the West's Great Basin and stuck up a sign announcing Purgatory."

I studied her. "Meaning?"

"Purgatory. 'A place for purging, for purification, for cooking the uglies out of you.' That's what you said, if I recall right."

"Sounds about right," I said.

"What it sounds," she said, "is like a place to redefine a person's identity. Which, applied to you, especially you out here, gets close to our talk about someone playing Indian."

"I guess I can see how Woody might make a wrong assumption," I said. "Or have a second thought or two. Still—"

"And by the way," she said, "you're the one who mentioned the word 'quest.' But never mind. My coffee mug's empty anyway."

"Tell me again why you came by this morning?"

"Again? Actually, I didn't say. I came to invite you to come with me to my class today. I'm inviting you now." She glanced at her watch. "We've time to make it."

After last night's sleep, the lack of it, and this morning's conversation, I figured little would come of my attempting to write. I stood and collected the coffee mugs.

"Give me a minute to rinse these."

Half-way to the Airstream door, I heard her speak.

"Of course, many times the person *on* the quest is the last person to realize that's what's going on."

14

Cars these days. What do I know? They all look alike. Judith Clearwater's wasn't spanking new, but of the breed and undistinguishable. Inside, though, looked and smelled like many miles. The dash was dusty. The backseat was crowded with stuffed files, books bristling with Post-Its, and soft bags of who-knows-what. A cloth version of the last she had lifted from the passenger seat and slipped behind the back of it.

She left the sunroof open, and once we hit the highway, the morning's air flowing in was still cool enough to refresh.

I settled back. Rather than pursue what felt like a losing argument about whether or not I was on a quest out here, I went after the question of why she'd dropped by this morning, assuming that she hadn't invited me to go with her now to encourage me to play Indian again.

She hadn't.

She told me that she wanted to find out what more she could learn from me, as she'd mentioned in our very first meeting. That surprised me, because it seemed to me that mostly I'd been learning from her. All that stuff about the petroglyphs or pictographs, about Paiute place-names, and trains chuffing along different time-tracks.

I told her as much.

She reminded me that she, too, was bending her efforts to write. In her case, she wanted to invoke an experience of Native life without using any western cultural framework. I was one possible member of her reading audience. Talking with me was a way to assess whether or how much her ideas might work or how to make them work, depending on what more I might tell her.

"But," I said, "I've asked more questions than I've related information."

"One can learn a lot from questions people ask," she said.

When Woody had said that Judith Clearwater was good at listen-ing, I hadn't grasped that she would listen to questions as closely as she'd pay attention to whatever statements I blabbed. It felt spooky, like I'd lost some vague protection. Sure, I'd used questions as a way to push the person I asked into revealing themselves and move the spotlight from me. But now, Judith Clearwater revealed that the opposite had happened. Immediately, I pulled silence around me, like wrapping myself in a new magic coat of invisibility.

My silence lengthened. She let it. The highway spooled away behind us.

"People underrate the quantity of communication in silence," she said, not taking her eyes from the road.

Spooky, indeed. "Like what?" I said. "For instance."

"For example, questions," she said. "Sometimes even more can be learned from questions *not* asked."

So, she listened to questions, she listened to no questions. It felt like a threat, but I doubted she meant it that way. Yet I wanted to challenge the control, or power, or maybe just some implied omniscience or omnipo-tence. Then she'd said she wanted us to learn from each other.

"Are you saying I didn't ask something in our previous conversa-tion?" I wondered. "Or that I'm not asking one now?"

"After our earlier conversation," she said, "it seemed to me that when our conversation stopped, you left something unasked."

"Okay," I said and drew a breath. She raised one hand from the steer-ing wheel to stop me.

"And," she said, "probably your question remains unasked now. "So, *both* your then and now possibilities are very likely true."

She was maddening. "Do you also know my *question*?" I asked. "The one unasked?"

She smiled and shook her head.

"At last," I said, "one thing you admit not knowing."

"Response depends on the question, doesn't it?" she said.

"But we're *not* talking about a question *asked*," I said. "It was silent space you mentioned."

She nodded. "People go on a lot about a question we don't ask to avoid the answer that we already know."

"Or suspect we know," I said, "and don't want to hear."

"Sure. Those unasked questions are a dime-a-dozen in our lives."

"So," I said, "what of it?"

"You don't strike me as a dime-a-dozen type," she said.

If that was bait, I wasn't taking it.

We sat, silent, for a while. She attended to all the complicated work of steering her car down the arrow-straight road. I counted the passing mileage markers. One mile. Two miles.

"There's another kind of question we don't ask," she said, both her face and tone of voice remained unchanged. "The one for which we're afraid there is *no* answer . . ."

Time for me to climb off my high horse.

"Purgatory," I said.

"The place where you posted your sign," she said. "Where your mobile home stands under the cottonwoods."

"I set up camp to figure out what made my country suddenly feel foreign to me," I said. "And also, to find some clue how I could now live in it."

"I remember," she said. "How's that going?"

"Slow," I said. "And painfully."

"'Getting to most things worth anything has some hurt,'" she said. "Woody told me."

"Okay. But return to the what-happened problem," I said.

"Yes?"

"So far, it seems to me," I said, "a different way of thinking, a different way of doing things overwhelmed the old ways."

"Winners won, losers lost," she said.

"Not a matter of winners and losers," I said. "This wasn't a tennis match. Or a war."

"Go on," she said.

"Those new ways, the different thinking, the different ways of doing things . . . they are *way* different. They are not in line with how the world actually works, according to the people believing in the old ways. For them, the new ways will destroy their society as they knew it, perhaps the world itself."

"If I hear what you're getting at," she said. "That's what made your country feel foreign."

"Yes. And over on your porch the other day," I said, "you'd told me about Natives getting overwhelmed by a way of thinking and a philosophy of life they didn't agree with."

She nodded and waited.

I was surprised by my hesitancy to put my question into words, say it out loud, particularly say it to another, and especially to a person who would or would not have an answer. I fought down my reluctance.

"What'd they do?" I asked.

"Who?"

"The Natives who were overwhelmed . . . What could they do? What *did* they do?"

Her eyes held mine, steadily, unblinking, the way one coolly considers another while gathering or sorting or weighing alternative possibilities. She shifted her gaze back to the highway that now bent to take advantage of a gentle fold in the geography.

"I assume you know," she said, "some basic facts."

"Such as?" I asked.

"Such as, early on, when faced with their food supply destroyed and prevented from getting anything to replace it, many Natives gave in, surrendered. They said that to do otherwise would lead to annihilation." Her voice had a narrative tone, almost a once-upon-a-time voice.

"What I know of that is probably a splinter off the tree," I said.

"And others" she continued, "said that to give up was only to die another death. They resisted."

"Another splinter," I said. "But the stories I got of this were told mostly from the other side. The telling was more splashy. Played with bugles and lots of galloping."

Her glance had changed from cool to glacial. "Either of those early paths led to many trails of tears, reservations, and tens of thousands dying along the way or after arriving."

She paused only long enough for me to nod. I knew more was coming.

"Your additional splinters of knowledge might be less," she said, "or at least have fewer details, about subsequent massacres of Natives for more of their land. About marrying their women and then murdering them for more of their land. Of forcing Native children from their land and parents. About forcing the children to live in religious schools, change their clothing, renounce their Native faith, stifle their language, and submit to assimilation, but only as inferior citizens." Her voice had exchanged any once-upon-a-time quality for one of not-so-long-ago.

"With few details, as you say, I've had a glimpse," I said, sounding to myself out of place in the context of her narrative. "I've remained . . .

insulated from the anguish running through those events. My ears are getting warm as I confess this."

"Is your embarrassment necessary?" she said. "Standard education—"

"I can't blame my sanitized history books or unaware teachers," I said.

"No?"

"I've known the history was there and haven't gone looking. Or when I have looked, my research has been superficial. I retreated at the first hints of the immensity of the tragedy."

"The stories can take one's breath away," she said, the way a nurse bandaging your slashed arm declares your wound had been ghastly, before the stitches.

"I suppose it has been easier for me to be outraged at other people in remote places who act similar ways to grab land, control governments, suppress dissidents, or steal profits," I said. "It is easier—especially in my lifetime—than looking in a mirror at what we have done in the process of *bringing democracy* to those supposedly in need. It's certainly easier than looking closely at what some are currently doing to others, including to Natives, in my name."

I'd walked myself into a dark pit. I shut up. She did nothing to break my silence. I felt like I was back at the base of the Pillars of Rome, facing the murderous end of a rifle and hearing that power is always everything and the arc of moral history is forever flat.

I changed the subject, if only for my relief. I related my encounter with Roger Stegman among the Pillars of Rome. When I was done, I returned to our—Judith Clearwater's and mine—starting place.

"I know there's a train of thought today," I said, "among those who overwhelmed Natives. They now say, 'We won, you lost, deal with it!' But how?"

"How? The Natives?" she said.

"Yes. After all, by deal-with-it, the winners mean assimilate. Assimilate as inferior citizens, as you said, was bad enough. But worse, how do you assimilate to a different way of life, which according to your traditional beliefs, threatens the entire order of the world?"

"Good question," she said. "The new way threatened a way of life that had ensured Native survival for ten thousand years. We believe it still threatens the true order of the universe. But I have to ask."

"Ask what?" I braced myself.

"Are you equating the Native history with the more recent events that made the country feel foreign to you? Really?" The intensity of her voice had taken an up-tick. "You're comparing the genocidal colonialism I just glossed over with what many see as only another phase of how this country practices politics? I'm trying not to sound outraged here."

"I take your point," I said. "I've wondered myself, even though you more or less suggested the comparison in one of our earlier conversations." Her mouth opened, and I held up my hand to forestall her.

"Truly," I said, "I don't mean my comparison to minimize the immensity of the Native tragedy over the past half century and continuing into present days." I waited for her to nod before I continued.

"On the other hand, I also do not want to diminish the present on-going damage to the entire country through modern variations of similar acts."

"All of which leaves you where?" she asked.

"It's an uneven parallel, granted," I said. "I believe it's something like thinking that my country might be in the early stages of being over-whelmed. Similar, say, to what Natives may have felt in the 1600s or early 1700s, depending on where they lived on the continent."

She nodded. "And maybe on whether their primary association was with the French, who were mostly trappers and intermarried with Natives and respected their ways. Rather than with the English, whom Natives hated for clearing the land and slaughtering all the animals."

"Also," I said, "it may make little difference to the overwhelmed whether those doing it are foreign invaders or enemies living within the gates."

"Okay. Go on," she said.

"So, if not assimilate, not get over it, not shut up, what *could* they do? Especially at the get-go?"

She braked to slow the car. The change of speed surprised me. The turn signal wasn't clicking, but we turned right anyway onto a secondary road. Not far along, we passed a sign: *Welcome to Numu Teepu*. "Welcome to Paiute Land," she said.

"Student of mine is from here," she said. "Told me others here, who'd never see a university door, would like to hear some of what I teach. She set it up."

Shortly, another series of turns took us among and through a collection of buildings. Another sign in a vacant lot that read, Pai-Sho Tribe, seemed to imply more than the lot's fenced space.

"We're getting close," she said.

We stopped in front of a large structure at the edge of rolling hills of sage. A sign announced in black on white: Wellness Program & Youth Center. The building's weathered boards were white, the windows not curtained. A few other cars and a pickup or two were parked nearby. She cut the engine and got out.

She walked around, opened the back door on my side of the car, and extracted the cloth bag she'd stuck behind my seat.

"There's two other bags on the back seat," she said. "Would you mind? Heavy. They're full of books."

By the time I struggled through the screen door and into a large meeting room, she'd placed her bag on a table that formed one side of a hollow square of tables. She freed a folder from the bag and motioned for me to bring my burden to her table.

In chairs around the square sat a collection of adults, mostly older women in dark blouses and long dresses. A couple of young women in denim shirts and pants sat side by side. One of them positioned pens and a pad of paper in front of her. I wondered if she was the student who'd arranged the program. I counted three young men dressed in work shirts and pants, without paper or pens but looking intense and bright-eyed for all that. They tracked my progress to Judith Clearwater's side.

I put the bags of books on the table.

"Sit here," she said, indicating the chair next to where she stood. "You can be my teaching assistant."

She scanned the room, looked through the door and window on the side of the building where we'd entered, came back to the young woman with pens and pad.

"Looks like we're all here," Judith Clearwater said to her.

The young woman nodded.

From the casual "good-mornings" and scattered nods from around the tables, I understood they were all familiar. A few glances bounced off me, but a general studied lack of scrutiny indicated I was odd man out.

"I brought a guest," she said. "He goes by Bitterroot Bob."

This won some nods and a "Welcome" or two.

"He's interested in our story," she added. The crowd looked unimpressed, a unanimous showing of good sense, I thought.

"Stories," an older women emphasized. "I hear more than one around these tables."

Several others nodded, including Judith Clearwater.

"Good point," she said. "Maybe I should have said history, in general. Anyway, our talk on the way here," she said, "his and mine, fits in with what I wanted to cover today."

That made me squirm inside. But I held still and breathed easier as she summarized.

Leaving out the he-said, I-said details of our conversation in the car, she framed the problem of Native ways being overwhelmed by another culture, a culture whose incomprehensible philosophy endangered not only their ways of life but also the stability of their universe.

"What could they do?" she said. "What *did* they do?

I saw a few small hand gestures, heard some muttering, none of which I understood. One young man lifted his chin a fraction, his eyes moved from her, drilled me, shifted back again. Perhaps I was not so much a teaching assistant as Judith Clearwater's visual aid.

"We might have been out-numbered, overwhelmed." he said. "But they didn't bury us."

"That's right," she said, "Natives continued. Early on, many leaders talked and reasoned and negotiated with the invaders."

When we turned off the highway, I thought, we crossed a border. No euphemisms here about colonists, settlers, pioneers. Here, in clear sight, was the other side of the rug.

She'd paused only long enough for my flash of thought. She continued.

"Others, mostly women to start with, wrote personal histories and stories like some of you are doing. Of course, as you know, one of the first women came from here."

Still holding the pen in her fingers, the young woman shot her hand up and down in one motion.

"Sarah Winnemucca," she said with a smile. "We have her books in our library."

She pointed to a long, three-shelf bookcase under the windows at the back.

Judith Clearwater nodded. "You do, and I saw two others there by Mourning Dove, another early woman writer. Both of them, in their stories and speaking tours, tried to describe, to explain, to correct misconceptions of Native ways in general and of Native women in particular."

The women shifted in their chairs and studied the tables' scarred surfaces. They shuffled their feet. One set her fingers soundlessly drumming on a table. The student-organizer held her pen poised over her pad.

"Even so, the invaders called us Squaw," one of the older women said. "They still do. A word not in a Native language." Judith Clearwater nodded.

"I know," she said. "Uphill work. You know because some of you are also writing in that direction. Let's look at the hill you face."

Around the room, everyone lifted their eyes and focused on her as if she were magnetic.

"Unfortunately," she said, "the words of those women, spoken and written, came after books that had already bent perceptions about Natives."

She motioned in the direction of one of the bags near me. I understood she wanted me to reveal its contents. After I spilled several books onto the table, she picked one at random and held it up.

"Here's an addition for your library. *The Deerslayer.*" She searched and found one more. "Here's another: *Last of the Mohicans.* These are only two of many in what are known as James Fenimore Cooper's Leatherstocking tales." She pawed among the remaining books. "I brought several other books about legends, about men like Kit Carson."

A rude noise set her looking around the room at rolling eyes, wrinkled noses.

"That killer led massacres of Native women and children." It was the other young man. "He helped starve out the last Navajos in the Canyon de Chelly. Those writers of his legends lied."

"They were scared, man," the first one said.

"Scared?"

"Sure. A few years before the Revolutionary War, our eastern and northeastern brothers had pushed the invaders from the Virginia and Carolina territories back over the Allegheny Mountains, all the way up into Canada. They were practically on the doorstep of Albany. Our southwest brothers and sisters had chased the Spanish back into Mexico. Native warriors were feared by all the invaders."

"Still," the man beside him said, "Why read one word praising someone like Kit Carson?" He shifted his eyes to put the question to Judith Clearwater.

"For one thing," she said. "it pays to do your oppositional research. Triggers your imagination for your own stories, among other benefits. But, a suggestion: read past the praise of the legends. Look for words like squaw, buck, you know them. And read past those, too. You're after the descriptions of the characters they refer to. How are they portrayed to serve the story? Note the stereotypes. Those have shaped your identity for the invaders. They've also affected how you see your own identity and your place in this country. Then ask yourself: what do you have to say about it?"

She pushed aside other books on the table in front of me to find what she was looking for.

"Here's a good case in point, as an example." She found a book, held it for the jury. "Karl May, a German writer. Never once visited America for a real experience. His romanticized fantasies of the American Old West and Native stereotypes were the most widely read stories of his day."

"His day? That was when?" The question came from the young woman wanting facts to write in her notebook.

"Late 1800s," Judith Clearwater said. "Thousands of his German and other European readers filled with his stereotypes immigrated to America and its western territories. Translations were also read by many people already here."

She paused to let that sink in, then added, "Of course, research of propaganda's effects finds that what is heard and learned first is usually what continues to be believed. And it's believed over whatever information is gotten afterwards. The accuracy—or its lack—of the first information doesn't matter."

"Except," the voice came from one of the bright-eye young men, the one who knew eighteenth-century Native history. "Except, maybe," he said, "the bigger the lie, the more likely it's believed." It wasn't like he was contradicting her. She appraised him.

"History of Propaganda course," he said. "Dartmouth."

"When do you graduate?" she said.

"I did," he said. "I hope to get my MFA by next year."

She nodded, adding a smile that said, Good for you. She swung her gaze across the room.

"There you go," she said. "What could they do? They—we—Natives kept on. In more recent years, some have become lawyers and worked to protect and recover Native ways and lands through the legal system. Others are doctors, politicians. But those professions are not for everyone. Many Natives, men and women, continue to write and talk of their experiences.

She'd brought other books. In the other bag. I emptied them out; she talked a bit about some. These were works by later and current-day writers. Some her class knew of, others they didn't. She had brought the books to add to their library shelves. She put down the last and turned to her class.

"Some of our current Native storytellers are in this room. Let's talk about your works."

The people around the table reached into their bags and backpacks. They took out folders or sheaves of papers. They found pens and pencils. The young woman who had been taking notes was the first to speak.

"I'm beginning an autobiography of Sarah Winnemucca," she said. "I know there are others, but I hope to capture what it felt like as a woman, particularly a Native woman, to try to work against the stereotypes we were talking about. Not so much what she said. That's been done a lot. But I don't know of anything about how she felt, her emotions during that time."

One of the older women revealed that she worked in the building, in the Health Center.

"With those recovering from alcoholism," she said. "I'm not sure Native alcoholism rates are worse than Caucasians, from what I saw outside during my training. But on the rez, our treatment resources are much less. So, opportunities for recovery are fewer. If you see what I mean . . . Anyway, I want to write about that."

The young man not from Dartmouth chuckled. "The best resource against alcoholism we have around here owns the Saloon up in Fast Buck."

The recovery worker nodded. But another asked, "Why? Does he refuse to serve drinks to Natives?"

"He doesn't have to," the man said. "Just his being there keeps the alkies away. Maybe they're afraid word will get back to the elders."

"Sometimes just the presence of a Native witness is enough," the recovery woman said.

Once again, Woody, I thought, another side you keep well hidden.

Several of the women were trying to write about their family histories. Others, their own stories.

"I just want to tell what it feels like to keep living on the rez as a woman," one of them said. "Why do it?"

Another wove traditional baskets with a group of women. She wanted to catch the spirit of their conversations while they worked.

"My great auntie is one of us," she said. "I think she's the oldest. She don't talk much. When she does, she talks about how when we work, we weave back together the tear in our world."

Judith Clearwater didn't push them, but her eyes kept going back to the two young men. In one of the longer silences, the one who had mentioned Woody finally shuffled the few pages he had. He kept his eyes on them when he spoke.

"I just want to show what it feels like to be in our own land now,' he said. "Not all that stuff about back in the day. Now." His voice had become heated. "Nothing about what got taken, stolen. But about what we have. Now." He made a dismissing gesture and took a breath. "What it means to me, anyway. Maybe do it with poetry. I don't know."

"Yeah, I'm with you," the Dartmouth man said, sitting forward and planting his elbows on the table. "I want to write a novel about the Paiute and Shoshone. Maybe several characters through generations. I'm going to start researching it next year. Let the characters show how our nations were maybe the least waring of all Native groups. Maybe because the others didn't want our land. But we didn't try to get theirs, either. Peaceful mostly, us. Take the story into the present day. Show that peaceful way is still here. How it works."

He stopped and looked around the group. "I know. I know. Not the Great American Novel. The Great Paiute-Shoshone novel." He shook his head. "Now you can all tell me how crazy I am."

Judith Clearwater pushed away from the table she'd been resting against.

"Nobody's going to say anyone here is on the wrong path," she said.

As all of them had talked, she had nodded, offered encouragement, often suggested Native writers they might read who had explored similar ideas. There were many. Most I didn't know about. Listening to her, I felt like shaking my head. My splinter of information on this or that! More like drifting sawdust than a few splinters.

"All our stories are important," she said. "They are part of our maintaining and strengthening our Native identity." She glanced at her watch. "Keep writing. Next time we'll read some aloud and talk about what works and how we might make them better."

15

After the class ended, I helped Judith Clearwater shelve the books she had brought into the long bookcase. My fingers ran along the spines of books already in place. They were not in alphabetical order by author: Elissa Washuta, Rebecca Roanhorse, Tommy Orange, Billy Rae Belcourt, Terese Maria Malhot, Cherie Dimaline, David Treuer, Tanelle Campbell, Daniel Heath Justice, Joshua Whitehead. So many writers I didn't know.

I stopped at a familiar one, pulled it out, and brushed a hand across its cover.

"N. Scott Momaday won a Pulitzer for that, as you may know," she said, looking over my shoulder. "You're holding his story that started the Native Literature movement back in the nineteen-sixties."

"And still, Momaday is hardly a household name," I said, "although I admit I've read this one, *House Made of Dawn*."

"I always liked what he said about creating stories," she said. "He wasn't talking just about writing them, but still . . ."

"What was that?" I asked.

"'Anything is bearable if you can make a story out of it,'" she said.

"That's good," I said and slid the book in between others and turned to her. "I think I've been asking the wrong question."

"The one about '*What* did they do?'" she said.

"Yes. I should have asked, what *happened* after they did whatever they did? What changed, in other words?"

She smiled. It wasn't much, but it illuminated her entire presence. It brightened the day.

"We can't know what things might be like now," she said, "if those people had not made the effort. Or for that matter, if we don't continue to try."

"But," I insisted, "are you saying there was, there is, *no* answer?"

"There," she said. "Now that sounds like the question you've been avoiding. You're afraid that Natives have no solution for their tragedy."

"Am I?"

"You're afraid of more," she said. "That you have no reply to Roger Stegman, his telling you that the arc of moral history is flat. You're afraid that you'll not find the words you came to Purgatory to find."

Maybe I looked blank. She went on.

"Our being here may seem a small thing to you or maybe you think it self-evident. But most people of this country talk and write and think about Natives as though their way of life is lost, gone forever, to be found only in history and anthropology books or museums or at public tribal festivals."

"And many folks attend those festivals. Still—"

"Which many people," she said, "attend and experience as an enacted museum exhibit." Both her voice and eyes sparked. "Natives are thought about and treated as an embarrassing historical artifact. But not as sovereign peoples living on over eighty thousand square miles of North America."

I waited.

"That's about the size of your state of Idaho," she said. "Yet many people believe we're to be swept under the rug."

"But they—you—haven't been swept," I said. "You're still here."

"Exactly," she said, "despite great odds, we're still here."

She paused, nodding, and then added in a quieter voice, "It's not over."

We walked together out to the car. She leaned on her hand against the car top.

"Ouch!" she said. "Open your door," she said. "This thing's a tin pot on a hot rock. Leaving windows open wasn't enough."

"You and Woody," I said. "You're both Natives." I opened my door.

She opened hers and studied me over the top of her sweltering car. "It's good you're not taking this class for credit. Obvious statements, no points."

"What I'm wondering about, are you both on the same side in this Native American thing?"

She looked past me, taking in the sparse buildings and the acres beyond the barbed wire fence separating our parking area from the beyond. Her faraway look seemed sad to me, but maybe she was just letting down after being on point in the classroom.

"The Native American thing?" she said. "How to be Indigenous, how to express it and live it, and what to do about it? *That* Native American thing?"

"It's in the ballpark," I said. "You and Woody seem to come at it from different angles."

"Points for noticing. Remember those different stories you heard back in the meeting room? These days," she said, "questions about the *Native American thing* get about as many answers as you have individual Natives."

She climbed into the car and shut the door.

The road back looked pretty much the same as it had coming. Here we are, I thought, rolling along while the globe rolls around.

"Once again," I said, "I seem to have learned more from your answering my questions than you have learned from me. In our exchange of me learning from you while you learn from me, it seems like you're on the short end of the deal."

She looked away. I thought she might argue it again, tell me what she'd learned from my silence and from my questions not asked or catch me off-guard again with other similar rigmarole. She stared into the distance so long that I wondered whether she was working out her grocery list.

"Okay," she said and brought her gaze back to me. "Just for myself, for the archive you might say, I've something I'm curious about."

"I'll do my best," I said, less than sure it would be enough.

She proceeded to remind me that we'd spent some time talking about stereotypes of Natives, the missing or misleading or false histories about them, even the stories invented from imagination rather than any experience of them or, at best, experience already tainted by faulty preconceptions.

"Sounds much like me," I said, "to a greater or lesser extent, depending."

"And so, my question. I'm going to make a big assumption," she said, "and ask it this way: what is your earliest personal experience you can remember with Natives?"

I had to think about it. "By personal, I'm thinking you mean other than playing cowboy and Indians or having an ancient man pointed out to me when six years old. He sat rocking in a chair across a room. I got told the man had met Sitting Bull."

"Nothing secondary, that's right. Your first-hand experience. I don't mean this as a challenge. I'm only curious."

I thought some more. There was my grandmother. Whom I'd visited and seen in her bedroom before everybody went to bed. Her black hair was in a single braid that fell past her hips. My grandfather had claimed she descended from the Powhatan. Other familymembers dismissed it as more of his silliness. Not a good example.

"I don't know if this would count as first-hand," I said, "but here's probably the first experience I had, or at least, the first I remember."

I told her that when I was growing up, somewhere in the early nineteen-fifties, I'd traveled with my mother and grandmother—the other one—from Idaho to Portland to see my uncle, who had brought the freighter he captained to dock there. For a lot of the trip, we drove along the Columbia River on the Great Columbia Highway, which wasn't all that great in those days, mostly just a well-traveled two-lane highway.

Along the way, somewhere near The Dalles, the adults decided to slow up for a closer look. There was a lake and a set of impressive falls.

"The Narrows known as The Dalles," she said. "You probably were at Lake Celilo and Celilo Falls. I know of them. They're actually a dozen or so miles downstream from The Dalles."

"Really? I never knew the names. I was just a kid at the time, so I guess I always thought the whole thing—falls, town, lake—was called The Dalles."

Anyway, I went on, the salmon were running. Maybe my mother and grandmother knew that, maybe that's why they decided to drive over to the falls. The Natives were fishing during the salmon run upstream over the falls.

At first, I thought they were using immensely long fishing poles, but when we got closer, I could see there was a net at the end of each pole. The fishermen, dozens and dozens of them, walked out to the edge of the rocks that formed the falls or onto wooden platforms they'd built over the drops. They scooped up the salmon with the nets as the fish eddied below the falls gathering strength and speed to leap up and over the tumbling waters.

"That must have been quite a sight for a young boy," she said.

"Yes. I remember being fascinated by the mechanics of the process," I said. "But it wasn't the strongest memory that stayed with me."

I told her that after we'd looped past the fishing, we stopped a little way below the falls to take in the scene from a distance, the whole panorama, although that word probably wasn't in my vocabulary at the time.

A white sunlight slanted across the falls and turned the men's figures and the wet rocks shining black against the bright, foaming cascade with its mist rising like smoke. The hundreds of jumping salmon glistened in the mist across the set of falls, were lost in the churning mass, reappeared in seconds leaping again, the men and their poles moved rhythmically back and forth at the edge of the water, nets dipping, poles swinging. The repetitive motion against the falling whitewater and rising haze was mesmerizing. Something about the whole business struck me as so primal—again a word I wouldn't have known then—that I felt, even then, I was witnessing something fundamental in my world. Until now, I've never tried to limit that experience in words, but its image rang so deep in me I still feel the truth of it.

Judith Clearwater heard me out without comment, the way one listens to a child tell a dream. I decided to go on.

"There's one more image, or maybe it's two, or a cluster of them, from that time," I said.

"Okay," she said.

On our way back to the highway, I told her, we drove through an area removed from the falls, where the women and children cleaned and packed the salmon in wooden barrels. Most of the adults ignored us as our car crept by their activity. But the kids didn't, at least the ones close to my age. They stared in at me staring out the back window of our car. I remember the distinct feeling of my being like the lions in their cages that I'd walked past in the main entryway to the Barnum and Baily Circus that once came to town. I felt I was more of a curiosity than the kids staring in.

"Perfect," she laughed. I thought I saw a sympathetic smile.

"What?"

"You and them: face to face, separated by glass."

"Not perfect to me. Not then," I said.

She shrugged. "Of course, it's all gone now."

I nodded. "I found that out when we also visited the building site of the Grand Coulee Dam later on that trip. Or at least I learned that it was going to happen." The backup from the dam, I told her, would eventually submerge, drown, and end that entire way of life.

"Actually," she said, "it was The Dalles Dam, closer than the Grand Coulee to Celilo Falls, that dealt the final blow. When they closed its final spillway, the Natives stood and watched the water rise. Their Celilo Falls disappeared. So did the salmon. Over five hundred million a year from the Columbia River, I've been told. Your memory is of a way of life that was already dying."

"You've reminded me of something else," I said. "Unfortunately, the memory comes accompanied by the words, 'fish out of water.'"

I told her that years later I had worked as a hospital orderly. One day I was joined by another young man who let me know he was a Native from The Dalles. He was training to be an orderly as part of an employment program for the tribal members.

"I never got to know him well. I left the hospital soon after he began working there. That first day, he struck me as depressed. Maybe it was our task. We were moving an old woman who had died in her room to a freezer in the morgue."

"Interesting," she said. "You were both learning the same skill."

"Hospital orderly?" I asked.

"The rite of transporting the dead from the midst of the living."

"I kept picturing him, as he walked in front of me and guided the gurney while I pushed," I said, "I pictured him in the mist of Celilo Falls, working his pole-net, one of many who were as much a part of that landscape as the leaping salmon."

I stopped talking. And what do you hear in *this* silence, I wondered?

"I don't know," I said. "I can still hear the river tumbling over granite shelves, a splash of jumping salmon, an occasional voice raised above the thundering. Maybe it was cry of joy in a catch. Maybe it was a lament."

"Beware," she said, "of sentimental nostalgia."

"Meaning?" I asked.

"Maybe the cry was a voice of defiance"

"Like, 'We're still here.'"

"Or, 'It's not over,'" she said.

"Maybe it had all the sounds."

"River, fish, the voiced will to live, all mixed together?" she asked. "How's that work?"

"In three stanzas," I said, "like a ballad."

16

For several days after the workshop visit with Judith Clearwater, I struggled to reconcile her sentiment of Natives "keeping on" with my search for a way to live with the reality of being overwhelmed by the unfamiliar and inimical. Make it into a story, like Momaday suggested? I felt obligated to act. But something more was necessary than blind optimism and symbolic demonstrations. Neither had prevented the country's current Pandora's box from being opened again. But . . . but . . .?

Needing a break from beavering away at my laptop, I decided to take a drive to blow the stink off. For lack of a better destination, I turned the Ranchero out along the road past her place, just to see where it went. Maybe, on my way back, I'd stop by Woody's saloon for a beer.

Maybe?

The road—surprise, surprise—took me through open miles of sagebrush and cheat grass. I wasn't in the mood for minimalist beauty. Having had enough, I turned around and headed back.

In the distance between me and Fast Buck, a thread of smoke trailed into the blue.

Minutes later I crested a rise and could see that the smoke wasn't that far away. And was more than a thread. Much more now. And dark nearer the ground, not white. This was a new fire.

Perhaps someone had cleared brush and was now burning it. Given of the fire's approximate location, the someone must be Judith Clearwater. That was puzzling because there had been no signs of brush clearing around her place last time I'd been there.

A controlled burn?

More miles of watching. The line of dark smoke widened. I dropped the idea it was a controlled burn. But I was certain it was close to her place.

Hoping that someone had noticed—was she even home?—I glanced down at my speedometer. The Ranchero was already moving faster. Maybe somebody was on it . . .

I skidded to a stop in front of Judith Clearwater's house. She stood on her porch facing the smoke, shielding her eyes with one hand.

"That yours?" I shouted through my open window, across the distance between us.

"No." She didn't turn toward me.

"Controlled burn?"

"No." Still scanning the smoke.

"You call it in?"

"My landline's out," she said, finally turning toward me. "What'd you see on your way over from Fast Buck?"

I got out and closed the pickup door. "Wasn't any fire, maybe a half-hour, forty-five minutes ago, when I drove by here."

"Hasn't been burning that long." The intensity of her voice fell off. She rubbed the side of her face with her open hand. "So, you don't know if the road's passable."

"No," I said from the foot of the steps.

"What's your take?" She asked. She shielded her eyes for another look. "At first the wind was pushing it this way."

I climbed onto her porch. "I think it shifted in the last five or ten minutes. The smoke is blowing away from here now."

"I wasn't sure of the highway," she said.

"Blowing away from it," I said. "Now."

She turned. Her hand dropped from over her eyes. She fingered a halter hanging over the porch railing along side a lead rope. "I was going to go, call from the Saloon, but the road," she said, gripping the halter. Her knuckles were white. "And I didn't want to leave my horse."

"I'll go," I said and started for the steps. I was part way down, when she called.

"No!"

I stopped and looked back at her.

"I'll be able to give the BLM better directions than you," she said.

"Woody can . . . I said.

" . . . or than Woody can," she said.

"Okay, but get a move on," I said. "That fire's closer than I thought. And the backside—"

"—I know, I know." She dropped the halter back on the railing. "Look, if the fire gets too close, will you move my horse? She'll come along easy enough with the halter." She took a second look at me. "Or you can just loop the lead rope . . . around her neck."

"I'll manage . . . and keep an eye here. Get going. Maybe I can do something in the meantime."

Already striding toward the stairs, she pulled her keys from a pocket. On the first step, she reversed direction, mouth open, looking startled. She ran to the screen door, swung it to her. The front door stood open. I could see her filled work table beyond.

"And I'll load your work papers in my truck," I said. "If . . . Scat."

She hesitated. "There are boxes under . . ." She pointed at nothing in particular in the house.

"I'll find them." I said. "Go, go."

She let the screen door slam shut and ran to her car. She wheeled it toward the highway, her rear wheels spinning gravel that pinged off my fenders and tailgate.

I went on down the steps to the Ranchero. Turned it around, nose out toward the highway. Early preparation is better than late haste. My water bottle on the passenger seat was now in the sun. I moved it to the floor.

Back on the porch, at the railing facing the fire, I could see there was more smoke. A burst of flame enveloped a clump of sage. At a guess, about a mile away. Better to walk than drive closer. Besides, the Ranchero might be handy to tie her horse to if I needed to move both.

I trotted back down the stairs and pulled my shovel from under the tarp. Thinking of the sage flaring up, I considered the ax. There wouldn't be time for that. I thought I'd have a better chance knocking the fire down than cutting a break. I slung the shovel handle onto my shoulder and set off.

After the shade of the porch, the sun stuck me harder. I hoped the water bottle in the Ranchero would stay cool.

Stupid!

I reversed my direction and went right back to the pickup. Opened the door, grabbed the water bottle, drained it in gulps, and tossed it back on the floor, empty. Not much, but it would be something against the day's heat. I slammed the door and started out again.

As I crossed the land near the house, I saw the horse in her shady spot, but head up now, facing the fire's direction, maybe showing a little agitation with her flicking tail and shifting weight, but not panicked. She looked my way and whinnied.

I kept going, wondering how long it would take for a fire crew to come.

Getting closer, I slowed, not wanting to walk into more trouble than necessary. It looked like I was near one end of the fire. It had burned away from the road in an arc that bowed toward Fast Buck.

For a while, I'd smelled the smoke. Now I could hear the fire, a snap here or pop there. But it wasn't raging. The breeze was steady, but not gusting. I grabbed a fistful of grit and let it stream from my hand. the wind was shifting a little, but mostly blowing from the road. Luckily, the far end of the curved line was the front of the fire. The end I was near was the back end, or near enough, and the flames were eating territory more slowly. Airflow angled across my left shoulder. If the wind held, I had a chance of cutting off enough of this end of the fire for it to miss Judith Clearwater's place.

A chance. How big? And again, how long it would take fire crews to get here?

Well, a chance was a chance.

I picked a place near the end closest to the road. The long line of calf-high flames stretched away until lost in smoke.

The chance looked more like impossible.

"Eighty thousand acres?" The remembered voice of Roy, my crew boss, repeating the reported size of the range fire in the Owyhee breaks. My first. He pushed his Allis-Chalmers cap back on his head, his brown eyes gathering all the wisdom of his twenty-five years. *"Big? Yeah."* He grinned. *"But think of it as a line of camp fires to smother."*

Now, at this Oregon fire barely started, I drew a deep breath and drove my shovel at the ground. *Ouff!* It was as hard as I remembered. I stomped on the blade and drove it deeper . . . a little. Enough to raise half a shovel of dirt. I carried it to the end of the creeping burn and threw it sideways along the line of flames. A foot or two flickered out.

A start.

Back to the tiny hole. This time it was fractionally easier to drive in the spade at the hole's edge. A larger shovel full. Spread across the licking flames. Another two or three feet reduced to smoke. Back to the somewhat bigger, softer hole. Dig.

Hole to fire, dirt across flames, back to hole, dig.

I was surprised but a bit pleased how quickly the rhythm came back. My old creaky frame oiled up and kept the pace steady. Breathing and heart rate up a smidge, but not bad. My awareness contracted to my motions, wind direction, double checking whether spot fires popped up across the line of smoking ash I was lengthening. A melody insinuated among my sparse thoughts:

The old grey mare, she ain't what she used to be . . . Hole to fire, dirt across flames, back to hole, dig. . . . *ain't what she used to be . . .* Hole to fire, dirt across flames, back to hole . . . *but she keeps amovin' on . . .* dig.

When the distance from the flames to one hole got to too far, I started a new one farther along the line of fire.

Even though the breeze was at my back and the flames relatively short, my face and body felt the heat. Fire, flames, heat. Who knew? For that matter, the sun overhead was a ball of fire. Also hot. How about that?

I thought maybe the wind had ticked up but couldn't be sure that it wasn't the draft created by the fire itself. As long as it kept smoke from my nose and eyes . . . Checking around, I saw that haze had obscured the road now, and although I was making fair progress, the flames had cut the distance to Judith Clearwater's buildings by at least a third.

Back to work. Hole. Flames. Hole. Dig. "The Old Grey Mare" became a faint tune, occasionally hummed.

"Crew's on the way."

I turned toward the voice. Woody strode toward me, shovel across his shoulders. Past him in the distance, I could see his Power Wagon standing near my pick-up. I hadn't seen or heard him drive in.

"They're just mopping up a burn over near Crane," he said. "Incident Command diverted a team to us. Ought to get here in less than an hour."

He gave me the full up-and-down while he talked. I could feel myself slick with sweat and must have been a sight. He looked past me along the black line I'd made.

"They're sending a water truck, too," he said. "Should help."

He checked the other direction and the flames eating their way toward Judith Clearwater's buildings and nodded.

"In the meantime, looks like you have a good idea."

He walked further down the burning line and started his own hole.

I went back to mine. I regretted that I'd stopped moving to listen to Woody. Every muscle complained, and each shovel of dirt weighed heavier.

After knocking down the flames up to where Woody had started, I walked along his smoldering line until well past him and started in again.

We carried on like that, lapping each other, same work as before, but I was aware of more progress. Good thing. The fire had halved the original distance to the buildings. Soon I'd have to decide about moving the horse, rescuing papers and anything else. Then I saw Judith Clear-water's car near her house, so I went back to digging and slinging dirt. I straightened after throwing a shovelful and my back twinged. Walking back to my hole, I ran my hand over the shovel blade. There was a time we filed them sharp at the start of every shift. So long ago.

I lowered the shovel. Dig.

At one point as Woody lapped me, he paused and leaned on his shovel handle.

"You've done this before," he said.

"Yeah. Sometimes the BLM was the only summer money for older teenagers." I was glad for the break to talk. My teens seemed lost in the smoke of time.

Another quarter hour of hole, dirt, fire, hole. The periodic *chunk* of Woody's shovel in answer to mine felt neighborly. I knocked down the last flames before Woody's extinguished line.

Walking on to lap him, I eyed the fire remaining that still threatened Judith Clearwater's place. "We're beating it!" I thought. And immediately: What was that, old man, a cry of joy? A lament for times past? Defiance? Or all three?

"We're getting there," I said as I walked by Woody. We're still here . . .

"Nuh, huh." He stomped his shovel into the ground.

The thing about hard labor, I reminded myself, is that its move-ments are often repetitive. The repetition develops a rhythm. The rhythm becomes mindless. Pain recedes.

Dig. Walk to fire. Throw dirt across flames. Return to hole. Dig.

I noticed my lips were stuck together and my mouth barely damp. Mindless, then, but not bodyless.

Another twenty minutes. Hole to fire, dirt across flames, back to hole, dig. I lapped Woody. I was pretty sure we'd done it, cut off enough of the fire line. Woody lapped me. My palms burned. Back and shoulders ached. Prickles spread up my neck, across my scalp.

I drove my shovel into the ground and leaned on it. Sparkles danced before my eyes. Not embers from the fire. Failing to blink them away and dizzy, I leaned harder and felt myself waver. A tingling wandered down the backs of my legs.

I slid my grip down the shovel handle and squatted before I tipped over. The wooziness lessened with my slow deep breathing while I kept my head lowered toward my knees.

A shadow fell across me, and a pair of boots stopped just where I could see them. A shovel blade bit into the sand. They were army issue boots, once well cleaned, new laces, now everywhere covered with dust. Had to be Woody. I looked up.

"You okay?" One more time of him with a question he already knew the answer for.

"Sure," and me with another truth needing qualification. "I just felt a little faint for a second."

"Uh-huh."

Straightening, I braced on the shovel handle. Blood plunged to my feet and rebounded. My heart made several great thumps and settled. I fought a wobble and won. After another deep breath, I added, "Just a touch of sunstroke. Maybe."

"I suspect." He wasn't going anywhere. And he didn't take his eyes off me.

"Don't start in about no hat."

Woody managed hurt, surprise, innocent, and concern, all with one expression.

"No percentage in telling a man what he already knows," he said.

"I'm fine, now." I pulled my shovel from the sand to prove the point.

"Sure you are." He shifted his gaze past me. "Hey, look who's come to town."

I turned to look the direction he indicated. A big yellow water truck, engine whining in a low gear, jolted over the uneven ground toward us. It rolled on by, across the burn line, headed in the direction of the advancing fire line.

A crew-cab truck, same color as the tanker, approached from the direction the other truck had come. The guys inside gave us a nod as they passed. There were a few more in back, already putting on hardhats and breaking out shovels and pulaskis from storage. One waved a greeting. Another grinned and called, "Thanks for the hand."

The carrier ground on down the burn line that Woody and I had been working. As it waddled on, they dropped off the truck, one by one, and set their tools in motion.

Through the smoke, now whiter and thinner near us, we could see across the burn to the water truck. The team had unlimbered their hose, and as we watched, a jet of water arced from the nozzle into the flames.

Woody turned to me. "Think we've earned a break?"

I nodded. "I've always believed in letting professionals do what they do best."

"True," Woody said, cradling his shovel across both shoulders and wrapping an arm around either end of the handle. "No need to show them up, either."

We set off toward the house, which was little more than a thousand yards away. A relief. Still, I wasn't in a hurry and glad that Woody kept his long stride deliberate. He tilted his chin in the direction we were headed.

"Seems we saved Judith Clearwater's place," he said.

I managed to nod. "Think she might give us a couple of glasses of water?"

17

Judith Clearwater's horse stood below the porch corner, her halter lead rope looped over the rail by the saddle and blanket. She turned her head to us to verify that the noise we made putting our shovels in the vehicles wasn't a creature come to eat her.

Woody and I clattered up the steps of the porch. Judith Clearwater came out of her house, backing against the screen door to swing it open. She turned toward us, carrying a tray with three empty glasses and a huge pitcher of iced tea.

"This might cut your thirst better than water," she said and set the tray on the porch's wide rail. The Appaloosa turned one ear toward the sound of pouring liquid as she watched her owner fill the glasses.

Woody and I guzzled them empty. She refilled both glasses.

"I saw what you two did out there," she said, casting a long look toward the fire. "Thank you. I don't need to get burned out right now."

Woody glanced at her and returned his eyes in the direction of the burn and smoke.

"If you want to schedule a better time, maybe it could be arranged."

He didn't look back at her when she frowned. She took her time responding. Maybe she was mulling the implication of his words.

"You think that was set?" she said. "On purpose?"

"Crossed my mind," he said, "seeing how it worked from the road."

"Could have been an accident," I offered. "Cigarette butt flipped from a car. Broken bottle glass magnifying the sun."

"Could be," he said in his flat, unconvinced tone.

We drank our tea, watched the rising smoke, each of us, I guessed, trying to judge from its color how the fire progressed or was getting knocked down by the fire crews. Meanwhile, I rode the mental teeter-totter of *accident or on purpose.*

Woody spoke first. "Think the crew's seen the fire across the road?"

"It jumped the road?"

Woody's sideway look asked, You believed that? No, given the wind direction, but fires can do the unexpected.

I tried again. "Maybe it was already burning but we missed it through the smoke. Wind might have held it near the road so it was slow to spread. Now that the fire on our side has moved along, we can see the other burn."

No one showed interest in my theorizing. The reality of the fire—now fires, plural—held us. We nursed our iced tea and silence. If their thoughts matched mine, the teeter-totter was teetering in the direction of *on purpose.* A *both-sides-of-the-road* kind of on purpose.

"Huh," Woody said. "Didn't see that before, either."

I looked where he was staring, toward the top of the bluff that rose between where we stood and my Purgatory on the other side. Up there, on top, had been Judith Clearwater's vantage point when she first looked down at me from her Appaloosa. Now, another lone figure walked along the ridge.

"More fire crew?" she said.

"Not wearing gear," Woody said. "And they wouldn't top a ridge a fire's about to climb."

Judith Clearwater went to the saddle on the far end of the porch railing, opened the case hanging from the saddle horn, and extracted her binoculars. After a long look, she walked back and handed them to Woody.

"It looks like that Roger Stegman," she said. "I've seen him only once or twice."

Woody took less time. "Yep. You're right." He passed the binoculars on to me.

Magnified through the lenses, Roger stood looking down toward the fire.

"That's him," I said, wondering whether he was merely curious or assessing his handiwork. I had also started to think he had something to do with Judith Clearwater's phone not working.

"What's he's doing?" I asked.

"Whatever, he's a fool," Woody said, pointing.

I looked the direction he indicated. The fire on the far side of the road had spread and neared the bottom of the hill. Woody swung his arm to motion Stegman away.

Roger didn't move. Woody swung his arm again. And again, making the motion look big and urgent.

I put the binoculars to my eyes. "He's waving back," I said. "No, he's stopped waving. He's walking off along the ridge."

"I can see." Woody's voice was tight. "Wrong way."

"Maybe he parked in that direction," I said.

"Well, he may not clear that gully in time."

Before I could figure out what gully he was talking about, a sound and motion distracted me from Stegman's situation. I looked around.

Judith Clearwater was off the porch and had pulled the horse's lead line from the railing. The sound I'd heard was the horse turning into the drive. She flipped the lead over the withers, and with a one-word ask, set the horse into a lope with her balled-up and hanging off the left side, both hands wound into the mane. Another second, and the pace went from lope to gallop. In a continuous motion, she dropped her legs, struck the ground with both feet, and spun up onto the horse's back. They were halfway down the drive before I drew another breath.

Woody and I turned to each other. My mouth must have been hanging open.

"Looks like she learned some trick riding," he said. He ambled over to the water pitcher and refilled his glass. "Maybe instead of barrel racing like other teen girls around horses."

I unslung my jaw. "What's she think she's doing?"

He took his time drinking before he answered with a shrug. "Couldn't have stopped her if we tried."

I looked in the direction she'd gone. The end of the drive was empty, but she reappeared as she came up out of the dip on the far side of the highway. She angled away toward the bluff, snaking through the sagebrush, possibly following some trail she knew.

I glanced at the ridge line where Roger strolled along before I swung my gaze across the face of the hill to find the gully Woody had mentioned. It took me a moment, because the fold in the hill was choked full with sage and veiled by a thin screen of smoke. The fire on that side of the road was steadily eating toward the bottom end of that crease. On the hill, Roger would cross the dip where the gully crested the ridge.

"Maybe he can't see the gully and where the fire's at," I said.

"More like, doesn't see it for what it is," Woody said.

He descended the porch steps to stand in the open and tried again to wave Roger in the opposite direction. If the fire reached the bottom of the gully at the same time Roger started across the top of it, he could be caught. I pictured the burn entering the gully, the fold of the hills funneling and sucking air into the fire. Its intensity would surge, turning the breeze into high wind, and the fire would shoot to the ridge before Roger could do anything.

Serve him right, I thought, if he fried in a fire of his own making. The grim thought warmed my heart. Why warn him off? I focused the binoculars on Roger.

"It looks like . . . I can't be sure . . . either he's waving back again or flipping us off."

"Doesn't understand the danger." Woody stopped his arm motion.

Roger continued walking in the same direction. I tried to measure his speed against that of the fire's burn. I gave the race even odds. I swung the binoculars away from his walking direction, back toward the rise of the bluff that Judith Clearwater had seemed riding toward.

Nothing.

Wait!

There she was, just cresting the far end of the ridge.

"She's up," I said to Woody, realizing as I said the words that neither of us had doubted where she had been going in the first place.

Her horse looked tired after the climb, but she kept a steady lope toward Roger. Was she calling to him? Could he hear?

I lowered the binoculars and joined Woody on the ground below the porch steps to watch.

She'd closed the distance more quickly than I'd thought possible.

Roger had a few dozen steps remaining before reaching the dip of the gully.

At the lower end, flames doubled their height when they hit the first heavy stand of sagebrush. We were watching a short fuse catch.

Judith Clearwater overtook Roger, rode past, and turned her horse to face him. He tried to dodge around her and the horse. They blocked him. He made a head feint and darted the other way. Horse and rider were there ahead of him. They herded him a few steps backwards. She pointed at the fire below them.

"Hope she's persuasive," I said. "For her sake."

"She'd better not cut it too fine," Woody said.

He glanced at the fire eating fast into the gully. A black plume of smoke rose like a warning flag. A tongue of fire flared into the rising soot and superheated particles.

Judith Clearwater's horse seemed to sense their danger. She pranced from one leg to another but didn't shift from where she was held in front of Roger. He reached up to lock his arm with the one Judith Clearwater had extended. She heaved him up. She was stronger than she looked, Roger in better shape than I thought. After a struggle, he wrapped his arms around her. Even before Roger was fully settled, the horse started trotting back the way she'd come.

Behind them, fire and smoke in the crease pulsed once, twice, and roared up the gully, thundering like an old-time freight train. Seconds later a fire ball blossomed over the top of the draw.

Judith Clearwater had slowed her horse to a walk. She pulled up, and she and Roger looked back to where he had nearly been incinerated.

After its race to the crest, the fire lost energy to burn further there, like it had blown itself out. Another line of flames continued to eat slowly through the brush further downslope. On the road at the base of the hill, two more fire teams had arrived and had already begun pinching off the burn on the far side of the road from either end.

"You think Roger set that second line of fire in hopes it would burn over the hill to my place?" I asked.

"Maybe," Woody said, with a last glance to the ridge. "If so, he's sitting on that horse pretty frustrated."

"Yeah, more likely that," I said, "than feeling grateful for getting saved."

Judith Clearwater asked her Appaloosa to walk on. They didn't go far but stopped close to where she had appeared on her way up. Roger slid down.

"What the . . . ?" I muttered.

"She's putting Togokwa back," Woody said. He turned away toward the porch steps.

That blasted snake again. *That's* removing him to where he can't do more harm? The thought had me feeling cheated.

On foot, Roger disappeared over the far side of the hill. Judith Clearwater turned her horse onto the trail that would lead down and back toward us.

I hadn't realized how tired I was until I sat down to wait for her to return. Woody disappeared with the near-empty iced tea pitcher into the house, leaving me with my thoughts.

Tired, yes. Out of gas entirely, I admitted. And emotionally exhausted. That evaluation, too, I immediately amended.

I felt stunned. The distance between my world and that of Judith Clearwater and Woody couldn't be measured. Passengers on separate trains? The cliché about being from different universes floated through my mind. Her dash to save Roger from getting caught by his own inferno—only to put him down again to walk away—left me empty. I was further than ever from reconciling her *keeping on* with my figuring out how to live in my world gone treacherous.

Woody returned from inside carrying the pitcher with a new batch of iced tea, frozen cubes rattling against the glass container. Down at the entrance to her drive, Judith Clearwater dismounted and walked her Appaloosa toward us. Both creatures looked pretty drained, especially her horse. Woody looked around for her glass, found, refilled, and set it on the railing for her near the saddle.

He turned toward me, and I told him what was on my mind. "I was happy to let him burn to death."

Woody took his time refilling his glass. He walked the pitcher over to me and offered more. I held up my glass. After topping it up, he made the commute back to the railing and set the pitcher by Judith Clearwater's glass. He watched her work her way toward our parked vehicles.

"Violent death, my experience?" he said. "Brutalizes all of us. Even those who find justice in it."

Judith Clearwater led her horse past my Ranchero and the rest of the way to us. When she got nearer, she glanced from me to Woody and back again. Perhaps she sensed from my face what we were talking about.

"His California company would have sent someone else anyway," she said. Spying the glass of iced tea next to her saddle, she added, "Thanks for the drink. But I should walk her out." She ran her hand down the horse's neck and wiped her wet palm on her pants leg. The inside of both her thighs were dark from the horse's sweat.

I pried myself from the chair. "I'll do it." I went down the steps and took the lead line. "I'll lock up myself, if I don't move some." Before I could get an objection, I led her horse toward the back of the house.

I found a watering trough and let her drink a bit. Located a hose with spray nozzle attached and ran the water down her legs and over her back. Found a scraper next to a tack box and scraped the excess water from her back and flanks. During all this, the Appaloosa stood quietly even though she was only ground-hitched.

I'd spotted a hoof pick in the tack box and thought while I was about it, I might as well clean her hooves. Each time I asked her for a hoof, she handed it to me. Her heavy horse scent enveloped me. Aroma therapy at its best. Working with her helped lower my emotions to a slow walk. Their plodding felt like regret about something I couldn't name.

I led the horse over to the tough for more water and brought her back for another spraying off. Judith Clearwater came out the back door of her place, walked over, and got a cheerful nicker and nudge from her horse in repayment for getting a scratch between the ears. Her hand continued down the face and around the muzzle that was still dripping from the water trough.

She checked me out standing there, hose in one hand, spray nozzle in the other. Saw the damp earth around us. She went over to the tack box, pushed aside the wet scraper, and grabbed the hoof pick. She didn't react to its damp handle. I left off spraying the horse when she picked up the near forefoot. She barely ran the pick around the clean frog, wiped her palm across the horseshoe, and let the leg back down.

"I usually don't let anyone touch my horse," she said. "If I hadn't been so tired . . ."

I nodded. "Sorry I was pushy . . . didn't think . . ."

After giving me and the horse a look that suggested I continue my waterworks, she traded in the pick for the scraper.

"Woody was telling me about your jumping on the fire before he showed up," she said, starting to scrape excess water from the coat where I'd sprayed. "It seems you also know something about horses."

I thought about that while I moved around to wet down the other flank.

"Seems to me I know mechanical bits and pieces about this and that. But know next to nothing about anything that puts a sliver of daylight between me and Roger Stegman."

Judith Clearwater ran her hands down her horse's front legs, stopping at the knees and pasterns.

"Let's see," she said. "He torches the countryside. You put out fires. It wouldn't take much pressure for me to see a trace of light between the two."

"He and I both thought seriously about participating in the other one's death," I said, "just because the other guy ran contrary to something the first one wanted."

"*You* did?" she said.

"I didn't even raise a hand to warn him off," I said. "Closer, I might have given a push. Between us is all the light of a sealed closet." I was sure she could hear the anger in my voice.

She straightened. The horse nuzzled her again. She rubbed the forehead, patted the arched neck.

"Good girl, Lappy," she said.

"Lappy?" I said.

She continued her rubbing and patting. "Nickname," she said. "When she was a long-legged filly, my uncle saw her prancing around in a field in the middle of a flight of butterflies. It looked like she was playing with them. He named her Lapwai. It means butterfly."

"Oh, Lappie," I said. "She certainly flew up that hill with you." I studied her a moment. "Did he, Roger, bother to say thank you?"

She smiled. "He shared his opinion that I'd gone to a lot of unnecessary work. He would have made it past the flare in time. All I'd accomplished was forcing him on a longer walk to his car."

I shook my head. Judith Clearwater gathered the lead. "I'll walk her out a little, and I think we're done. Thanks for your help." She led the horse to the trough for another drink.

I shut off the water and coiled the hose under the bib.

Before Lapwai could drink too much, Judith asked her to knock it off, and when the horse raised her head, gave her affectionate scratches along the jaw.

"Please have more iced tea," she said. "I've long believed that deep thinking or decision making when dehydrated and exhausted doesn't add up to much."

I found Woody in the kitchen, back to me as I entered, at a big table. He'd laid down a line of bread slices on the table's surface. Large jars of mayo and mustard stood open near a stack of still-wrapped bread loaves, packaged salami and cheese, and boxes of sandwich bags. With his practiced motions, he seemed at ease and at home as he bent to his work. He finished slathering the last of the slices with streaks of white and yellow and looked up.

"She said she figured it'd take the BLM a while to divert supplies to the crews here," he said. "Before she hustled back from Fast Buck, she whipped through Doris and Fred's place and cleared a shelf of bread loaves, grabbed a few jars of mayo and mustard and snatched up what was in the deli cooler. We can drive some sandwiches out in my truck." He tore open a package of sliced salami. Picked up a second and tossed it meaningfully on the table near me. "Cutting knife's in the long drawer, left of the sink," he said.

I refilled my glass at the sink and took a long drink. Refilled it and set it on the worktable. I washed my hands, noticing that cool water felt best. I saw the palms were beginning to blister in several places from my shoveling. I gently dried them, got a knife from the drawer, and walked to the table. Opened the plastic pack. Dealt salami slices onto one prepared bread slice after another.

Fires, horses, and sandwiches, I thought. That's me all over again. But while it was something, my knowing how to do those things was not enough.

We completed a cheese layer, and while I sliced, stacked, and bagged the finished product, Woody opened two more loaves of bread and filled the spaces as I created them on the table.

Our silence, broken only by the scrape of a knife against a glass container or bread crust, the tearing open of more salami and cheese packs, me swallowing water or Woody clearing his throat, lightened my mood.

Maybe the arc of moral history running a straight line was pretty good after all, given unrelenting pressure to drive it to hell by the Roger Stegmans of the world. There was a thought he had wanted to con me from seeing. Maybe that's what *keeping on* accomplished.

What to do when overwhelmed by a way of life you believe dangerous? Control the fires to salvage what you can. Cool the horses. Make sandwiches for those fighting on.

Maybe doing what you can was more than a start.

Fires, horses, and sandwiches. Might be me, okay, but now I felt I had something to build on.

MOTION

===== *18* =====

Over the following days *fires, horses, and sandwiches* brought little peace of mind. Neither did *salvage what you can*. I worked to invest in the ideas, to cheerlead them forward. I wanted to believe. But *Move Togokwa* got in the way.

My feelings swirled around what Roger had probably done, what he was liable to be planning, what he'd probably get away with. I couldn't stand it that he would never feel remorse or shame for his actions. Another feeling also badgered me: I should do more to stop him. But with what? How?

Two evenings after the fire, I was sweaty and sticky, as if from the boiling pot of my conflicted emotions. But what I thought and felt—as always—weren't the biggest items in the overall scheme of things. There was the weather: still, close, and hot. We'd had some hope of rain, but the sky remained clear, and today the still air hadn't cooled as usual with the setting sun.

I escaped my baking Airstream and prowled in circles under the cottonwoods. I kicked a downed branch hidden in dead leaves and shadows. Picked it up. Leaned on the dried wood, realizing I wanted to hear it crack and break. I sure wanted to break something. It didn't. Where its desiccated bark had fallen away, the underlying wood was smooth. It would make a good hiking pole.

That gave me the idea of climbing to the top of the bluff in hopes of finding some breath of relief.

Breath? Standing on the ridge line above Purgatory, I leaned on the cottonwood branch and laughed at myself. The only breath at the top carried the stench of char rising from acres of burn that stretched away from the base of my hill.

It was easy to imagine the abrupt rise of the bluff as a hulking ship riding on a dark sea. Below me on one side, the Airstream, shack, Ranchero, and cottonwoods eddied like flotsam near the hull of my ship. Down on the other side, a block of light glowed from the porch of Judith Clearwater's house, a golden marker floating at this blackened rim of the burn.

Well beyond her place, a snaking line of flickering colors marked the last phases of the firefighters' work. The fire had been mostly extinguished now. In the fading light I could just make out a thin rise of pale smoke. Soon, all that would remain of fire crews would be a small mop-up team left to cut smoldering embers from the bases of burnt sage before sparks could blow up and restart a burn. My gaze and thoughts lost themselves in the distant horizon.

After my climb, I felt even more prickly. Hearing a faint rumble, I cocked my head. Maybe we'd get rain after all?

A glimmer attracted my eyes to a space above the distant hills. To the left another flicker came and went in seconds. I waited. Less than half a minute later came a grumble of thunder followed by another. Meanwhile, other glimmers and flickers jigged here and there among the clouds in the darkening sky. I had a feeling no rain would come. This looked more like an electrical storm. Several fine threads of lightning danced and squiggled over the hills as if to confirm my guess.

Not only was no rain likely, but now lightning strikes became probable, which could start other spot fires.

My lightshow continued. The flashes now illuminated larger and nearer swaths of sky. A brighter bolt spiked vertically between heaven and earth. A thunder crack arrived more quickly than had earlier reports.

Maybe it was a more compelling reason than the heat and climb for my feeling prickly. There I stood, the tallest object on a hill. And holding a taller wooden staff. Knowing I'd wished for Roger to burn, would Woody and Judith Clearwater think my getting struck by lightning was ironic?

I dropped the makeshift walking stick and sat. An observer might have thought my pole had gone hot and that my legs had failed me at the same time.

Not that I ever thought it a good idea, I always enjoyed watching electrical storms, at least as long as they remained distant. Reluctant to abandon my excellent viewing post, I leaned back on my elbows, kidding myself that my lowered profile would protect me.

Sniffing, I smelled the burn but not any ozone, which further reassured the pragmatic nag telling me to go back down the bluff. Besides, the glimmers and streaks of light still looked a dozen miles away.

As it happened, the whole show fizzled and moved on in less than ten minutes. I sighed and levered myself to standing, still stiff from shoveling sand at the fire. All my movements felt awkward. The darkness had deepened, despite some stars and a three-quarters moon filtering through the thinning clouds. To steady my way down, I leaned over and picked up my walking stick.

Instead of the smooth cottonwood branch, I grasped a telephone pole and marveled at its lightness as I straightened. *Grasp?* A telephone pole in one hand? How can that be? There was no logic to it. I felt a jolt as if struck by lightning but recognized—not the tingle of electric current—but my stab of fear. This was my nightmare. And I was awake.

My reflex was to drop the stick. Fighting it down, I steadied myself by driving the wooden end against the ground.

I heard my ragged breath. My heart hammered. Its pounding in my ears sounded like Lapwai's hooves galloping up the drive. I waited, but my distorted sensation didn't pass.

Staring hard at the branch, which looked very much like any other stick picked up for walking, I shuffled my feet, which now felt like they filled two tug boats. Looking down, I saw my boots, which, except for the sepia haze swirling about them, appeared normal.

And still the frightening sensation of a telephone pole in my hand.

In my mind, I heard a fleeting voice: *Look around for that young boy.* Judith Clearwater.

Maybe now? But if I looked, I knew I wouldn't find a child of any age. So now what?

If I didn't see him, perhaps relive him? Is that what she meant?

What had he done on that staircase many years before, when startled by the handrail's unreal size? With that thought, I was standing on the staircase next to him, watching.

He lets go of the railing. And then he forces himself to grab it again. This time, his sensation is normal. The waking nightmare, gone.

But back on this bluff, I still held my cottonwood branch. I'd not let go. And I still felt like I held a telephone pole.

Slowly, as if afraid the wooden thing would leap at me, I brought my other hand forward also to grasp the walking stick.

One by one, the fingers of my second hand wrapped around the cottonwood. The feel of the smooth surface was familiar as the coarse denim of my pants. And this felt dimension of the staff—by this hand—was normal. No telephone pole in the second hand.

I exhaled my pent-up breath in a single rush.

Gradually, the normal sensation spread to my other hand. Although a feeling, it was as if I were watching a movie's special effect transform one object into another. I shifted my gaze from the pole to my feet. The swirling sepia also dissipated. The tugboat sensation had disappeared, and my boots were only boots.

I tried several steps back and forth just to enjoy the mundane movement.

Yet my every nerve was as sensitive as a sandpapered fingertip.

The odor of burned grasses and sage remained sharp, but now I also smelled the plants still alive on the unburned side of the hill. The wood of the cottonwood stick was silky smooth, even soft where worn a bit. In my mouth was a dry taste of grit that had risen from where I'd scuffed the sandy soil.

Turning slowly on the bluff, I was acutely aware of no sound, then a bare whisper of sage and grass, which increased as a stronger breeze kicked up, possibly a ripple in the air from the passing electrical storm. And then another sound I couldn't identify, a faint, fluctuating hissing, as if from a steam valve a block or two away. Yet it was close.

I cocked my head. I knew that sound from somewhere.

Yes. From an even dryer desert. Death Valley. I recalled standing on the dunes toward the northern end of that sunken land. As it often does, a wind swept over the sandbanks. Twisting veils of sand flowed just above the surface, across my boots, dropped over the ridges. And from those strands, came a sound. This sound I now heard: the faint hissing. Like the "s" in whisper. Like the sound of silk drawn across rougher fabric.

And now, on the bluff above Purgatory, similar grains drifted across my boots. I struggled to bring another word to mind. Not susurration.

Not a word for naming the sound at all. It was the word for what caused the sound.

Saltation. From the Latin word for leaping, I remembered. And where did I get that? From one of the folded pocket guides rangers provided throughout the valley.

I started to pick my way down the slope to Purgatory and wondered why all this came to mind. And because I was working my way more by feel than by sight, my mind's eye was free to wander.

It replayed a visualization of saltation, so clearly described by the Death Valley information pamphlet. The trajectory of each grain, blown up and forward, eventually declines and the grain crashes into the dune. The crash looks like that famous kiss of billiard balls. The moving grain chips a stationary one into the air, the beginning of a "jump." Wind blows it up and forward until it, too, falls to kiss another.

Saltation is the mechanics or process of the jump, flight, and kiss. A miracle of scientific observation and description in its own right. But here's where I really got interested. Each "kiss" makes a "click" of sound on a minute scale like that of colliding billiard balls. What's heard as a million whispered "s"s is a gazillion grains of sand repeatedly kissing one another into flight. Again and again, over and over.

The remembering of images from my mind's eye got me to the bottom of the bluff. I turned and looked back up.

Clouds had pulled apart, leaving a mostly clear sky. Stars stood out like sparks on a dark blanket. As many stars as grains of sand someone once said. Who's to say whether all planets, solar systems, and stars are not also part of a celestial saltation happening in a timeframe and scale that defies our comprehension? We could be in flight to our next *click*

The bluff's ridge cut a black silhouette against the starry backdrop. How long did I stand and stare? Long enough for the moon's ascent to induce my feeling the earth's turn. Long enough for me to imagine the constellations' wheel from that evening until dawn. I felt myself tilt and took a side step to catch myself.

For a moment longer, I was aware only of motion. Everywhere. From the beginning to forever.

I thought this was either unusual clarity or an echo of my dizziness from days ago.

A heavy metal door slammed from the direction of the shadows under the cottonwoods. I jumped and turned.

"'Evening, Bitterroot Bob." It was Woody's voice. I barely made out his figure.

"Jesus, Woody!"

"Saw you were out," he said. "Waited to see if you showed up."

"*If?*"

He walked out of the shadows into the moon and starlight. "Thought I'd check on how you're doing after all our work."

"Ah nuts," I made the sound dismissive. I was touched by his concern. "No need to make me your business."

"You had no business working a fire in the sun," he said. "Without a hat. You're no spring duck, you know."

"Chicken."

"Chicken?" he said.

"Spring chicken," I said. "The saying is about a spring chicken."

He stopped his amble a few steps from me. He cocked his head. "It seems to me the key word here is '*spring.*' As in, *Spring* is what you're not." He rubbed his nose. "Duck, chicken . . . makes a difference?"

"I'll give you this, Woody. You're a strange duck," I said and turned in the direction of the Airstream.

"Been called worse," he said.

"Mind if we sit?" I motioned to the chairs under the awning. I'd put the table away. "I've had a climb."

"Yeah, I dialed you in when I heard you about half-way down. Sitting's good. Been on my feet all day."

I watched him drop into a chair and stretch out his legs. He crossed his ankles. I noticed the boots were once again as clean as if they'd never walked a fire line. Clean shoelaces, too. They lay perfectly flat between the eyelets. I was curious whether he'd bought new ones or washed the old. Did he iron them?

"I think I got some lemonade," I said, craving a beer myself.

"Water's good, if you have it," he said. "Prefer it to anything sweet."

"Ice?"

"Even better."

Leaving the lights off and the door open, I went on into the galley. Broke out a tray of ice cubes, added some to two glasses. A lemon sat near the water faucet. I whacked off a couple of slices and added one each to a glass and ran the water after.

Outside, I watched him drink. He took a second look at the glass.

"Straight lemon, I said. "Not sweet." I pulled my chair to make its position more conversational.

"Good idea," he said.

We drank in silence for several moments. Woody rocked the foot on top and tapped the side of one boot against the other. *Tap . . . tap . . . tap . . .*

"You okay?" he said.

"Is that connected to your '*if*'?"

He nodded once. "There was stopping the fire," he said. "And since then, I haven't seen you for a couple of days."

"I've been trying to get some work done."

He made a show of peering through the dark in several directions, as if looking for improvements to the landscape or buildings. His eyes came back to me.

"Fire, and you not coming around," he said. "Taken together."

"Yes?"

"That's the connection to my '*if*,'" he said.

"I detoured around my being touched by your caring," I said. "Thank you. Should have said it sooner. But, thank you for your concern." Maybe that would divert him from this probing.

His gaze didn't waver. "Fire, plus your absence. And also, what I saw while sitting in my truck in the dark over there." He pointed his nose at the cottonwoods.

"You saw what?"

"You," he said. "After you got to the bottom of the bluff."

"A man in the moonlight. You think I was Roger Stegman on a night mission?"

He shook his head. "Knew it was you. By the way you moved coming down."

"I move funny?" I asked.

"You move like you," he said.

"So, you're a student of how different people move," I said. There may have been a note of disbelief or sarcasm in my voice.

"Everybody's a student when life depends on it." He sounded like he was speaking from half a world away. "Anyway. You stared into space for a long time."

"Oh," I said and shrugged. "Night sky . . . stars . . . moon. You know."

"A long time."

"Well, maybe so."

"A long time," he said. "And every now and then, you kinda wavered, shifted like. Maybe catching your balance."

"Once, maybe," I said. "Not because I was dizzy, though."

"So, are you okay?" he asked. "Should I drive you over to Burns? The clinic there? For a quick check, to be safe?"

"Nah, I'm fine. Thanks anyway," I said. "Waste of your gas and time."

He studied his glass. Drank again. He rolled the glass between his hands, watching the half-melted ice cubes shift. Their soft tinkle seemed artificial in the sounds of the evening.

"Night sky," he said. "Up there on a fair regular schedule."

"Pretty much. Good to have something you can count on these days." Small talk wasn't Woody. I was curious what direction he was headed.

"Stars . . . Moon. You mentioned them, too," he said.

"Yes?"

"Also up most every night," he said. "Suddenly, tonight, you're fascinated?"

"Ah, well," I said, "you started it with your tale about Togokwa."

He leaned forward. "You get bit up there?"

" . . . "

"Would have been strange at night," he said. "Getting snake-bit."

"A lot gets strange at night, if you ask me," I said. "Like you and me, right here, right now. This conversation."

"I asked if you were okay," he said, relaxing back into the chair. "What's that got to do with Snake and you staring at a night sky?"

I took a deep breath. I wasn't getting very far trying to shake Woody off. "Actually, it has more to do with *moving* Snake," I said, "than about Snake himself."

"What about moving Togokwa?"

"I don't like it."

"The story? It's about how to keep mean power from doing harm," he said. "You don't like it?"

"I like the idea of moving power away, to where it can't poison us, rather than killing the darn thing outright."

"You're thinking of Judith Clearwater and Roger Stegman," he said. "Up on the ridge."

"I am. She picked him up, got him away from the fire. Then put him down. You said she moved Togokwa."

"I did," he said.

"But was he moved away from where he could do more harm?" I asked. "To me, it looks like she only moved him *over*."

"Our story doesn't tell us a distance or a direction for *away*," Woody said. "For that matter, the telling doesn't promise that Snake will not appear again."

"Seems temporary."

"Temporary?"

"We have to move that darned snake—the original or a different one—again and again," I said. "We're stuck with doing the same thing over and over."

"Over and over," he said. "Yep. That's often the universe of our stories. Your universe, too, when someone stops to look carefully. Lets it register." He leaned back, as if allowing time for his words to sink in. "But maybe I got that wrong."

"You do. In my universe we like to fix a problem and be done with it," I said.

"The happy ending."

"Yes. No over-and-over nonsense. Again and again? Not for us."

"Uh-huh," he said, looking toward the bluff. "Tonight, up there, your moon and stars. Again. Repeating all their other agains. Maybe why you stopped and looked tonight?"

I shook my head. "Let's not get starry-eyed here. We're talking Roger Stegman. Here on earth. We can't just move him over. He'll come again."

"Okay," he said. "Where is *your* away? What distance guarantees our safety forever? Besides, it's like one of your stories . . . a fable about the cat."

"What cat?"

"The one about who will bell the cat," he said. "Aesop . . . that fable. Who will move Togokwa to your place that's far enough away?"

"The three of us, you, me, and Judith Clearwater."

"Didn't she do her part already?" he asked.

"None of us reported we think Stegman set the fires," I said. "That would be a start."

Woody cleared his throat and took another swallow of water. "DMV arson inspectors will not find an accelerator," he said. "Roger's not dumb. He used matches, or a lighter, or one of those gizmos guys use to start their barbecues. At most, a paper spill that's burned and long gone."

"But we can tell the inspectors what we saw," I said. "And tell them all about Roger Stegman. What he's up to around here. What's he's done.

That stunt at the Pillars of Rome for one. His motives . . ." Woody let me wind down.

"Let's see," he said, "the Inspectors. They get their information from? An *Indian* who owns a bar and is suspected of PTSD, from an *Indian woman* who lives alone, at least when she's not doing her liberal professor job."

"But also from me, a *white* guy, if I catch your drift."

"Yeah," he drew out the word, "a *not-from-here* guy, who's well past Spring, camped out in the desert and who sticks up a sign saying Purgatory."

"You hear the arson inspectors laughing," I said.

"You don't?"

"I do," I said. "I'll be right back."

I got up. Went back to the galley. Pulled a jug from a cupboard. I emptied the remainder of the ice cubes into it and tossed in sliced lemon. After filling the jug with water, I carried it outside. Woody emptied his glass and held it out for refill.

I did. He thanked me. I refilled my glass. I set the jug on the ground near my chair.

"You know, a part of me wished we'd left Stegman to the fire," I said. "Satisfy my blood lust."

Woody took his time answering. "That path leads to an infinity of mirrors," he said.

"Yeah, My being anywhere near a reflection of Roger? That's what holds me back from stepping gladly into that funhouse."

I watched him breathe. In and out. I could have counted to five before he spoke again.

"Not the only thing, your wanting not to be like him," he said. He let that lie there a moment, then added, "My guess."

The tempo of our conversation was slowing. Maybe it's a western thing. Maybe something tired people do. But the decreasing cadence was familiar. Silences getting longer than what's been spoken. Pauses extend, it seems the subject's done. Tapped out. Then someone else chimes in with six words more.

"Mirrors," I said. "That your Aristotle again? Did he have mirrors?"

"People have had mirrors since they looked into still water," he said. "But the infinity of mirrors comparison is not a quote from Aristotle. It isn't new from me, either."

An image came to mind: me facing Roger Stegman. Me creating him creating me creating . . . Where does it start? Does it have an end? This infinity of mirrors wasn't pretty. No wonder we confuse who we're dealing with.

"Speaking of Aristotle," I said, "when I run the world, ethics training will be mandatory in schools. Educate the Roger Stegmans of the world."

Woody nodded. "It would be handy to have wider concern than our personal self-interests, that's true."

All our ice had melted. Woody studied his glass is if some crystals remained to tinkle. He took a drink.

"You look unconvinced," I said.

"Ethics," he said. "About which Aristotle did have some words."

"No doubt," I said.

"One thing he wrote. You can't teach ethics to children," he said.

"Why not?" I asked.

"Because they're too young to have any," he said.

"I thought that was the point," I said. "Teach them, so when they grow up—"

He shook his head. "You also can't teach ethics to adults who are not ethical in the first place," he said. "Same idea. Different ages."

That gave me pause. It lasted longer than my previous silences.

"'Houston, we have a problem,'" I said.

"Yes," he said.

"Let's start with Why not?" I asked. "Those unethical adults, why can't we teach them?"

"Because they have moral *beliefs*," he said. "Nothing more. They're not interested in a system to weigh conflicting choices, especially those including other people. According to my philosopher."

"Beliefs sound good," I said. "At least good beliefs."

"The goodness of the belief doesn't matter," he said. "The person without ethics will act against his moral belief when personal gain is at stake. Believe I should treat the other guy like myself—but I take mine first. And maybe take more, as well."

"They will?" I asked. "They do?"

"That's why people act against a wider good that would benefit them, too," he said. "That's what he says, Aristotle."

"Cheerful reading, your Aristotle guy," I said.

"Your Houston has another problem," Woody said.

"Because of course it does," I said. "Go on."

"Most of us are without ethics, by Aristotle's standards," he said. "But maybe I got that wrong."

"I'm sensing a catch-22," I said. "Maybe that was Roger Stegman's point."

Woody asked, "Remember Zeno?"

"The guy with the arrow?"

"Yeah. The paradox guy," he said.

"Because, if I remember what you said over by the Pillars of Rome, neither side of the argument is winnable."

"That's right," he said.

"Even by Aristotle."

"Yes."

"That should have made his day," I said.

Woody raised his eyes from his water glass.

"That's all I got," I said. "Remind me."

"Unwinnable, the arguments," he said, "because either side of the disagreement is based on beliefs that can't be proven."

"How could I forget? That's some of what's been bothering me," I said.

"Bothers lots of folks," he said. "Through the centuries."

"Opposing beliefs," I said.

"Not winnable because not provable," he said.

"Yes, yes. I kept up with your there, and my short-term memory isn't that short," I said. "But . . . it seems like when it becomes obvious to both sides that their beliefs are unprovable, that's the time when people on both sides crank up the volume. They shout louder."

======= *19* =======

Woody set his empty glass next to his chair and stood. He nodded by way of saying his thanks and also that maybe for the time we should be done with chasing my preoccupations through shadows. I followed him to his Power Wagon standing under the cottonwoods.

It hadn't moved an inch from where it had been when he had climbed out of it and shut the door. When I registered that it was the vehicle's immobility that had nabbed my attention, it struck me that I'd descended to where irrelevant constants in life reassured me.

The door squeaked when he opened it, a sound I hadn't noticed when he'd gotten out earlier.

He frowned at the door hinges. Maybe he hadn't noticed either.

"On the other hand," I said, "to hell with Aristotle."

He swung the door back and forth. There was a squeak in each direction. "Okay," he said.

"I mean, to hell with Aristotle's ethics."

Woody moved his head closer to the hinges. "Up to you." Glaring from one of the hinges to the next, he rocked the door one way. *Squeak.* And back. *Squeak.*

"I won't make teaching ethics mandatory," I said.

He glanced my direction. "When you run the world," he said.

"Correct."

"Shortens the school day." He looked back to his hinges and put a finger on one and slowly moved the door wider until the hinge squeaked.

"No," I said.

Woody swung the door back. *Squeak.* "Ha! Gotcha!" He rubbed his diagnostic finger and thumb together. He picked up a red cloth folded on the seat next to him and cleaned finger and thumb.

"Look," I said, feeling a touch exasperated by his fascination with door hinges. "I probably have a can of 3 in 1 oil in my cupboard. If it will help you out here."

He shook his head. "I've a tool chest back home."

"You going to rebuild the entire door?" Somehow with Woody, my question wasn't as bizarre as it sounded.

"Inside the tool chest," he said without missing a beat, "there's some WD40."

"Okay then. No doubt an improvement on sewing machine oil."

He rested one hand on the open door. "No?"

"No, what?"

"Not teaching ethics won't shorten the school day?"

"No. Teach rhetoric instead," I said. "And rules of logic."

He nodded. "Get 'em young. Teach 'em how to think. Good luck with that."

"At least have students rub up against some problems and principles of inductive and deductive inference," I said.

"I hear heads hitting desks,"—he stepped up into the driver's seat—"as your students fall asleep."

"Not all of them," I said. "But I wait to hear—from his high seat in the Power Wagon—the oracle speak."

He wiggled the gear shift to be sure it was in neutral. "Your oracle's advice? Call Houston again."

"Again? Just, why, please?"

Woody left the door open and gazed through the windshield, although he couldn't have seen past the pool of light falling out the Airstream's open door.

"In the first place," he said, "some of your students—and they might be the bigger percentage of those who stay awake—will deliberately abuse those principles of rhetoric and logic to trick the others."

"Others?"

"The others with their heads on desks, sleeping," he said. "Or who skipped your class entirely."

"Presumably, the deceivers are my students lacking ethics," I said. "Don't you think guilt would slow them up some way?"

Woody tapped the steering wheel with his index finger. The finger stopped, and he dropped his hand into his lap. "Consider their possible adult occupations." His deadpan face and voice foretelling wreckage ahead. "Advertising probably tops the list, not just because it begins with A. Then there's politics, although there's not much difference between the two professions these days."

"There goes your alphabetical ordering shot all to heck," I said. "Unless there's nothing between A and P."

"The finance and legal professions get fat on logic and rhetoric tricks." He scratched the side of his nose. "I could go on, but are you really hearing anything new here?"

"It's an old song," I said. "Although you carry the tune just swell. I've done enough hack writing for your alphabet companies and organizations to know I've deliberately misled, deceived. And so?"

"Looking around? I don't see guilt slowing your students when they grow up. And already, that's a ton of people. A lot of guilt with missing brakes."

"And you didn't mention statistics," I said. "I should have named teaching that, too."

"More logic, but with numbers, seems to me. But maybe I got that wrong."

I asked, "What's number two?"

"You want a longer list?"

"My oracle started with 'in the *first* place,'" I said. "What's in the *second* place?"

He paused as if to think about it. But I doubted he had to search much. "In second place are another few of your students who also managed to stay awake."

"You mean a separate group of students who stayed awake, but who *do* have ethics?"

He shrugged. "Maybe. Maybe not. Maybe they only have moral beliefs. Just a different set of beliefs from the first bunch."

"But they stayed awake. They learned. And they point out the logical errors, the rhetorical tricks of the devious students. See?" I said. "That's what I had in mind. That's the fix."

"More trouble," he said. "Maybe bigger."

"Because?" I asked.

"Because then, the folks who want to throw sand in eyes will question the premise of the argument that shows them up."

"The premise being something that the awake-but-principled students begin with and insist on being true."

"Ah. You stayed awake in class," he said.

"Something true. A fact," I said "Or facts."

"Or fake news. If you're on the other side," he said.

"So, then the two sides argue about the truth of truth," I said, "The original subject disappears."

He nodded. "You got ahead of me there." A new warmth in his voice let me think he could be pleased with my progress. "Each side," he went on, "disbelieves the other side's fact, then discounts the source of the fact, then dismisses as mere politics the information used by the discounted source who stated the disbelieved fact, which itself, each side believes of the other's, is not true because . . ."

"All for the house that Jack built," I said. "Except not a house. Talk about a truth gets changed to talk about opposing beliefs about where the truth came from or how to interpret it. And because each belief is only a belief and ultimately unprovable . . ."

"Yes," he said. "Down that road, discussion ends. Just like between Zeno and Aristotle."

"I thought Zeno had only one arrow."

"Aristotle didn't say that," he said. "I don't think I got that wrong."

The air stirred. The movement brought no relief from the heat.

"It's curious," Woody said. A small furrow between his eyes made him look troubled for the first time that night.

"The nature of a paradox, I would think."

"Not the paradox, not the ending of discussion," he said. "That serves a goal clearly seen."

"Easy for you to say."

"Nah," he said, "you see it, see the danger of reaching the goal."

"I do?"

"Otherwise, why do you want those courses taught?" He asked. "Logic? Rhetoric? Break them down. Logic . . ."

"What you might call the standards of thinking," I said to his prompt. "Still . . ."

"A tool, then," he said, "to separate true from false."

"Sure."

"And your rhetoric?"

"More or less an extension of logic. Rhetoric being how to accurately communicate a truth and warnings about how a thought gets twisted into something it isn't," I said. "In other words, an elaboration of your logic tool to distinguish between fact and fiction."

"Which—distinguishing between fact and fiction," he said, "is how we get closer to knowing the reality of experience."

"So, if discussion ends," I said, "so does opportunity to use the tools to figure out the world. And everything on it."

"And that makes it easier for folks to get led around by the loudly powerful who claim to have a lock on what's real. Particularly, when they have the guns. See?" he asked, "Ending Discussion? Dead easy to spot the goal for that."

"Didn't feel easy," I said. "But what do you find curious?"

"Killing discussion ends more than your chance to figure out reality," he said. "The purpose of discussion is using the tools to know reality so as to be able to survive. Right?

"Yes, I think that's where all this talk got us."

"So, using the tool," he said, "is why talking to each other exists. Why words exist."

"The reason for language, in other words," I said.

"Killing discussion," he said, "taking away its purpose, eventually kills the language of the society."

"'Lose a language, lose a way of life,' Judith Clearwater says. You're thinking of what happened, is happening to Native languages," I said.

"Not just the languages of Native people," he said. "There's plenty others."

I looked away as if to see everything lying in and beyond the darkness outside the pool of light from the Airstream. "You mean," I said, "all the languages the slaves weren't allowed to speak? The Irish, the Welsh, one side or other in the Balkans? It's a long list of conquered people. What of the German or French who couldn't speak their dialects in the Alsace-Lorraine, depending on who won the most recent war?"

"Yes," he said, staring with me through his windshield. "How many endangered languages are there in the world?"

"We'd have to ask Judith Clearwater."

"How many are endangered because of edicts from conquerors? Doesn't matter."

"Is this where it gets curious?"

"No. This is not curious, either," he said, shaking his head, whether sadly or emphatically, I couldn't tell. "Makes sense. Want to grind the losers into dust? Make them disappear?"

"Take away their language?" I asked.

"Happened over and over," he said. "Tried and true."

"Seems like," I said.

"And *there's* the point this gets strange, curious."

"Yes?"

"Makes sense to kill the other culture's language: it kills the society, your enemy, who uses it," he said. "Or at least it puts them on the endangered list."

"Go on," I said.

"Why would any sane person kill the language of their own society?"

"You say when *our* discussion dies, *our* language is endangered."

"I do," he said.

"So, the survival of our own society, right now, is endangered," I said.

"Or civilization." Woody reached out and pulled shut his door. "But maybe I got that wrong."

I stepped closer to his open window. "Maybe you do," I said.

He turned his face my way. "Do what?"

"Have that wrong," I said. "Endangered. I'll give you that."

"I accept."

"But your ultimate doom and gloom? Consider a fact," I said. "You and I are still talking."

He blinked as if startled by my newfound optimism. "Uh-huh." He started up the Power Wagon. "But you're working with a short time-frame there." He set the truck in gear. Before he let out the clutch, he rested his crooked arm on the ledge of the open window and gave me a long look.

"For the third time," he said, "you okay?"

"I thought it clear that the first time was one more than enough," I said.

"Your cranky seems normal enough," he said. "I'll leave it there."

He rolled from under the cottonwood canopy and into the night.

I stared after Woody long after the glimmer of his taillights disappeared and the stink of exhaust dispersed.

Boy, he'd done a job. Ethics. Rhetoric. Logic. Statistics. All my cherished protections shattered. They were the overlapping iron plates, I now realized, that I hoped would make it possible for me to live in my alien world. I imagined a clatter, somewhere out there, as they hit the ground like a suit of armor discarded piece by piece. I should feel, if not devastated, stripped bare.

But I didn't.

Now *there* was a curious fact. Possibly not provable to Woody or Aristotle's cast-iron skeptic, Zeno. But good enough for me to believe. Ah, there it was again: *belief.*

In fact—this might be fact number two or simply a positive way of stating fact one—I'd felt calm throughout my conversation with Woody. Either way, how could he or anyone deny the "factuality" of my feelings? To be fair, he hadn't denied it, and to be honest, I was as startled as he by my optimism. Why was I now aware of this fact or these facts, even if they were only beliefs?

Because, composure, what I now felt, had not been the case since I'd decided to come looking for it in Purgatory.

I thought back over the past several weeks. I had come wanting to find out what had happened to make my world alien to me. I also wanted to learn why something had changed. Figure out (A) what was different, and (B) why the change, I'd reasoned, the answer would become clear to my biggest question: (C) how to live, what to do, within a society where A and B are true.

Now, in the dark under the cottonwoods, I laughed to myself. I *had* staked out a territory as Judith Clearwater had accused me. Instead of naming it ABC, I'd dubbed it Purgatory. I ambled back to the Airstream and sat in my abandoned chair. In the other seat, Woody remained a presence, nearly palpable.

Thanks to your object lesson, Woody, I learned on my canyon hikes that a map is not the territory. Words leave the truths they represent elusive. Stirring that in with Judith Clearwater's stories, I'd gotten a better bead on A, on what had happened to make my world alien: all that stuff about being dominated by beliefs not shared. Roger Stegman's belief that greed, possession, and power ruled everything, for instance, was not my belief, despite his attempted object lesson at the Pillars of Rome.

But even with the A of my ABC in hand, my composure had stayed away. I moved on to B. Why had Roger's belief had become dominant? By uncovering Doris and Fred's dissatisfaction and hearing more of Judith Clearwater's stories, I'd come to understand the country's domination by unshared beliefs had followed a resurgence of hate, which often masqueraded as simple intolerance and resentment.

A plus B. What of that? Big deal. Still no composure like I felt tonight. Worse, my A and B did not make C, how to live where A and B are true, as easily apparent as I'd hoped.

Pumping Judith Clearwater about *what'd they do,* the Natives, how did they manage to live in their altered world, had not brought me satisfaction.

Woody's myth about Togokwa had offered promise. But that snake slithered away among my shattered armor, among those bits and pieces I'd imagined as my C.

Meanwhile, my uncontrollable nightmare sensations—experienced asleep or awake—continued a threat.

Until earlier tonight, when they vanished almost like magic.

That they ceased was a fact, and though perhaps transitory, my belief they were vanquished was enough for me. What had changed?

Fact: at the time I climbed the bluff, nothing had changed. Fact: at the top, I experienced my waking nightmare. Perhaps that could be disputed by some witness of me at the time. But I know for certain I experienced as reality a cottonwood branch, simultaneously, as looking like a stick but feeling like a telephone pole. I couldn't—still can't—explain how that was true, but there was no denying my terror while experiencing the contradictory realities of my eyes and right hand.

Until, fact: I'd acted as I had as a child to reconcile the two conflicting realities. How? Not by hoping the true one would reveal itself to me. I'd used myself—this time with my left hand—to add its testimony to the right. It wasn't that the left hand had a better grip on reality than the other hand. More important was that I'd stopped being at the mercy of the nightmare, which always demanded: freeze! Stay afraid, stay very afraid until I release you. Instead, I moved, picked up the branch with my right hand and gripped it with my left. All this explanation, however, raised the question: why had I moved instead of remaining frozen in place? That, I couldn't explain. Any more than I could explain how my right hand and eyes experienced two very different realities.

Nevertheless, once I forced myself to move my left hand onto the branch, the frightening sensations ceased. Why, I have no idea. But they were gone.

A fact.

Perhaps unprovable to your unethical students, Woody, or to Zeno, and therefore, only a belief. But I did trust the improvised walking stick to support me as I went back down the hill. So, fact enough for me.

As was hearing the click of sand grains enough for me to believe in saltation.

As was seeing the stars and moon, there every night as Woody observed, enough for me to believe I would see them another night.

What did Woody once quote from Aristotle? *To understand reality, begin with the physical world.*

And somewhere between the top of the bluff and the slamming door of Woody's vehicle, my composure had returned.

Fact?

Enough for me. Enough, in fact, to drive my optimistic response to Woody's concern for this endangered civilization. I felt hope.

The trees stirred. I felt a breeze pushing against one cheek. The temperature was finally dropping. The fresh air felt like swimming in an ocean and passing from a warm current into a cooler one. The scale of the water's movements is beyond comprehension. But it is a fact.

I looked at my watch. How long had I sat there? The face was too dark for me to see its hands. It didn't make any difference, because I hadn't looked as soon as Woody had pulled away. I'd have to make a stab at what seemed a reasonable amount of elapsed time.

Back inside my aluminum home, I removed my phone from its storage cubby and plugged it into the landline. I raised the receiver to check for dial tone. It hummed. A sound texters on cell phones never hear these days. I hung up and waited.

I listened through my open door to coyotes yipping from distant hills until enough minutes by my dead-reckoning had ticked away. I dialed.

"Hello," Woody answered.

"Maybe we've got it backwards," I said.

"Well, you did tell me you had a phone in your place," he said.

"Legacy of a forward-thinking uncle," I said.

"What's backward?"

"Or incomplete. Or inside out. Or something," I said. "I can't dig up a metaphor."

"Too fancy for me anyway, that stuff," he said. "Don't dress it up."

"Your snake story," I said. "We're in a new age."

"Myth. Not story," he said. "Like legends. Get to be myths, because they last through many ages."

"Still, maybe there's another . . . perspective, another way to go at it."

"Can't this wait until morning?"

"May be a few days before I see you," I said.

"The rest will do me good."

"I just wanted you to know."

Woody stayed silent.

"Because you wondered about me being okay," I said, "and all."

"Whenever you show up, the beer will be always cold," he said. "The glass always spotless . . ."

". . . the bar polished and glowing bright. Good night, Woody."

I hung up and closed the outer door and turned off the light. I was asleep before my head settled into the pillow.

20

F ind A and B, get C: understand what changed and why, be able
to figure out how—or whether—to live with it. I'd been wrong
about that. Despite my developing explanations for A and B, my
bits of armor for the all-important C had been stripped away by Woody.
Logic? Rhetoric? The rest? Forget about all of it. But a negative result
is also information, I figured. But as with much new information, the
annoying question was what to do with it. Especially when, as in this
instance, the new information showed that my original equation was
wrong.

For instance, after Woody had left last night a surprise C had come
to mind that was not based on A or B or their combination. Considering
the incorrectness of my original formulation, how could I be sure about
this alternative C? Would my *belief* continue to be *fact* enough for me?

The composure I felt with Woody last night might prove fleeting in
the heat of the dawning day. Although I noted with satisfaction: so far,
so good. Another detail was more worrisome. Whatever had vanquished
my waking nightmare might not operate in a different context. In either
case, I didn't want to consider walking back my optimism telephoned to
Woody.

Mulling abstract thoughts would come to nothing. Of that, I *was*
sure. Action was needed. And the needed action needed to come from
me. It was necessary to test the new C. Would it work or prove useless?

At my Airstream table, I thumbed my list of addresses and telephone
numbers. Another confirmation of my Luddite ways.

I flipped pages while conjuring the merry face of my lawyer, Earl
Hoffman, after he'd perpetrated some trick in high school that had led to
our becoming friends. I remembered he'd looked equally jolly years later

while he drafted my will and living trust. Now I found him listed under "L" for lawyer. His assistant answered on the second ring. Earl kept me waiting a long three seconds.

"Good Goddess," he said after we'd done our hellos, "you sound like you're calling from outer Mongolia. How many bars do you show?"

"Not a cell phone. Landline."

"You *are* in Mongolia."

"A very old landline. I'm less than five hundred miles from you."

"And in the bottom of a well." He was not one to yield a position easily. "What's up?"

"Remember my will and trust you drew up?"

"You hardly needed me. Could have done it on the back of an envelope," he said. "I felt bad taking a fee."

"Hell you did," I said. "You wrangled about nickels and dimes over milkshakes when we were kids. Remember my uncle's fifty acres that came to me?"

"Natch," he said. "Middle of that goddess-forsaken desert. Oh. Ah-ha! That's where you're calling from." I remembered Earl itching to get out of Dodge for the big city. Any big city. I pictured him now, behind his desk in San Francisco. With a bridge-to-bridge view of the bay from his office.

"I need papers for the land, the deed," I said. "And some of your so-called free advice."

"Get what you pay for," he said. I heard the click and rumble of a file cabinet opening. "Probably, you also need an address that I'll give you."

The office of Javier Cruz sat in an area of Burns where streets named for presidents gave way to naming by letters of the alphabet, and all were crossed by streets named for trees. Elementary education in a grid.

A wall of metal file cabinets, a credenza holding a computer printer and world globe, the standard wood-veneer desk with computer and telephone, and two tired leather chairs in front of the desk furnished the place. I slid one of the chairs forward on the linoleum floor.

I saw on the desk the deed for my acres lying on top of an opened FedEx envelope. It seemed a long three days since I'd telephoned Earl.

Across from me, Javier—"*Javier*, please," he'd said over the phone to my, "Mr. Cruz"—spun in his chair away from his printer, from which he'd extracted several pages, and faced me over his desk. He spread the pages between us.

"Hot off the presses," he said. "Earl let me know you are rushed to get these."

He showed me where I was supposed to sign and write the date, where other notations and signatures should go.

"Comes time," he said, "those'll have to be witnessed and notarized." He pulled a seal stamp from a drawer and set it to one side. "Happen to be a local notary, too." He smiled.

I smiled back, gathered the pages, and tapped them on the desk to square the edges. I laid three fifty-dollar bills where the documents had been.

"Thanks," I said. "I'm rushed and have a way to go."

"Anything for Earl," he said. "He sure was a kick in law school."

My hand was on the doorknob before Javier finished putting his notary seal back in the drawer. Looking back, I saw that my three fifties had vanished.

Approaching Woody's saloon the next morning felt like coming home.

Really? I thought. *I've been out here too long,* and climbed the boardwalk steps.

Or in this saloon too often. I walked through the open door.

Woody finished polishing a glass and slid it into place alongside others. He saw or sensed—I was never sure with him—me enter. More likely, he'd seen me park outside. He pulled down a cooled glass and carried it to the draft taps.

I was surprised to see Judith Clearwater sitting near one end of the bar. The end closest to the door and window, as if staying as close to out-of-doors as possible. Even so, the quiet and lack of physical tension between those two gave me an impression of a couple long accustomed to each other's presence. I had wondered about that possibility since watching Woody peacefully making sandwiches in her kitchen.

I walked to my usual mid-bar stool and sat. Woody placed a coaster on his bar and installed the beer-filled glass precisely in the center.

The legal-size manila folder I'd carried in I slid onto the bar next to my beer. How would these two react to what was in the folder?

Judith Clearwater gazed out the window. A fly's buzzing was punctuated every time it butted against the pane. Woody rinsed another glass and applied his towel. It made a slight squeak against the pristine surface.

After a minute, what the saloon lacked came to me: a grandfather clock. The pendulum's slow *tick . . . tock* might spur someone to speak, if only to override the metronome.

I cleared my throat. The others turned their heads and bodies a degree or two in my direction.

"Surprised to see you in here," I said to Judith Clearwater. Her eyes narrowed, but she said nothing. "I didn't see your car outside." That sounded like what it was: an explanation made up on the fly. An excuse for my being nosey. "Or your horse." Not an improvement.

"Lappie's around back," she said. "In the shade." A hint of a smile twitched the corners of her mouth. "I was out for a ride in this direction and came by to learn if Woody had seen you recently."

So, she hadn't been here overnight. Not that it was any of my business. Or that it mattered.

"Had a nice drive to Burns yesterday," I said.

"You mentioned you wouldn't be in for a while," Woody said.

"Over and back," I said. "Actually."

"You being here now," Judith Clearwater said, "we could guess a round-trip."

"Maybe," Woody said. "Maybe not." I expected them to exchange conspiratorial glances about teasing me. But her gaze held steady on me, and Woody had shifted his eyes past her to the splendors of Fast Buck beyond the open door of his saloon. "Would of had to do the math," he said, sounding absent from his words.

I took a sip of my beer and returned the glass to its coaster. "When you folks are done clowning around, you might be interested in what I've got in this folder." I gave it a meaningful tap.

I felt as much as saw the light change in the place. Judith Clearwater must have, too, and looked over her shoulder. I made a quarter turn on my stool toward the door.

Roger Stegman stood a few paces inside. He'd crept in on his little sneakered feet. His Range Rover wasn't outside. Woody had probably been watching him walk across the highway from the motel. I glanced at Woody just in time to see him visually frisk Stegman.

He covered the distance between the door and us but stopped a few steps short of the bar stools. He stood halfway between me and Judith Clearwater, directly across from Woody.

"Well, well, well," he said—theatrically, to my ear. "All the usual subjects. In one place. Good. What I've got to say, I want all of you to hear."

The other two said nothing but kept their eyes on Roger. He hadn't shaved for a couple of days, maybe returning to his LA mask.

Isn't chance wonderful? I thought. This is working out just dandy.

"Whatever you have in that folder of yours can wait," Roger said. "I won't take long."

"You do seem the kiss-and-run type," I said and slid down off my stool. Roger stepped back. I held both hands up as a sign of peaceful intent. "No, no. I meant that affectionately. It's just we ought to do this right." I dropped my hands and walked past him and out the door.

Both windows of the Ranchero were open, so it was still cool inside when I opened the passenger-side door. After pulling the small ice chest from the passenger seat, I nudged the door closed with one hip.

As I reentered the saloon, Woody had gone back to polishing glasses and Judith Clearwater to gazing out the window. Only Roger shifted from one foot to another like a horse held at the starting gate. He jerked up one arm and looked at his watch. The fly, intent on a more vast reality than any of us except, perhaps Judith Clearwater, still buzzed and butted at the window.

I carried the ice chest to the bar and set it next to my folder. As I did it, Woody's eyes narrowed for a fraction of a second. He drew a deep breath and remained standing where he was, dishtowel in hand.

I didn't want the fly's frustrated ambition to be a harbinger of my project. I picked up the manila folder, walked to the window, and used the folder to herd the fly away from the glass. With my free hand and the folder, I hazed the little buzzer toward the open door, through which it finally made its escape.

Our performance had riveted the others. They had not moved an inch by the time I returned my folder to beside the ice chest. As if exploding from his center, Roger threw up both arms, hands spread and fingers curling like he wanted to grab each of us by the throat.

"Alright," he said. "Listen up."

"Not now, Roger," I said. "You'll get your chance." I pointed at the cooler. "If you'd give me a hand, Woody?"

He flipped his towel over one shoulder. Keeping an eye on me, he lowered the ice chest to the counterspace on his side of the bar. Then he concentrated on wiping the bar surface where the ice chest had been. After a final swipe or two, he looked again at the ice chest and then at me.

"A donation for the saloon?" he asked.

"Sort of. Would you open it and do the honors, please?"

While Woody snapped open the catches and removed the top, I turned and spoke to Roger, who'd lowered his hands and stood glowering, working his pursed mouth as if chewing his unsaid words.

"I want you to know you're never far from my thoughts, Roger." Other than the line of his mouth tightening, I thought he looked unaffected. I pressed on. "While I was in Burns, I picked up something for you. Well, I picked up several things you'll be interested in."

I heard the rattle of ice against glass, a gentle slosh, and looked over to see Woody pull the towel from his shoulder again. He applied it to a bottle.

"When you've wiped that down, Woody, please open it for Roger."

Woody nodded, solemn, but I thought I caught a glint in his eyes. He took his time with the towel and kept it wrapped around the bottle while he popped the cap. The contents foamed a little over his hand, which he took care to dry.

"Sorry, Roger," I said. "Road's a bit rough in places coming back from Burns. But this should be cold enough. I got ice from Doris and Fred's as soon as I got back, and it hasn't all melted."

Woody stepped over in front of Roger, set a bar coaster, and positioned the bottle on it.

"Green," Woody said, forever true to noting the obvious. He turned the bottle so that the Heineken label faced Roger. Woody reached to his shelf of glasses and set one on a bar napkin beside the bottle. He didn't pour for his customer.

Roger's upper lip twitched in and out of a sneer. He stepped to the bar and grasped the bottle like he wanted to choke it. Taking his time, he raised it and drank directly from the bottle. Forever manly. He replaced the bottle and wiped his hand on his cargo pants.

"You think you're so smart," he said.

Woody's gaze shifted from Roger to the doorway just a moment before I heard the clatter of feet on the boardwalk. Roger frowned and turned with Judith Clearwater and me.

Fred and Doris, side by side, came through the door like a team of mules long paired in the traces. They halted, still beside each other, just short of the space separating Roger and me. Fred nodded his greeting to everyone but sort of skipped past Roger. Doris said her general hello and went right on.

"Mr. Stegman here was just now over to our store," she said. "Floating another offer to buy. Bigger this time." She winked at me, not bothering to shade it from Roger.

"More like giving it his last go," Fred said. "We'd already told him we weren't selling."

"You're not?" I asked. Even Woody and Judith Clearwater exchanged looks.

Doris shook her head, lips pursed. "Nope. Mr. Big Business here made out like he'd give us so much it'd be Easy Street once we moved nearer our kids."

"But we done your research," Fred chimed in with another nod to me, "and then some. And some adding and subtracting. Shoot . . . that cost-of-living thing, or whatever you call it, down to where the kids live, would put some serious barbed-wire in that feather mattress Roger's dangling . . ."

". . .be living *with* the kids before we could turn around," Doris said, "instead of *near* them. Wouldn't they be jumping-up-and-down happy to see us coming?"

"Besides, Dor and I decided," Fred put his arm around her shoulders, "we decided we liked the folks hereabouts"—he cut his eyes to Woody— "well, I had more deciding to do than Doris, and we'd gotten the hang of it here, the store and all . . ."

". . .feels like home to us," Doris said, moving closer to Fred as if to help him over the rough spot with Woody. "We'd be out of place anywhere else." She looked at Fred. "And our staying might help Millie hang on."

"As long as some big-box store don't set down some place near like Burns Junction," Fred said, "we'll do all right." He gave Doris a squeeze.

"I'll drink to that," I said and raised my glass to them.

"Want anything?" Woody asked them, adding an open-handed gesture along his bar that included the drinks menu over the back counter.

"Mr. Big Business said he was leaving town," Doris said. "But when he saw Bitterroot Bob pull up to the saloon, he cut off talking to us and took out over to here. We came over to be sure he didn't get up to more funny business. But it's never too early to party. What's he having? The green thingy." She pointed at Roger's bottle. "Would I like it?"

Woody hesitated and glanced at me.

"Up to Roger," I said. "All his now, to keep or drink. But gentleman that he is and considering the occasion, I bet he'd be delighted to offer."

Everyone looked to Roger. He blinked several times as if to gather himself. He raised a finger and drew a deep breath, his eyes shooting needles.

"Not yet," Roger." I said and pointed my chin at the cooler. "Remember your western hospitality."

He exhaled in a gust and made a half-shrug. "More than happy," he said to Woody. "Give 'em a beer, for all I care."

"Not for me," Fred said. "Dor is the sperimen'er with food and drinks. I'll stick with my usual."

I gestured to Woody that I was good. He dried a bottle from the cooler for Doris. Went through his coaster, bottle routine. On a bar napkin, he placed a glass and poured it half-full for her. He pulled a tap beer for Fred and set it before him. Woody put a glass of water on a napkin in front of Judith Clearwater and slid his own from a shelf under the bar.

"What'll we drink to?" Doris said.

I raised mine. "How about to Doris and Fred . . . home, home on the range."

As we drank, I noticed that Roger hadn't picked up his bottle again. His near-sneer, which seemed always to hover just behind his mask, turned into a real one.

"As I said, you think you're so smart." He looked at me before sweeping his eyes across the others. "You *all* think you're smart. Sure are smug. Believe you're getting one up. Losers from the start, all of you."

"How do you figure?" I asked, as much to stem his stream of insults as anything else. "We get your diagnosis. What do you see as symptoms?"

"Like you care," he said.

"Be surprised," I said. "Let's say, we're curious."

"Money," he said. "I offered you money. Good money. More money than you'll ever get from anyone else, no matter how long you wait for appreciation. And you turn all that money down. That's just plain stupid. School dropouts slinging dope on a Compton street corner can do better math, probably faster, than all of you working together. Losers."

He grabbed his bottle and took a vicious swig. Plunked it on the coaster so hard drops flew from the mouth. "See what I mean?"

Expressionless, Woody toweled the moisture from his bar.

"What I see," Judith Clearwater said in a conversational tone from her end of the bar, "or, more accurately, what I *hear* is money, money, money, money, money."

"Exactly." Roger spat the word. He reached again for his bottle. Judith Clearwater continued as though he'd said nothing.

"You *offered* money, but what we *chose* to buy, to invest in, to use your bankers' term, is a way of life. Seems like a smart bargain."

Roger clenched his bottle halfway to his mouth, turning one way then the other to glare at us. When his eyes got to me, they narrowed.

"I do recall mentioning," I said, feeling cheerful, "that your stack of money fell short of the sun, moon, and stars."

"Ha! Don't you get holy," he said. "Especially not you. I showed you more than money. I took my time to demonstrate how you could partici-pate in progress. Be the future."

"The future, maybe," I said. "Maybe even progress, in the sense of something going forward, changing. But change for what? Yours was a crystal picture of how I could contribute to an ecological disaster from the Yukon to Mexico. Some progress! Hardly the deal of the century."

"We should sit down," Doris said to Fred. "This'll take a while."

He looked about, found two chairs at a nearby table, turned them facing the bar. "Front row seats, Dor."

Doris sat. She sipped her beer and wrinkled her nose. Fred brought her bottle, his own glass, but stopped short of setting them on the table. He handed Doris the Heineken bottle. She turned it to read the label and adjusted the distance from her eyes for best focus. Meanwhile, Fred retrieved the coaster and bar napkins, which he put on their table. He sat and looked at Woody.

Woody nodded his approval.

"Well? Mr. Stegman?" Doris said. "Deal of the century?"

"Much better than the alternatives," he said. "I warned Bitterroot Bob he didn't know who he was dealing with."

"You did," I said. "Tarted that up with your cute demonstration at the Pillars of Rome."

"Yes . . . that could have . . ." Roger turned his head toward Woody, who, arms crossed, leaned his backside against the wall counter "If it hadn't been for this self-appointed sagebrush sentry . . ." Roger shook his head.

Woody selected a toothpick from a bunch stuffed in a shot glass. He twirled the wood in his fingers and stuck it like a blade of dried grass between his teeth.

"And you were, what?" I asked Roger. "Playing Wild West as the Sheriff of Fast Buck? Vigilante? Bounty hunter? Think of your gun, do you, as The Preacher?"

"Gun?" Doris turned to Fred. "I told you that boy would get in trouble with what he had hanging on the rack in his . . . thingamajig parked out there."

"I think *that boy* is the one bringing the trouble," Fred said. "As I understand it."

"Anyway," Roger said, "that was just for fun. No big deal."

"Always easy to say," Woody observed, "easy for the man with the weapon." He drew the toothpick from his mouth and inspected it. "But maybe I got that wrong."

"Speaking of fun, Roger," I said. "I'll bet any packets of your money that your kind of fun includes lighting matches."

He stared at me. "I've no idea—"

"And setting fires?" I asked.

Fred and Doris looked at each other and leaned toward us.

Roger drank from his bottle, making a show of going slow and easy. He wiped his lips with the back of his hand. "An unexpected shift in the wind . . . Too bad . . . " All the time he looked at me. "Anyway, I've always thought you and Old Stone Face here were more than a little whacky." He upended his drink. "Well, I'm out of here, like the lady said." He put the bottle on the bar to one side of its coaster. "I'm gone. But not until I tell you this. There's—"

"Not yet," I said. I pointed from the ice chest to Roger. "Open another for him, Woody. This celebration is barely started."

"Oh, goody," Doris said and sat back in her chair and crossed her ankles.

I drew the manila folder to me.

21

Woody removed Roger's spent bottle, wiped up its wet ring on the bar, and tossed it into the empty bin under the counter. He pulled a new one from the cooler, worked his towel, popped the cap. While he transported the Heineken to the dead center of Roger's coaster, I pushed aside my half-full glass. Woody returned and ran his towel across the surface.

"Better now?" I asked.

His nod seemed to imply we two had accomplished something of grave importance. I put the file on the wiped surface and opened it.

"In here," I said, riffling pages, "I've a legal paper or two." I surveyed the group. All eyes were on me.

I set aside three pages. Explanatory information prepared by Earl and given me by Javier Cruz. I ran a finger down the fourth page. "This one here's a document." It seemed right to include Roger, especially, so I sent him a beaming look. "Documents are big in your world, I suspect."

"Get on with it," he said.

"Right. This one's about Purgatory. Well, not actually about Purgatory. That's a Johnny-come-lately tag mostly unknown and unnoted outside the people in this room. This document concerns my fifty acres in and around Purgatory."

Roger moved in my direction, but I raised one hand, and he stopped. "I thought that'd get your attention," I said. He retreated to grasp his fresh bottle.

"Now here's the thing," I said. "There's another page or two in here"—I tapped the open folder—"the deed for those acres, which I will eventually attach to this handy-dandy document. If you'd please take a look, Woody, I'm going to need your help."

Woody pulled the toothpick from his mouth and flicked it into the waste bin. Folding the towel from his shoulder into a smaller square, he came over. Roger shifted from one foot to another.

"Not you," I said to Roger. "Woody's the man of the moment. But I'm sure you'll be entertained anyway."

"Me, I sure am," Doris said at the same time I heard two chairs scrape the floor as she and Fred pulled them closer.

I rotated the folder a quarter turn on the bar so Woody could lean over it. When he did, I pointed to the document's title across the top.

"You'll notice this bunch of legal words that announces a transfer of land."

Woody nodded.

I moved my finger down the printed lines. "Down here, it states the land involved. It's my fifty acres. Now I've been told, I'm going to have to get a little more specific about the boundary descriptions here."

"Why?" Woody asked. "Looks plenty specific to me."

"Yeah, but your people have only lived around here for ten thousand years or so," I said. "You're not gum'ment authority."

"There's that," Woody said. "But . . ."

". . . because it seems there is, or could be, some confusion about exactly where my fifty acres lie."

"I guess it's a stretch," Woody said, "to know they're out there below that bluff." With one hand, he drew in the air an arc that took in pretty much everything to the east that lay between the north and south extremes.

"Details are the problem," I said. "There's a county line. That's detail one. Or maybe it's two details, because it separates Harney and Malheur counties."

"Without survey equipment, the line gets vague in the sage," Woody said.

"Exactly," I said. "'Vague in the Sage,' sounds like the title of a romance novel."

"Or of an odyssey about self-discovery," Judith Clearwater said to no one in particular, although I knew where her comment was aimed.

"But the boundaries of my acres," I said, "the ones we got in the original document, are so old that it's also vague whether they are in one county or the other or straddle the boundary line."

"Huh," Woody said.

"The problem can be fixed, I'm told, with GPS coordinates."

I looked at Roger. He glowered. "Seems to me," I said, "I remember something that looked like GPS coordinates next to a picture of my place you've got in your laptop. Maybe—"

He took a vicious swig from the bottle. "Don't see why I should help."

"Right. Information is power," I said. "You'd believe that, worshiping power as you do. Stick to your guns, hoard every scrap of knowledge. Own it. We admire your consistency."

Turning back to Woody, I said, "I've got a GPS gizmo that'll get close enough. Earl, my lawyer, can refine details with your folks and the counties.

"My folks?" Woody asked.

"Representative, spokesperson, whatever they're called." I flipped a page and put a finger on a blank line. "Agents, maybe, administrators, I need their name or names here. You tell me, or tell me who to ask for them."

"I missed something," Woody said, leaning again toward the document.

"Ah, of course, this part here," I ran my finger up to a preceding paragraph. "See? I'm giving, donating my land to the Paiute-Shoshone Land Trust. Like you did with the saloon and all. So maybe the same people involved, their names, will still be familiar?"

Woody turned his head to look at Judith Clearwater.

She was leaning on her forearms against the edge of the bar. With no change to her noncommittal expression, she looked from Woody to me and back again. She raised one shoulder and turned both hands palm up, fingers spread: *Don't look at me. I had nothing to do with this.*

True. Or, on second thought, partially so. But I didn't feel a need to debate percentages at the moment. At any rate, she probably hadn't influenced my decision more than any of the others in the saloon, including Roger.

He was shaking his head. The look on his face would match that of a mother at her child who just tipped over the glass of milk for the third time in five minutes. At the corner of my eye, I saw Doris and Fred lean forward. She raised her beer glass.

"'s funny thing," she said. "At first, I thought Mister Stegman's Hinkerman stuff—"

"Heineken," Roger sighed. "Heineken, Heineken, Heineken . . ."

"Yes, your green-bottle stuff," Doris said. "At first, I thought it tasted sort of bitter. Didn't care for it much. But as talk here goes on, I'm changing on that. I'm liking it more and more." She shot Roger a sharp look that should have shaved his stubble.

"So anyway, Woody," I said. "Once I get the GPS numbers and fill in the other blanks with your information, we're set. I'll telephone the information to Earl, my lawyer in San Francisco. He'll make the final draft. All I'll have to do is drive over to Burns to get the signatures witnessed and notarized and then deliver the thing to the County Land office. I may also have to drive all the way up to the Malheur County Land office in Vale to drop off a second copy.

"Witness?" Fred asked. I looked over. "You said witness?"

"I did," I said. "I'm sure Mr. Cruz's office assistant can act as one."

"I'll do it," Fred said. "Be the witness."

Fred really had done some stout thinking and deciding, I thought. "Like I said . . . "

"I'd be glad to do it. In fact, I'd be honored if you'd let me put my name to it."

"Make it a 'yes,'" Doris said to me. "We'll close the store. Fred and me can drive up together. Make a swing by See's Candies while we're at it. Restock my chocolates."

Fred nodded and smiled. "Maybe get some extras, too. Unless," he looked from Doris to Woody, "unless you prefer we pick up something else for you."

"Chocolates, land . . . all this is coming fast," Woody said. "Never thought there was much to 'In the Big Rock Candy Mountains.'"

"Rock Candy Mountains?" Doris said. "That old folk song always gets me thinking of See's."

"I was thinking about the line about where the handouts grow on bushes." He rubbed his nose, a faraway look in his eyes. "Also, the song's the background of a book title by an author I never could bring myself to read much."

"Tell you what," Judith Clearwater said to me from her end of the bar. "If you need a notarized copy taken to Vale, I'll drive it up. I want to go north to see family before the school year starts again. I've an uncle, works in a county office there. He'd love to have me drop by and say hello."

"Okay then," I said, at a loss for better words. "Seems like we have a group project well started."

"Project for what?" Roger asked, his derision dripping. "This is about? Social responsibility?" His eyes bored into me. "Guilt does this?"

"No. Even though," I said, "there's some sense of setting things right."

"One of those liberal things, then. Quality-of-life and all," he said. "Think some sort of ethical good deed makes you feel better, like 'to do good for others.'" Roger actually drew the air quotes with his fingers. "A kind of self-denial? Your type, monastically hermiting away out here? Maybe it's penance."

"Penance?" I asked.

"Alms. Giving money," he said. "Sacrificing, preferably on some jerry-rigged altar. Paying for salvation. Wasn't that a problem with Purgatory? The rich could pay their way out?"

"Sounds like *your* sort of game," I said. "But, no. That's not what's going on here. Just my own idea of keeping the world in balance. Or maybe rebalancing it. Putting something back where it belongs."

"Power verses power keeps the world in balance," Roger said. "I thought we did that."

"Power, huh?" I said.

"That's right."

"That would be your powerful who decreed one hundred and sixty acres as the perfect allotment for a homestead," I said. "The right amount of land to sustain a family."

"Homestead Act," Roger said. "Fine example of balance. Allowed people to make good use of land that Indians let go to waste."

"Except," I said, "except—and I've noted your crack about lazy, wasteful Indians. I'll get back to that. Except, when the original allotment of acres proved not enough, your powerful doubled the number of acres to three twenty."

"An adjustment," he said.

"Which still wasn't enough. So, your authorities upped it again to six hundred and forty acres."

"Power in action," he said.

"And when your powerful find that entire section still isn't sufficient," I said, "they tell the government to switch up. Instead of adding more land, they figure they'll add water."

"Irrigation," he said."

"Another adjustment?"

"Yes. And because more settlers coming into the area meant more mouths to feed so that the area had to be made more productive by adding water."

"More people . . . reminds me of a story," I said. "Part of *my* oral history."

"I *do* like stories," Doris said.

Roger pursed his lips. "If you must," he said to me.

"I keep hearing a lot of them," I said, "stories, out here. Thought I'd take a turn." Roger kept mum. "So . . . had a chance to talk with an anthropologist in my youth. He'd lived with Natives in these parts for some time. Studying them. Asking questions so he could learn how they live, day to day. Subject comes up in such a discussion with them about how this territory can't support a whole bunch of people at any one time."

"There you go," Roger. "What I said. This place needs water."

"You did. I'm just doing background here," I said. "So, the anthropologist asks his informant, 'What's the answer to being unable to feed more mouths.' I'm paraphrasing here," I said to those around the bar, "to fit the story to our immediate conversation."

"We get it," Roger said. "Go on."

"Well, the informant tells the anthropologist, 'Have fewer children.' Now remember, these were pre-pill days. Pre-lots of things. My anthropologist says he thought about the informant's answer for a minute or two. Mostly trying to figure out how to ask his next question. Decides on the direct route and asks, 'How do you manage that? Having fewer children.' Gets one of those *are you dumb, or what?* looks. Playing stupid, as I understand it, is one of an anthropologist's tools, so my guy lets his question ride. Finally, from his informant, he gets, 'Don't have sex.'"

I shut up and waited for Roger's reaction. One by one, everyone else turned to look at him.

"What?" he spat. "What's your point? Stupid story. Besides, why would anyone choose to go without sex?"

"Because there happens to be an alternative policy to your *adjustment,* Roger," I said. "Another 'A' word."

"'A'?" he asked.

"*Adaptation,*" I said. "Unlike your power philosophy, which is to make adjustment *on* the land. Native philosophy is to adapt *to* the land. Then you don't have to add more water to get by. You adjust to live *with* what's here."

"Nuts," Roger said. "And go without sex. No thanks. I'd rather add more water and—"

". . . and more, and still more water. Until—or more properly—and theeennn . . . along comes Roger," I said.

"You surprise me," he said. "I didn't think you were paying attention."

"And now?"

"You're proving my point. Power—"

"Your power . . . Here's the point. Your powerful are," I said, "and always have been, just nibbling around the edges."

"Nibbling? Our irrigation and reclamation projects are the grandest works ever undertaken by man." Roger drew a big breath. He was only getting started. I thought to head him off.

"A wheel of cheese looks grand to a rat," I said. "Not enough land? Look out the window, for god's sake."

I pointed. Roger looked.

"The fly that was in here had more sense than you and your powerful. There's plenty of land out there," I said. "Used properly."

"But . . ." Roger said.

" . . . not enough water?" I said. "There's enough. Not in the right place? Rivers run the wrong direction? Empty into the ocean?"

"Needs adjustment," he said. "Adjustments."

"Your dikes and ditches? Nibbling," I said. "More nibbling. And myopia by the powerful. Look out there, your problem is not land, not water. It's the mountains."

"Well, yes. That's why," he said, "have to . . ."

". . . pump over, drill through? Oh, please stop with your everlasting nibbling," I said. "You've even got the wrong mountains. Instead, all those ranges to the west? There's your problem. They're in the way. And too high. Need to knock them down. Let the moisture from the coast flow in. Level those suckers. While you're at it, better stitch up those overlaps of the continental plates. Otherwise, they'll push those mountains right back up."

Doris was getting the giggles. Roger glanced at her, frowned, came back to me.

"You're being ridiculous," he said.

"You want to play God?" I said. "Get at it. Show us works that are worth the awe you aspire to. Unless, of course, you and your power-wranglers fear the competition."

"No sense talking to you if you aren't practical," he said.

"Alright. Let's get practical. What you have out there"—I swept my hand toward the window all beyond it—"all the acres framed in that glass could never sustain an individual. Didn't evolve that way, how I see it. Not support a person alone, not to mention a family, clan, tribal nation. And you and yours promote entire cities, whole states."

Roger nodded. "With enough water . . ."

"Sure, water, water everywhere," I said. "You wanted practical . . .
you said. Practical, that would be the Natives. Known to you as the Lazy,
Wasteful Indians. Told you we'd get back to them."

"I only said they didn't use the land, develop it," Roger said. "I never
called them—"

"Close enough," I said. "No, they didn't *use* the land. *Own* it. *Fence*
others from it. They didn't live *on* a piece land. They were *practical.* They
lived *with* the entire territory. Nomadic according to seasons. Sharing
resources as needed. Interdependent through trade and marriage across
the entire space around them. They adapted."

"That time's long past," Roger said. "Now . . ."

"Now? Time?" I asked. "Your sense of time . . . Do I have to bring up
that buzzing fly again? The Natives survived here for thousands of years.
How's that for practical? *Your* powerful bunch have been here barely two
hundred and are on the verge of making everything in sight unlivable.
They got an early start on it by destroying the pinyon pine forests, from
which the Natives had harvested nuts for centuries. *Your* bunch cut them
all down for timber to shore up mine shafts. Exactly where all that timber
is wasting away now. Where's the practical food harvest?"

Rattling off all this Native stuff, I felt uneasy and glanced from time
to time at Judith Clearwater and Woody, hoping to see when I was getting out of line. Although their expressions gave away nothing, the two
watched Roger and me as we harangued each other and the light never
left their attentive eyes.

"Well," Roger said. He took a step back. "This . . ." He scanned the
group around him. "I can . . . Never mind." He straightened and knocked
back a gulp of beer. "Not going to make any difference."

"What's not?" Doris said.

"What difference?" Fred cocked his head.

"This . . ." Roger flapped one hand toward the folder between me
and Woody. "This . . . Bitterroot Bob's grand gesture. His giving his acres
to the Indian trust."

"Because?" I asked. "I know you have a *because* back there. And
you're just itching."

"Has been since he walked in here," Woody murmured in my ear,
cleaning imaginary dust from the bar.

"Because I told you, one way or the other," Roger said, "we'll get the
land."

"You did," I said. "Maybe you can throw piles of money at the trustees. Threaten them? Burn them out? That's the big thing you stomped in here to tell everyone?"

"One way or the other Your trust donation doesn't change a thing. We'll get your land," Roger said. "Push comes to shove, a drought goes long enough, we'll invoke eminent domain. Get everyone's acres for pennies."

"Maybe," I said. "Meanwhile, I can hope."

"Hope? More of your Pollyanna optimism," he said.

"I don't mean that kind of hope. Mine's more long range," I said. "Happens while doing good. I've heard it called living well. It's like the hope you have planting a tree for future generations. A storm, a fire, a guy with a chainsaw may come and take it down. But right now, there's hope for the tree and people to come. And given the thousands of years of the Natives' success in this territory—as opposed to our bare two hundred—I have hope those fifty acres will survive longer."

I rubbed my finger along my nose and drew a breath. "At least, the donation will make your maneuvering more difficult. Assuming you'll try what you say."

"So why do it?" Roger said. The furrow between his eyes made him look sincerely perplexed. "Why do you . . . ?"

"Other than the reasons I mentioned?" I said.

"There's got to be more to it."

For once he was right "Has to do with that stuff your powerful folks go on about: life, liberty, and the pursuit of happiness."

"But if we still get—" he said.

"That will be then, Roger. Right now," I said, "making the donation gives me pleasure."

"Pleasure?" His voice squeaked.

"Me, too," Doris said. "A real glow." She toasted Roger with her glass. Fred raised his with hers.

"Pleasure?" Roger had regained his normal tone. "That's it?"

"Pleasure," I said. "Another word for happiness. As in, life, liberty, and the pursuit of?"

He still gaped at me.

"Pleasure. You know—as in pleasure and pain," I said. "Our instinctive Go and Stop lights that we use in the world to survive. See, I weigh the survival record out here of your powerful against the survival record of Natives. And, by the way, they're still here. I imagine selling my acres to you and your powerful gang. That idea gives me a pain. A big red light. But donating the land to the Native trust? Pleasure. Green light. That's my instinct telling me that survival of the acres, perhaps our own survival, has a better chance in their hands."

"I don't see . . . " he said, blinking more than usual, his eyes staring hard.

"No, you don't," I said. "Your idea of how to survive is different from mine. But I don't have to disprove yours, nor do I have to convince you of mine for me to get pleasure giving my acres to the trust. So, *your* losing or *my* winning our debate doesn't matter."

Roger said nothing.

"Pleasure—now there's the sun, moon, and stars as far as I'm concerned," I said.

He took a deep, deep breath and squared his shoulders. "You think, all of you think—" he looked slowly from one to the next of us—"you think I don't value survival?" Anger flared deep in his eyes. "I have family. Two children, a boy and girl, both still young enough to need protection. Often, I lie awake like any father worrying about what could happen to them My wife and I have families of brothers, sisters, uncles, parents and grandparents. I'm out here in this heat and waste to protect their survival. To ensure it. Why else would I tolerate not being with my wife week after week? Money? You diss me about love of money? How dare you. For me, it's a tool. A weapon. To fight for my family's survival. You don't approve of my methods." He swept us once more with a contemptuous look. "But I care as deeply about our survival as every one of you."

He seemed to have reached an end. Even for him, it was a long speech. His eyes dimmed and face went slack, as if the effort had drained him. I nodded. "I believe you." His mouth tightened. "Yes," I quickly went on, "I really do. Maybe next time around, instead of leaping to our personal versions *how* to survive, we could begin with asking what do we *mean* by survival. Or maybe explore whether we *should* survive. I don't know. Except we need better questions to begin our discussions. Like, what are we willing to *give up* for survival?" I thought another moment. "Or better still, perhaps we should start with asking what our children, what your kids would be willing to give for their survival. Because in fact, your kids' survival is a big part of why *this* donation"—I tapped my open folder—"makes me happy."

He reached for his bottle and emptied it.

"I'm done." He set it next to the coaster. "And out of here."

"I'll get your beers," Woody said. "There's three left. I'll bag them."

"Don't bother," Roger said. "There's plenty where I'm going."

He turned about and marched toward the door.

I watched him in the mirror behind the bar. He paused in the doorway and looked back. Shaking his head, he went out. After he descended the steps to street level, I lost his reflection.

Woody chuckled. He shook out his towel. After picking up Roger's empty, the coaster, and unused glass, he ran his towel over the vacated space and wiped it dry and spotless.

I emptied my glass and raised it toward Woody.

"How about another for everyone?"

22

In the saloon, only Woody was in motion. He trashed Roger's bottle in the recycle bin, set the glass in his sink, restored the coaster to its stack. After another moment to straighten it, he moved to the cooler, pulled up another bottle, gestured with it to Doris.

She shook her head. "Changed my other mind," she said. "I'm back to thinking the green stuff is bitter. I'd prefer what Fred has, if it's all the same."

Woody selected a clean glass and pulled the beer. Fred went to the bar to get it, bringing his own glass for refill.

"Move on up, you two," I said and gestured at the unoccupied bar stools. "We're practically family now." I felt bubbly.

They chose a couple of stools between me and Judith Clearwater.

"Actually, I apologize," I said, looking from Woody to Judith Clearwater. "I didn't mean to presume . . ." She flicked one hand and shifted her gaze out the window again.

Woody said, "No one thought . . ." He glanced at Fred and Doris and back to me.

". . . about the family thing, yes," I said. "There's that, thanks. But also, all that talk about Natives in the third person. Roger and me. Like you two weren't here, like . . . and so on."

"'s okay," Woody said. "We're used to hearing white invaders talk about us like they know something."

That brought Judith Clearwater back from the window with a smile and nod. Doris and Fred's heads had been going back and forth as if watching a tennis match.

Woody replaced the Heineken in the cooler and reached for its lid.

"You keep the beer," I said. "Diversify your stock."

"See, Doris?" Fred said. "Diversify. That's what I've been saying for us. Get more things on the shelves that will appeal to all those bird watchers that come through."

"Okay, Fred. Okay," she said. "Just so it's not more of those bird whistle mugs."

"I'll drink to that," he said.

We all did.

Judith Clearwater stepped down from her stool and excused herself, saying she ought to check on Lapwai. I watched Woody's eyes track her as she went out the door and disappeared around the corner of the building.

It wasn't long before Fred and Doris asked to see the documents that would turn my acres over to the land trust. I pushed the copy along the bar to them. They bent their heads over the pages and pointed out items of interest to each other.

In the meantime, Woody extracted the remaining three bottles from my cooler and upended it into his sink. He dried the bottles before putting them in the undercounter refrigerator on the back wall. After closing the door, he reopened it, retrieved one of the bottles, and carried it to the chalkboard that listed his offerings. At the bottom of the list, he printed the brand name, checking his spelling against the label of the bottle held in his other hand. He scanned his work, then added a price: $2. Without pause, he wrote at the bottom: *(limited supply).*

He went by me on his way back to the refrigerator.

"Limited supply?" I asked. Maybe he hadn't heard me.

He opened the fridge door, replaced the bottle, and closed the door. "What?"

"Is 'limited supply' a description only about the green-bottle stuff?" I asked. "Or something more?"

His face betrayed nothing. "Eye of the reader," he said. "But maybe I got that wrong."

Judith Clearwater came back through the front door from seeing to her horse. As if answering the question that Woody or I may have allowed on our faces, she said, "Lappie's fine. She's got water, shade, and all the time she wants to nap. She's content."

Doris pushed the land transfer document over to her. She ran her eyes down the cover page, flipped to others, slid the thing back in Doris's direction with a nod and smile. Fred handed it back to me.

The unsettled weather became a compelling topic. Fall was on the way. Maybe an early winter.

Doris and Fred asked me to let them know when they should make the drive to Burns. They finished their drinks and said they'd better get back to the store. They wanted to avoid a long line of impatient customers. Both fell out laughing in each other's arms.

After they left, the saloon felt cavernous. No ticking grandfather's clock. Yet something simmered. How could I feel that? Judith Clearwater had returned to her vigil through the window. She and that fly, apparently drawn to the beyond of beyond. Woody bent to his sink and glasses. I worried my beer, straightened the papers in the folder, and closed it. Woody glanced over, pointed at my file.

"That what you meant on the phone? The other night?" he asked. "About you and me having things . . . something-or-other?"

"Or inside out, or upside down," I said. "Reversed . . . Still don't have it quite . . .

"*That*, I got," he said. He went after a glass with his towel.

Judith Clearwater turned from the window. "You're both code-talking as much as I can tell."

"Sorry," I said. "It's related, in a way, to you and Togokwa."

She flicked her eyes to Woody.

He explained about telling me the legend of Snake, about not killing him but moving him to where he wouldn't do harm, about her similar act when she let Roger Stegman go after saving him from his own work of arson.

"We argued," I said, "Woody and me, about whether moving Togok-wa like you did was as effective as the legend pretended."

"We talked," Woody said.

"The idea sat sideways with me," I said. "Couldn't make peace with it."

"You two," Judith Clearwater shook her head. "I barely know that particular legend, let alone gave it a thought."

"Too busy," Woody said to her, "For any kind of thinking . . . my experience." He slid a dry and polished glass onto its shelf. "Bitterroot Bob, though," glancing at me, "out there, pondering away in the dark after I left. Plenty of time."

"Maybe too much time," Judith Clearwater said. "Upside down, inside out? Sounds like you tied your thoughts in knots."

"Not just that night. I'd been worrying it ever since you helped Roger out."

"You wished I'd left him to burn, if I remember right."

"Yeah, but doesn't help. Brutalizes everyone. Woody is right. So okay, move the snake."

"I wasn't thinking about that," she said. "I told you."

"Even so, seems a better deal than making a mess for whoever has to clean it up."

"His problem," Woody said, "Bitterroot Bob's? You didn't move him far enough."

"Lapwai was tired," she said. "I wasn't going to work her any harder than necessary for Roger Stegman." She said the name as though it tasted sour.

"Doesn't matter," I said. "The other night, Woody wanted to know how far away was far enough. Left it to my decision."

"Where was it?" she asked. "Canada?"

"Unfortunately, Roger's plans reach into Canada," I said. "Bigger problem is that I couldn't come up with *any* location that would be far enough away for me."

"This must be where your back to front, up to down part comes in," Woody said.

"Right. I'd climbed to the ridge above my place, watched the lightning storm, heard the billiard-ball clicks of blown sand . . ." my words tapered off. I was unsure I could reconstruct my thoughts and feelings.

"Don't know about any poolroom sand," Woody said, "But your fascination with the moon and stars . . . I watched that."

"Yes. I came back down. We had our talk. And later I got to thinking, what if, or how about, or—"

"Don't start again." Judith Clearwater shook her head.

"Okay. Okay. Somehow, after being on the bluff and later, talking with Woody, it came to me that moving Togokwa away from the territory wouldn't work," I said. "But we could move the territory away from him."

"*Away.* That'd be into the land trust," Woody said.

"Yes."

"And when, like he said, his company wins a future eminent domain ruling," Judith Clearwater asked, "what then?"

"I don't know," I said. "If and when? World will have shifted. I'll have to think again." I stopped myself. "Actually, that's incomplete. I felt something about getting . . . about having a different perspective. But it's not a simple matter of look and look again. It's more like keep looking and allow what we see to penetrate. But right now, I don't have a plan."

"It's not over?" she asked.

"Well, you told me that stories don't end," I said.

She looked at Woody. "Stegman got one thing right today."

"Which was?" he said.

"Bitterroot Bob pays attention," she said.

"He's good at something else," Woody said. "Pretending he's not."

She nodded. "Just when you think he's somewhere else, he surprises you."

"Are you two done?" I asked.

"Not quite," Judith Clearwater said.

"Why am I'm not surprised?"

"See?" Woody said to her. "He pays attention."

She ignored him. He reached into the sink. Came up with nothing. He pulled a glass from the shelf and held it up to the light. Grabbed his towel.

"You mentioned a climb up the bluff by your place," she said.

"It was that hot, sticky evening," I said, "a couple of days after the fire by your place."

"You spent time up on that ridge," she said. "The one by your place, by Purgatory."

"Yes."

"Watching lightning, communing with nature . . ." she said.

"Communing . . . ? That's more fancy than . . ."

"Whatever happened, did it include your childhood self?"

"Umm . . . not exactly."

Her gaze held steady on me. "*Approximately* is hard to imagine," she said.

I looked over at Woody.

"Don't mind the dishwasher," he said. "The dust around here . . . got to stay ahead."

"She and I, we're talking at this moment about knowing what's real. And from my point of view both of you have been around that issue with me," I said. "Unless I got that wrong."

He made a slow take of Judith Clearwater. She rubbed the back of her hand across her mouth. She hadn't drunk from her glass. Her eyes, sparkling at him above her hand, seemed to say: *Yep, you had that coming.*

"Fair enough," he said. "I don't remember digging into your childhood. Fill me in."

"Alright." I nodded. "There I was, that evening you dropped by, up on the bluff, and . . ."

"Nuh-uh," Woody said. "Nope. You gonna tell a story? Got to start at the beginning."

"Seems arbitrary," I said, "just where the beginning begins."

"True, your choice. But otherwise, the story doesn't make sense. According to what the elders say. And it feels like, your story, it didn't start on the ridge."

Judith Clearwater had turned on her stool. She leaned on one elbow, facing me. Why had I looked at her? Because Woody's comment reminded me of her talking about my train starting from the Garden of Eden.

"Many of the stories from *your* elders seem to begin back when people walked out of the forests," I grumbled. "A bit far back. And telling my story from that far back would take up too much time right now."

"You see a clock?" Woody asked. "All the time in the world. But you can move it closer, your beginning, than once-upon-a-time. I won't complain."

"You did . . ."

"Just get off the darn ridge," he said. "I don't trust high places."

"How about this," I said, "You both know I came to this corner of the world to be alone."

Woody paused his toweling. "There was something about your finding your *own* words."

"Yes. To help me feel—if not at home, at least able to live day to day in a country that had become unrecognizable . . . to me."

"So very unrecognizable, as I remember," Judith Clearwater said, "that other peoples' words didn't match what your senses registered. Sort of like what you believe caused your childhood nightmare."

"Right," I said. "That's where the reality part comes in. Knowing what reality is." I gestured at Woody. "Also, you and your so-called hikes and your stuff about *the map is not the territory.*"

Woody nodded and reached for another glass. "Go on."

Gulping my beer, I felt a wave of fatigue. My ebullience after Roger left had fizzled. What I was saying, what I had said was . . . now . . . all of it, so . . . I hunched over my glass and sighed.

"Don't you have something stronger?" I asked, rousing myself to point at my glass and look at Woody.

He nodded his head toward the back shelves of bottles and waited.

"I don't care," I said. "As long as some Kentucky's in it."

He pulled a bottle, poured a shot, placed it on its own bar napkin in front of me.

"Ranchers, truckers stop by here, partial to this," he said. He refilled my beer and returned it to the coaster. "Compliments of the Saloon. Contribution toward repaying the Heinekens. Whatever."

I took a slug from the shot glass and gasped, chased it with beer.

"Thanks," I said. "That helps. It's just that . . . " I ran my drinks routine, more cautiously this time, and shook my head.

"*Solitude.* So grandiose," I said. "*Reality.* So noble," I said. "*Alien country, nightmares, synesthesia, maps . . .*" I said, shaking my head through the list. "All of it. Very pretentious, vain, self-absorbed . . ." I spread my hands to them. "Foolish."

"But," Woody said, "it . . ."

"I make a big deal about *not* believing in America's myth about the western rugged individualist," I said. "And then buy into it, big time, with my Solitude act. Think I'm some Lone Rider."

"But didn't take you long," Woody said. "Figuring it."

"*Alone?*" I was still wrapped in my rant. "*Me,* alone against the world? I couldn't have knocked down enough of that range fire without your help." I paused and stared at him. "Wait! 'Figuring *it*'?"

I gaped at Judith Clearwater. "You, too? *Figuring it?* Both of you?" I asked. "All this time you saw my ridiculous . . . and have been . . . ?"

I looked from one to the other and back. Noncommittal, even neutral to my words and turmoil, the two of them. Waiting me out.

"Jesus," I said, covering my face with my hands.

"Now," Woody leaned toward me, both hands on the bar, "*this* feels like a story beginning."

Down at her end, Judith Clearwater slid from her stool. She picked up her water glass and bar napkin.

"Where are you going?" I said.

"Sounds like you're working uphill at this." She sat at a stool just off the far side of Woody, leaving one between her and me. "No need to make your telling more difficult by distance."

Woody gave me a nod, as if to nudge me on.

"Solitude," I said. "Big pretentious word."

"*Pretentious* aside," Judith Clearwater said, "solitude: defined as the state of being alone, remote from society."

". . . which I said I wanted, yes—needed—for my . . . *thinking*," I felt awkward again. "Sorry, that word, too . . . can't cough up one more accurate."

"And getting back to your big word?" Judith Clearwater said.

"Solitude, yes," I said. "I tried to get it by coming here . . . setting up Purgatory. Struggled to keep alone. Wanted to drive away Roger, you . . . everybody, just to leave me be."

"You did," Woody said.

"And hey, boy, was I wrong," I said. "Solitude wasn't what I needed. I needed what I got."

"Company," Woody said.

"I haven't been alone since I got here," I said. "Really alone. Even when tapping away at my computer, going to sleep, I've been surrounded by the people in the tales you've told me. Even those of Roger, who tells his own kind of tall tale."

"All those words aside," Judith Clearwater said. "What about *your* words? The ones you came here to find?"

"*My* words," I said. "Another thing I've been wrong about."

"You didn't need them?" Woody asked.

"Oh, I needed my words alright," I said. "And don't get me wrong. I wrote plenty. Set the keyboard smoking, I did. Words and more words. Some of them pretty good, I thought. But *my* words? Looking them over, I saw they came from, or *through* someone else: Native storytellers. Aristotle and the others you told me about, you two, Roger, his sales and PR people, his powerful backers. I only ordered and arranged all those words on a page. Words. A question of ownership, I'm starting to think. Or simply, questionable. Does anyone, *can* anyone own a word? Can say that one, *that* one right there, is *mine*?"

The spiel made my throat scratchy. I took a long drink of beer.

Woody pointed at my file of documents.

"That stunt there, your inside-out, other-perspective move with the land trust, something of an original flavor to that."

"Original? Hardly," I said. "Came through you straight from your buddy Aristotle. That business with Zeno's arrow."

"One of you philosophers going to help me out here?" Judith Clearwater said.

"Woody's the one for that," I said. "All I remember is an unwinnable argument because both sides of the squabble are based on unprovable beliefs."

Woody nodded. "And now you've quit trying to get Roger to agree that what *you* believe is going to make you happy."

"Like Aristotle suggested," I said. "Just do your good and let the other guy see your happiness that comes from it. Maybe it'll get him interested enough to take another look." I sipped the shot. Shook off the jolt. "Although I'm not sure that part worked on Roger."

"Oh, he's thinking on it," Woody said. "At least thinking about you and what happened here. When he walked out? That's the most puzzled I've seen him since he first marched through the door."

Judith Clearwater tapped her fingernail on her glass. A slow tapping. Woody topped up my shot glass.

"Feels too easy to me, your explanation so far," Judith Clearwater said. "Too logical. Something's missing."

"What's missing?" I said.

"*I* should know?" she said. "Our local saloon keeper may not trust high places, but something happened up on the bluff that night. Something that included more than thinking. Maybe what's missing is more emotional . . . maybe it revolves around a child long since grown and his nightmare?"

"Well . . ." I sipped the shot. "Well . . ." Chased it with my beer. "Feels slippery . . . hard to get a hold . . ."

"Yeah," Woody said. "You're not alone now, either."

"Okay, okay," I said. "There was an electric storm while I was up there. I went flat to watch it . . . kidding myself . . ."

"Tsk, tsk," Woody shook his head. Judith Clearwater raised one finger, and he stopped.

"It was distant," I said, without conviction. "Anyway, when I stood up, I grabbed an old cottonwood branch I'd used as a climbing stick." I went on with the rest—about the branch feeing like a telephone pole, about my tugboat feet, about watching my childhood self back on the staircase.

As she listened, there was a glow behind Judith Clearwater's eyes.

"See, it was a kind of remembering," I said to her. "Not really like finding my lost child."

"Never mind," she said.

From there on, I struggled to describe my reenacting what I visualized of my younger self's reaction on the childhood staircase, how the dissolution of my synesthetic nightmare demonstrated that even my senses didn't work in solitude but complemented and corrected each other. And if sight and touch of a right hand were out of sync, a left-handed touch could reconcile the previous two sensations.

Judith Clearwater nodded. Woody had stopped polishing glassware and leaned against the back counter, both hands wrapped in his towel, its action stilled for once.

"Sorry not to be more clear," I said. "It's not like any of my thoughts came as flashes in the dark. More muddled and messy. They grew on me over time. I'm not sure I had the pieces until after I'd telephoned Woody about a different perspective. Sort of filled in the blanks after the fact, if you get the idea."

"Of course, you've been describing more than just thoughts," Judith Clearwater said. "The world's more than thoughts. Logic isn't everything."

"Even so," Woody said, "makes sense. In its own way."

"Gets worse, though," I said. "There's probably no way to explain how I linked those thoughts to your Aristotle story. Although somehow connected is his suggesting a person should act on what makes them happy."

"And without also having to convince the guy who holds the opposing argument," Woody said.

"Yes. And one more thing I've been wrong about. My simple mantra that people such as Roger Stegman are a symptom, not the disease."

"The disease being . . . ?" Judith Clearwater asked.

"Greed, dominance, fear," I said. "And any of their enablers: hatred, envy, wealth as proof of being chosen, race superiority, anger. Not an original list and incomplete in any case. Been around since before such things were written down."

"You were wrong about what?" Woody asked.

"What to do about the disease. Like what to do with Togokwa," I said. "I believed it was important to control it—stamp it out where possible. At least, immunize oneself against it."

"Let me guess," Woody said, "win the argument for your belief to disprove the opposing belief."

"And that way of thinking frames the disease as the Bad Guy. But listen to those words," I said to Woody. "*Win. Disprove.* In them are the seeds of aggression and dominance. Working that way, I'm already infected. And I am. If nothing else, I'm fertile ground for the disease. Look how I was here, today, with Roger. I didn't want to be angry at him, diminish him. But I was and did. I'm not skilled at my so-called *other way.* Where, just maybe, someone with more practice working from your Aristotle's point of view would do better."

"Roger Stegman isn't immune to the complicated world," Judith Clearwater said. "You can sense the pain of his confusion in all that anger."

"And in the violence behind his arguments," I said, "as well as his desperation to make the indifferent high desert compassionate."

"I hope he finds peace of mind," she said.

"Me, too. I'm just not as good at helping him along as you are."

"Physician, heal thyself," Judith Clearwater said. "Thinking back to front, if I hear what you mean."

"Yeah, I guess," I said. "But I don't want to make too much of that angle. It's only part of the mix. Sometime, in that evening after Woody left, I also came to some hazy understanding, or at least my interpretation, of the importance of *not* killing Togokwa."

"Not to maintain the balance of the world?" Woody said. "Like the elders claim?"

"More like how killing Togokwa *would* imbalance the world. Because you can't. In some form, he'll always slither back."

"You mean, kill a Roger Stegman with his gun or fire," Judith Clearwater said, her eyes narrowed as she puzzled it through from my view, "and someone with, say, an eminent domain ruling will show up."

"There you go, sooner or later," I said. "Killing Togokwa, believing you have, creates an *illusion* of safety. Safety forever. Then, with that illusion the world *is* out of balance and therefore dangerous. If you only remove him to where he can do no harm, the balance is maintained because you remain alert to his return."

I drained my shot. Woody moved toward the bottle. I waived him off. My beer stood nearly empty. I drew a vertical line with my thumb through the condensation on the outside of the glass.

"My apologies, once again," I said to somewhere between the two of them. "I've been pontificating." I fussed with my folder of papers to make a show of getting ready to leave.

"Funny thing about your name," Woody said. "Your *assumed* name, Bitterroot Bob."

"I know, I know: a flower," I said. "Told you I made up the name thinking of the mountain range, not pansies."

"Some people from where I come from?" Woody said. "Know the bitterroot, the root itself, and use it as food, sometimes a medicine.

"Further north and east, my territory," Judith Clearwater said, "people had an aversion to bear attacks. For protection, they ate the bitterroot."

"Some pansy," Woody said, straight-faced.

I gave both of them the iciest appraisal I could manage, hoping to chill their blood. They did me the favor of not laughing.

"The two of you," I said and shook my head. "I provide you far too much entertainment."

Beyond Judith Clearwater, outside the window, an eighteen-wheeler rumbled by. Its noise soon disappeared. The hills of sage, the blue sky, and its flowing rafts of cloud were never the same in temperature, color, and, if you waited out the centuries of wind sculpture, in contour.

Inside the saloon, the other two waited for me to go on. The glass pane really didn't separate them from the outside. They seemed to have always been there.

"All I know," I said, "is that I stood on a bluff one evening. I heard an endless ocean of air sweep grains of sand across my boots and into collisions, one after another. It was part of the earth's elements in perpetual movement. At the same time, I, with them, rode one grain in similar movement with other hurtling planets and stars."

I drank the last of my beer.

"I came here as a perturbed and frustrated old man. I can't change the old or the man parts, but at least now I'm in motion."

23

Over the following days, I felt not so much in motion as in simply being swept along.

In the hard blue of a cool morning, I trod the turning planet to pace off and record the approximate boundaries and GPS coordinates of my acres. I stood at one corner and marveled that the line of numbers calculated on my device was made possible by data from multiple satellites twenty thousand feet above, orbiting a globe caught in its galactic vortex. I walked on to the next corner through a flood of air that somewhere downstream would, according to some, be stirred by the wings of a creature flapping up a storm that might break a continent away.

I lost count of my paces from the last coordinate and had to re-step them.

Woody had also been diligent. He called me within twenty-four hours after my saloon showdown with Roger Stegman to say he had the names I needed for my transfer deed. I dropped by, supposedly to get the spellings right but really for the beer he pulled. I stopped the glass halfway to my mouth and stared at the last printed name.

"Elwood?" I asked.

"A name in my family from mission-school days. Legally correct," he said. "More so than Woody."

Javier Cruz proved obligingly flexible. I let Fred and Doris know Javier could see us and gassed up the Ranchero. We made the trip to the Burns office the next day and got the signatures notarized. Fred beamed when he handed the pen back to Javier.

Doris raided See's for her chocolate assortment. Back in Fast Buck, Woody, straight-faced, accepted his gracefully as always. I did less well, showing surprise when she handed me a small box.

"Not really a going-away present," she said. "More like a come-back-soon invitation."

It didn't take me long to prepare and close up the Airstream and get it towed to a storage lot at Burns. Woody had reassured me that I could repopulate Purgatory any time I wanted. Whether Purgatory existed anymore was open to speculation.

I'd wiggled the signpost free of its hole. Knocked off my hand-lettered placard. Cut and split everything to pieces. They generated a pleasant warmth one evening for the three of us, Woody, Judith Clearwater and me, sitting around a small campfire of the wood scraps on my last night at the old shack. Evenings came earlier now and were decidedly cooler.

And then, as easily as turning a page, I was driving south, my few travel items stacked in the passenger space next to me or lashed under the tarp in the Ranchero's bed. During my drive, the early fall sun bored through my windshield from midmorning to sunset. A vacant highway most of the way to Winnemucca was the perfect setting for my mood as the miles increased between me and the folks in and around Fast Buck. Even the rise to the Donner Pass over the Sierra didn't lift my spirits as it usually did.

Finally, traversing the ridges north of Vallejo and the Carquinez Strait and bridge, I sighted the first silvered strip of the bay. But the greater confirmation that I was back in the Bay Area was the scent of water. Interesting what we forget we're missing until it's registered anew by our senses.

And now a second day of rain. Low clouds and falling water obscured the city across the bay. Drops pinged from time to time against the windows of my work room. On the desk to the left of my keyboard lay a book by Epicurus, *The Art of Happiness.* My future choices for happiness, for pleasure, weren't going to be as easy as figuring out what to do with fifty acres of high desert. Likewise, it was not second nature for me to come up with questions like those I finally asked Roger Stegman about survival. But that was the best way to find out what people can learn from each other. I had much to practice. It would be a long haul. But more immediately, I had loose ends to tie up.

On the panes, rivulets lengthened their crooked streaks, disappeared, were replaced by new ones. I imagined I could smell the moisture through the glass. Not the desert now, Toto. It was good to be home. At the same time, I felt part of me had yet to arrive.

The outline of what I had seen, heard, and taken part in had blurred, due not so much by time and distance as by sharp contrasts. This grey flat sky rather than white cumulous piles in endless blue, rain instead of desiccation, and wearing a jacket, not shirtsleeves, all softened the details of past months and gave my memories a dreamlike quality. Did Fast Buck exist? Were its people, Doris and Fred, Woody and Judith Clearwater characters of fact or my fantasy?

What remained that I could put my hands on were the pages I'd written on my laptop, scraps of notes, information recorded and sifted for . . . what? Reading through them often left me groping for something just out of reach.

Around the low flames eating away at letters of Purgatory on my splintered sign, Judith Clearwater had turned her face to me. "End of your Purgatory, Bitterroot Bob?"

"Doubt it. Besides, Woody said I can come back."

"Any time," Woody nodded, "Sign or no."

"Purgatory, you once explained, was a place to burn out the uglies," she said to me.

"Sounds like me."

"Did it?" she asked. "Burn them out?"

"Not entirely. More like singed around the edges."

True to their usual way, the two of them allowed me to lapse into silence. I was grateful. Yes, I had managed a limited victory over Roger Stegman. There was my resolution to do what felt best where others were considered without trying to convince the likes of him of its rightness.

All of which, I continued to wonder, left me where, exactly? Where should I go from Purgatory? Return East? Where I would also be an outsider? To Europe, where I'd be classified as a foreigner? Besides, my *going* had the same problem as *moving* Togokwa: how far away would be enough?

Now in my rain-assaulted study, watching the drops trace their kinetic art down my windows, I reflected on that conversation and my thoughts around the fire.

The question of where to go had resolved simply. I returned to this outpost on a frontier of the colonial power that had taken the territory, often from previous colonial powers—France, Spain, Russia—and also from its longer-term residents. Taken from the latter more by overwhelming numbers than by guns or germs. And stolen additional territory by self-serving laws, broken treaty promises, and raw deception. By outright murder as an additional tragedy.

Many weeks ago, I had left my windowed study for the desert, only to be reminded that my colonial roots lengthen each year. I am still an immigrant, a colonist, an outsider. After my return, I've thought now and again, usually in my darker moments, to petition a counsel of the First Nations for asylum. Perhaps someday, assuming I could learn and promise to honor their laws, traditions, and customs, I could win dual citizenship? Would they consider such an animal? Perhaps all U.S. citizens should do the same. But why just in the U.S.? Over the centuries, millennia, in so many places around the world, people have come as immigrants, then as invaders and colonists on other peoples' lands. Many of their descendants should petition for asylum and dual citizenship. Come that improbable day, hope could be reborn for peaceful, respectful coexistence and for groping toward a shared comprehension of how to avoid planetary extinction.

Applied to me, that idea wasn't a plan or a goal, I realized. It was a direction. At best, a static thought contemplating motion.

The rattle of rain against my panes took on the sound of Doris's giggles, this time at me. More ridiculous, impractical ramblings from Bitterroot Bob.

"Again, you're right to laugh," I said, mentally projecting my unspoken words through the wet panes facing me to Doris as I saw her last—happy at Woody's bar with a glass in her hand. "I'm walking into one of the oldest traps, aren't I?" I continued. "Don't like the current reality? Seek an alternative that has different rules and traditions for making collective decisions, ones that flatten or eliminate pecking orders and high poohbahs. Can't find an alternative to suit? Invent your own. A utopia, a city on a hill, a new world order, an etheriam. Or emotionally return to an imagined great version in the past. What a laugh, right?" In the wet window glass, I saw Doris nodding. "Because," I told her, "so far no one has designed a version of perfection that can be maintained according to the blueprint. Another reality, the *real* reality that eludes us all, always pulls the imagined design to pieces. The new design isn't an alternative, it's only a facet of the larger one. The question isn't *where* to live—or in which to live—but rather remains, *how* to live in what we got. Whatever that reality is, it's as merciless as the high desert. We'd better adapt.

The silence among the three of us around the burning Purgatory wood had extended that final evening. I tossed a branch of cottonwood in the fire, which popped and threw a few sparks. Judith Clearwater stirred.

"Well, Bitterroot Bob, you came here hoping to learn how to live in a world you found alien," she said.

"And somewhere along the line, you tagged my looking as a quest," I said.

"I did. You'd said you hoped to find a way. Did you? Have you?"

There was no hope in trying to divert her. I sighed and reversed the cross of my ankles. Besides, if I owed anyone an explanation, these two people topped the list.

"First of all, I resist being included among the other odysseys of Ulysses, Aeneas, Don Quixote, Leopold Bloom, Huck Finn, Frodo Baggins . . . think of it, mythical heroes of how many in other cultures . . ."

"Not bad company," Woody said.

"All outrank me exponentially," I said. "And the many other questers, with their searching languages of math, sciences, music, fine art. Your philosophy, Woody."

"You expand the quest idea."

"*Expand*?" I asked. "There's a sea of inquiry around us like the moving sea of air . . . a searching will to know that's not interested in imposing a reality but to understand a reality bigger than our present comprehension, a consciousness seeking to live within that greater realm.

"And did your quest find a way?" Judith Clearwater asked.

"You are one tough audience," I said, coming down from the clouds. "And my answer is simple. No."

Neither Judith Clearwater nor Woody turned or looked elsewhere. They never did. Their way was not arguing or confrontation. They used their physical presence and engaged awareness to allow a person choice of movement. They waited in the flickering light from the fire. In their unwavering eyes I read expectations of more.

"Quests, searches," I said, "they all start with a question. That one of mine? How to live in a world gone alien? I hoped that figuring out what had happened and why would lead me to the how. I was wrong. It didn't. For that matter, I was not only wrong about the equation, I was wrong about my original question."

"Wrong?" Woody said. "How do you mean wrong?"

"The world hadn't *suddenly* turned *alien*."

"No?"

"No," I said. "What I thought was alien had been there all along. I hadn't paid attention. And everything familiar and friendly? It hadn't vanished, either. It is still here. Again, I hadn't been paying attention." I stopped to correct myself. "Actually, it was worse. I looked away."

"Togokwa lives among us," Judith Clearwater said, "just as we live among all Togokwas. Is that what you're trying to fit your idea into?"

"I suppose. But if so, that's your story line, not mine."

"So, what's yours?"

"I don't know. I may need a few thousand more years to develop one. Oddly enough, I think my culture has been working on it for several thousand already. It was more than seven hundred years from the telling of Ulysses's Odyssey to the telling of another odyssey taken by Aeneas. The search of both characters starts from the same city: fallen Troy. But some people think that in the intervening seven centuries, the odyssey story line shifted from Might is Right to Might Wins, But That Doesn't Make It Right. Somewhere along the line, our human fascination in the self-righteous grievances of one man broadened to a concerned awareness for others, a *responsibility* to others, and recognizes massacring the opposition morally warps everyone who massacres."

"Okay." Woody said. "Who were you thinking of massacring?'

"Roger Stegman? By extension, his company. Everyone who enables any of them. Extend that further, the word massacre isn't big enough." I poked at the fire with a cottonwood stick I'd picked up. "I recognize the urge."

The fire fluttered to life before subsiding again.

"You also see the damage it can do," he reminded me.

"Yes. Yes. Somewhere along this seven-hundred-year story line, western civilization went beyond recognizing opposing urges: one instinct for selfish, personal preservation and another instinct of self-sacrifice for the larger group. Both impulses are always there, poised to act, in ourselves and in society. Mine versus ours. Total individual freedom versus honoring collective agreements. But finally, the Aeneid implied the question that asked how to live within this contradiction."

I turned to Judith Clearwater.

"That's my story line to date," I said. "So far, I have a language that can describe or defend one side or the other of those two opposing instincts. And we're now a few thousand years from our first telling of Ulysses. I was wrong about what I've said before, about needing to find my own words for how to live in a world that felt alien. Now I think I'm searching for words for how to live in a way that acknowledges both drives are always present. Maybe I'm looking for new words that unite the two urges rather than pitting them against each other."

"*Unite*?" Woody frowned.

"Maybe reconcile," I said.

"*Reconcile*?" Judith Clearwater wondered from her place near the fire. "Really? Can they be?"

"Okay," I said. "Maybe come to terms with." I thought again. "Or perhaps this is another one of those words that hasn't been found yet."

I tossed the stick into the embers and sat back.

"Thousands of years up to now, this search?" I said to the fire. "What's a couple of thousand more?"

"Aristotle always claimed his ideas were works in process," Woody said.

"I remember," I said. "And thanks to you, I'm more aware than ever that so many of our so-called facts are only theories. We're constantly revising them. Even then, it's not so much through disproving some *fact* as it is including something *in addition* that makes the world more complicated and interesting than previously believed."

I turned to Judith Clearwater. "I also remember you said that a story never ends." She nodded. "One of the psychology wizards of the last century maintained that accurately naming something changes it. In recent days, I've wondered whether our everlasting storytelling is actually our search for accurate names to what disturbs us."

"Forget 'quest,' then," she said. "We'll call yours an ongoing story."

"I think so, or something like it," I said. "Among all our factions, I sense a longing for something. But our languages, all those languages I listed, lack the vocabulary to come to grips with it. It's like I'm hoping to find a part of myself, and I'm looking for a language that's not mine or any one's I know of. My search, our searches, attempt to create it. I'm also aware that my actions are neither resistance to something nor any pretense at leading the way or setting a marker, drawing a line. All I'm sure of is that we are living in and have always lived in the Garden of Eden. That story wasn't history. It was cautionary. Every time we presume to act like a god, we throw away a handful of the garden. We lose it, bit by bit, until now, when we may finally throw away the entire thing. Our Eden? No one owns it—or more accurately—we all do. And we should greet it daily with wonder.

"Meanwhile," I said, "the search, and all else we do, is part of living among other members of a herd grazing across the landscape. We're all in motion aboard a swirling world. An action taken by one—perhaps simply finding a word—affects all others."

The fire was nearly out. I took in Woody and Judith Clearwater.

"So, I thank you both," I said. "My search for whats and whys and hows? That's done. I'm no longer sure any more about their implied cause and effect. Perhaps humanity's changes are more like a slide and glide of emotional tropisms. It's just that hate, being fueled by adrenaline presents a greater danger for addiction." I drew a breath and exhaled. "Anyway, one can find words to approximate the social and political landscape. But it's a lot more difficult, isn't it, to find words for the havoc of seething emotional currents underneath? More important, maybe, is believing that living well really is the best revenge. Where *well* doesn't mean high on the hog. It means living ethically, doing good for as many as possible. Whatever *that* means for each person, it involves the heart, which means emotion, which means basing our actions on happiness. Which in turn means to allow what you see and hear—both before and after you act—*to penetrate.*"

As I talked, Judith Clearwater had stared into the fire and continued to do so as she spoke. "I must say, from you I now have a different view of Purgatory."

"And as I learned from you," I said to her, "*It's not over.*"

"Of course," I said, turning to Woody. "Maybe I got that wrong."

I wondered if Doris and Fred, all the way over in Fast Buck, heard us laughing.

On our evening lost in the when of yesterdays, Woody and Judith Clearwater stood to leave the campfire gathering. The fire had burned to cinders, their glow pulsing dimmer. She turned to me.

"I'm thinking of lines from a country song," she said. "About not telling how the story ends."

"I can't," I said. "Even though I want to."

From somewhere, a breeze moved across us, on its way to further on.

A gust of wind blows a cascade of water against the windows of my study. It reminds me of the torrent over Celilo Falls and the cry I'd heard above it. Perhaps that had been a cry of joy. Perhaps lament. Maybe a shout of defiance. Perhaps all three at once. How could the three work as one? Judith Clearwater had asked. As a ballad, I'd replied. In three stanzas.

And I listen for that remembered cry. Perhaps the cry I now hear is my own. A cry struggling to be heard before my Purgatory experience shifts and drifts away like so many grains of sand. A ballad of new hope.

And so, I begin. I lay out three sheets of paper.

On each, I write one word.

SPACE. TIME. MOTION.

Acknowledgments

I am indebted to the creators of the many secondary resources that enrich this story. Those works suggested For Further Reading merely scratch the surface and are offered only as starting places.

I am very grateful to many friends and fellow writers who read the manuscript of *Endangered: The Ballad of Bitterroot Bob* and offered their suggestions. My thanks to the numerous readers of the Berkeley Branch of the California Writers' Club Saturday Critique and Support Group; to James N. Frey and his writing workshop members: Cara Black, Margaret Cuthbert, Susanna Solomon, Ken Freeman, James Fant, and Eric Seder for suggestions that helped shape the story and characters early on; and I particularly thank CWC's Crawford 7: David Baker, Risa Nye, Francine Howard, Gerry Marmion, and Anne Fox, whose copy editing was especially useful, for their generous time and support as chapters and characters came to life. Many times, I did not want to hear their invaluable critiques. They made them anyway. Most often they were right. Additional thanks to Michelle Cozad of the Owens Valley Paiute-Shoshone Cultural Center in Bishop, California and to Stacey Burns, Language and Cultural Coordinator and her Elder Resource, Ralph Burns at the Reno-Sparks Indian Colony for their time and generous assistance with the several Paviosto/Numu words and spellings Bitterroot Bob encounters. Thanks also to Matthew Wimer, Managing Editor at Wipf and Stock Publishing, for his support and direction throughout the publication process.

I am especially grateful to Ann Campbell, who lived with the me as well as read the manuscript, for both her encouragement and unflinching honesty.

All errors in the story are mine.

For Further Reading

Boethius. *The Consolation of Philosophy*. Translated by P. G. Walsh. New York: Oxford World's Classics, 2000.

Deloria, Philip J. *Playing Indian*. New Haven: Yale University Press, 1999.

Ellul, Jacques. *Hope in Time of Abandonment*. Translated by C. Edward Hopkin. 1973. Reprint, Eugene, Oregon: Wipf and Stock, 2012.

———. *The Political Illusion*. Translated by Konrad Kellen. 1967. Reprint, Eugene, Oregon: Wipf and Stock, 2015.

———. *Propaganda: The Formation of Men's Attitudes*. Translated by Konrad Kellen and Jean Lerner. New York: Alfred A. Knopf, Inc., 1965.

Havel, Vaclav. *The Power of the Powerless*. Translated by Paul Wilson. 1979. Reprint, London: Vintage, 2018.

Lear, Jonathan. *Aristotle: The Desire to Understand*. New York: Cambridge University Press, 1988.

———. *Radical Hope: Ethics in the Face of Cultural Devastation*. Boston: Harvard University Press, 2008.

www.ingramcontent.com/pod-product-compliance
Lightning Source LLC
Chambersburg PA
CBHW070223030726
47505CB00006B/1797